Simply Wicked

By

Lisa G. Riley

Parker Publishing LLC

Noire Passion is an imprint of Parker Publishing LLC.

Copyright © 2008 by Lisa G. Riley
Published by Parker Publishing LLC
12523 Limonite Ave., Ste. #440-438
Mira Loma, California 91752
www.parker-publishing.com

This book is a work of fiction. Characters, names, locations, events
and incidents (in either a contemporary and/or historical setting) are
products of the author's imagination and are being used in an
imaginative manner as part of this work of fiction. Any resemblance
to actual events, locations, settings, or persons, living or dead, is
entirely coincidental.

ISBN: 978-1-60043-050-3
First Edition

Manufactured in the United States of America

Cover Design by Jaxadora Design

Dedication & Acknowledgements

This book is dedicated to all of those women who believe in going after what they want.

Thank you to my mother, Gloria B. Riley (1938-2000) for loving me, supporting me and encouraging me.

Thanks to all of my sisters. You guys are always there for me. Thanks to my nieces, who helped me to remember how the mind of a six-year old works.

Thanks to D.D. and RHH for being willing to read and offer such great suggestions.

Chapter 1

Six-year old Cassidy Edwards stared out the car window as her best friend's mother navigated the narrow streets that made up their Chicago neighborhood. It was a perfect spring day, and the neighborhood of modest Ranch homes and manicured lawns was fresh with newly bloomed flowers.

I wish this car had wings, or even that Mrs. Rodriguez would go just a little faster, Cassie thought in excitement, *one or the other; it doesn't matter. I just want to get home.*

Long and brown, she pressed her thin, leotard-clad body against the car door as if that could somehow make the car move faster.

Cassidy sighed. Come on already, Mrs. Rodriguez! Of course, she'd never give voice to her thought, but oh, she wanted to. She started counting in her head like her mom had taught her to. She was supposed to count whenever the ants in her pants — she giggled helplessly and broke her concentration. *Ants in the pants, it just sounds so silly*, she thought with a shake of her head. It was a struggle, but she finally controlled the giggles by picturing a quiet beach with nothing but sand and water — another way her mother had taught her to keep herself under control.

Cassidy sighed again. There were so *many* ways, but she knew she needed them because like her mommy and daddy said, she was almost always inches away from getting in trouble because the ants were almost always in her pants and crawling to get out. And when she said something she wasn't supposed to say, or did something she wasn't supposed to do, that was their way of getting out, and that's when she got into trouble. So, when she felt them itching and scratching, that was her clue to start counting or to start imagining quiet, still places.

She looked out the window again. It seemed to her that they were no closer to getting home than they had been a few minutes before. Filled with energy and mischief, she was rarely still, and now was no different. Her toes tapped out a melody only she could hear as her fingers tattooed that same beat on her knees. She closed her eyes and made another picture. This time it was of home.

Cassidy smiled as she thought about what was waiting for her at home. Tonight was the night that she and her father would put on a stage production for her mother. It was called "*The Princess Who Ate the Pea, Instead of Laying On It.*"

It was her own title, and she was proud of it. She'd made it up because she'd made up the story herself with some help from her father. She couldn't wait to get started. They'd build a set and wear costumes and everything! She would never tell her mother, but she liked it best when it was her father's turn to help her write and produce a play. He just showed more imagination. Cassidy believed it was because her mother was just a little bit too serious sometimes. *But still*, she thought as loyalty and love kicked in, *I always have fun with Mommy, too.*

The Edwards family had been entertaining each other for the past two years—ever since they'd taken Cassie to see "Annie," and she'd proclaimed that she wanted to make up stories and "act like the little girl on the stage with the funny-lookin' orange hair."

Cassidy's smile turned into a grin. She loved to hear her parents tell that story, about how she'd been so stubbornly sure that she was meant to act that they knew they had to do something about it just to keep her quiet. They'd put her in the local theater group and indulged her with their family productions. She giggled again. Her daddy even had a name for her.

"Cassidy Marie Hamilton Edwards, Girl Actor," she whispered as she continued to stare out the window.

"Whatcha smilin' at, Cassie? I wanna know. And did you just whisper? What did you say? Come on, tell me."

Cassie turned from the window to look at her friend, Laura

Rodriguez. She was her best friend, but she was also just a little bit whiney. *Whenever I'm with her, I know why Mommy tells me it's not good to whine. It's so annoying,* Cassie thought and tried not to frown and let the ants overtake her. "I wasn't smiling at anything outside. I was just thinking."

"'Bout what?"

"Nothing." Cassie decided on the spot to lie. If she told Laura, then Laura would ask her mother if she could stay when they dropped her off, and Cassie wanted her parents and her play all to herself. She shrugged. "It was nothing. I was just thinking about that new step we learned in ballet class today. It was cool, huh?"

"Yeah," Laura began eagerly. "I didn't think I'd get it at first, but Teacher said…"

Cassie let her friend ramble on and turned her attention to the window again, absentmindedly twirling some strands of hair that had escaped her ballerina bun. *I think I'll wear the red princess dress tonight,* she thought, and wished impatiently that Mrs. Rodriguez would hurry up and get her home.

"Okay, Cassie, we're almost there," Mrs. Rodriguez said as she turned onto their block. "In case I forget, remind your mom for me that she has ballet carpool next Saturday, will you?" she asked as she slowed by the curb.

"Yes, ma'am," Cassidy said and opened her door, not taking notice that Mrs. Rodriguez was preparing to get out on her side. She was more than halfway up the cobble-stoned walk when she heard her call her name. Still impatient, she turned, but kept backing toward her house. "Ma'am?"

Mrs. Rodriquez's face showed hesitation for a second before it cleared and she started to climb back into the car. "I guess I don't have to go in. Just wave to me from the door once you're inside so that I know your parents are home, okay, honey?"

"Yes, ma'am, but their cars are in the drive—"

"Just wave, Cassie."

Cassidy shrugged. "Okay, Mrs. Rodriguez. See you later, and thank you for the ride! Bye, Laura," she yelled over her shoulder. She was already on the porch. The main door was open, so she opened the screen door and went inside. "Mommy, Daddy, I'm home!" she yelled as she started to move toward the back of the house. At the last minute she remembered her promise, and opened the screen door to wave at Mrs. Rodriguez. "They're home. Bye!"

She dropped her dance bag on the floor, and immediately picked it up again. "Your bag goes in your room, Cassie," she reminded herself happily as she started toward the back of the house again. "Mommy, Daddy! I'm home," she yelled again and did a little turn before skipping to snitch a piece of candy from the dish her mother kept in the dining room. *Just one little piece*, she thought guiltily as she bit into the gooey center. *My appetite will be fine*. Hurriedly swallowing it, she kept moving towards the kitchen, calling again as she went.

"Where are you guys?" she asked in a small voice when she was confronted with an empty kitchen. She frowned in confusion. One or both of her parents always met her in the living room when she came home from ballet.

Why didn't they answer? Panic began to creep in and she started backing out of the kitchen. She heard a strange pop followed by a loud thump. It all came from above her, and she threw her head back in reflex, staring at the ceiling as if she could see straight through it to what was going on. Guessing that the sounds had come from her parents' room, she decided to check upstairs. She left the kitchen for the front of the house again where she ran up the stairs.

"Mommy! Daddy! What was that noise? Why don't you answer me?" Her voice was quivery with fear and she wavered at the top of the stairs. There was something wrong. She just knew it. Usually by now her dad would be picking her up and swinging her around, and her mom would be smiling and holding out her arms for her turn, but today...today there was nothing.

What she didn't recognize as dread settled in Cassie's chest as she stared at the door to her parents' room at the other end of the short hall. The door was partially opened, and to her, seemed to represent all of her nightmares rolled into one. She wanted her legs to move, but they wouldn't. "I want my mommy," she moaned and tears splashed down her cheeks.

Fear made the short walk to her parents' room a slow and arduous one. "Be brave, Cassie, be brave," she mumbled the mantra to herself as she walked. Once there, she couldn't make herself push the door open, only being able to peek through the narrow opening. The sight of her mother lying on the bed immediately caught her eye, and a glad cry escaped her mouth as she dropped her bag and rushed into the room. *Oh, you're sleeping! That's why you didn't hear me!* "Mommy!" she cried and began to shake her awake. "Why are you sleeping? You're never sleeping when I come home. Wake up Mommy," she demanded, shaking her mother harder when she didn't get a response.

"Are you sick, Mommy?" she asked in a voice that sounded thoroughly confused.

"It's okay, I'll take care of you," she assured her and moved to the phone on the bedside table to call for help just like her mother had taught her to do if something was wrong and she couldn't wake her. "No ants, stay away...*stay away*," she pleaded through tears and tried to conjure up something peaceful while she dialed.

Breath hitching from suppressed sobs, she started talking as soon as her call was picked up. "You have to come now," she told the operator who answered. "My mommy's sick. I can't wake her up. You have to come. *You have to come!* I think there's bad sugar in her blood." She continued to talk, not pausing for breath as she gave the operator her address. "Come now, please. I have to hang up because I have to take care of my mommy. You come now," she said again before hanging up and dialing another number, as she'd been taught.

"Granny?" she cried, breaking down when she heard the familiar voice. "Oh, Granny, Mommy's sick. Please, you have to come. She w-won't w-wake up, and I can't find Daddy!" she wailed. "I called the 'mergency people. They're coming and you have to come, too. Come now, Granny, please." It was difficult, but she forced herself to hang up. She just had to help her mother.

Remembering what her mother did for her whenever she was sick, Cassie ran into the bathroom where she made a cold compress. "Here you are, Mommy," she said as she smoothed her mother's French braids out of her face and carefully laid the compress on her forehead. "You'll feel better soon," she promised as she took her hand and kissed her cheek. To comfort both herself and her mother, she began to sing the song her parents had been singing to her since as far back as she could remember.

"My brown-eyed girl. You're my... brown-eyed girl..."

As she sang the Van Morrison classic, she didn't notice the blood soaking through the dark, multi-colored comforter that covered her mother's body. Nor did she notice her father's body on the floor on the other side of the bed. She didn't see the young woman who was dying on top of him, either.

Cassie walked down the stairs in her grandmother's new country house, knowing that she wouldn't be heard. Her grandmother and uncle were arguing again. It was almost all they ever did since her mommy and daddy had gone to heaven. They usually argued about her and where she was going to live. They never asked her what she wanted to do. If they ever did, she could save them the trouble of arguing because she'd just tell them that she wanted to go to heaven with her mommy and daddy.

She wanted to just tell them that on her own, but she never did. She'd get bored thinking about it. What did it matter? Nothing really mattered any more, really—not even ballet or theater. She sighed and crept closer to the entrance to the small living room where her family argued. No one was yelling, but their voices were just...heavy with feelings they were trying not to let out, and they both sounded tired.

Fixing her eyes on a painting of a bowl of fruit whose pears were the exact same color as the walls, Cassidy listened.

"It's for the best, Charles," Jessica Edwards told her son.

She sat down heavily on the plaid sofa. Lord, she was just so tired, and angry. She was so angry that every morning she had to pray to God to help her to forgive.

"I can't do it anymore, Charlie. I just can't," she said. "That lunatic killed my boy, and we barely got to mourn him and Victoria because of all the attention from reporters and them saying that he did the killing." She paused to gather herself because thinking about everything made her want to scream.

"She killed my children, Charlie," she said calmly now. "And when the truth finally came out and they arrested her, the crazy woman had to go and kill herself in jail, which brought the reporters back and after my grandbaby…trying to track us down. I think I saw one at the market the other day, though how he knew that we had come here, I'll never know."

Charles Edwards studied his mother. She had always been a beautiful woman who wore her age well, but since the tragedy, as he'd come to think of it, she looked like she'd aged a good ten years. There were lines where there used to be smooth dark skin, her hair had more gray and her once lively brown eyes were now dull and flat. He felt helpless as he sat next to her on the faded sofa.

"I wish there was more I could do, Mama." He took her hand in his. "I thought renting you this house for the summer would help, but maybe not. Why don't you let me hire a housekeeper? That way, you wouldn't have to go into town for groceries and things." He was at a loss as to what else they could do.

Jessica looked at her youngest son with his handsome face and dark worried eyes. This child of hers had always been the one eager to help, to make things better. It was always difficult for him when he learned that there were some things he just couldn't fix. Sighing, she squeezed his hand, kissed his cheek and patted it before releasing him. He and Cassie were all she had left in the world.

"Oh, baby, I know you're trying to help, but there really is no perfect solution for this mess. No housekeeper, okay? I can take care of Cassie and myself, and I won't hide. What about Cassie? She's already withdrawn. She needs to be able to go out, and run and jump and play like normal kids. I won't deprive her of that."

"But that's just the point, Mama. Things aren't normal for Cassie right now. A psychotic girl who fancied herself in love murdered Cassie's parents. Why should we try to act like things are normal when they're not?"

"I know, that, honey, but she walks around here like a ghost. She barely eats anything, and she never talks. The only time I really hear her voice is when she has a nightmare, or on the rare occasion when she asks for something, or answers me."

"What does the therapist say?" Charles asked.

Jessica's lips thinned with disappointment. "A lot of hooey, that's what!"

"Come on, Mama," Charles said and was surprised at the urge he had to smile.

"Don't you, 'come on, Mama' me. I'm serious. All that therapist says is to give her time, and let her mourn in her own way."

Charles shrugged. "It sounds reasonable to me."

"I guess," Jessica said reluctantly. "I'm not being fair to her, I know. I expected her to give us our old Cassie back, you know?" she asked. She huffed out a breath in resignation. "She did say one thing that made sense to me, though. She said if I could get her back in ballet and maybe the theater, those things would help. Which is why going down south makes sense. I could do those things there."

Charles sighed, reluctant to agree to another move. "Are you sure you saw a reporter?"

"I don't know. What I do know is that I don't feel comfortable here. This is not my home, Charles, and Cassie doesn't know the place, either. It's lovely, but I feel as if we've been exiled. I think it's best that I take Cassie and go to Georgia, where I grew up. Cassie loves it there. She's been twice before. We'll go until the end of the summer. Then I'll bring her back to Chicago and register her at a different school. Things should have quieted down by then."

Charles was silent for a while, before finally saying, "All right, Mama. I'll miss the two of you, but if you think it's best." He wanted them with him. He knew that Cassie needed him.

"I can only go with what I feel at this point. That's what we both have to do, seeing as how we've been thrust into the situation."

"Okay, but I want you to think about the other thing. I want Cassie to live with me. I want to take care of her."

Jessica cupped his face with a gentle hand. "I know you do, baby, but we've had this discussion before, Charles. You know that wouldn't be a good idea with all the traveling you do. She needs stability. I think it's best if she stay with me—"

"I love her just as much as you do, Mama. You know that."

"I do, sweetheart. We both love her, but we have to look at what she needs right now, at what's best for her."

"Yes, I know, but —"

"Please don't fight!" Cassie had run into the room and now she threw herself against her grandmother. "I don't like it when you fight. Just send me to heaven, Granny. I want my mommy and daddy!" She looked at her uncle who looked so much like her daddy that looking at him sometimes made her want to cry. With a child's innocent faith, she knew if anyone could get her to heaven, it would be her uncle Cha-cha. He could do just about anything. Her daddy had always said so. And besides that, he couldn't resist her and he spoiled her rotten — her daddy had always said that, too.

She looked hard at him, unaware that the misery in her wide, brown eyes was breaking his heart. "Take me to heaven, Uncle Cha-cha. You can do it, I know you can!"

"Oh, God," Charles moaned in pain as tears filled his eyes. He picked her up and held her tight, pressing his face in her hair. "Oh, my poor baby girl. My own little Sweet C. I can't do that. And even if I could, it would break my heart to lose you, too." When she continued to sob uncontrollably, he looked helplessly over her head at his mother.

Jessica rubbed her back. "It's okay, Cassie. We all miss your mom and dad, and we all wish we could have them back. You know…we can't see them, or be with them the way we want to, but they're looking down and taking care of us — especially you. You can talk to them and they'll hear you, but the biggest thing is that they'll do their best to make sure you're all right. That would be the most important thing to them — to know that you're all right and safe. If you went to heaven, that would mean that you weren't okay, and your parents wouldn't be happy. They'd be so sad."

Cassie didn't answer. She let herself be lulled by her grandmother's soothing hand and soft voice as she began to sing. When her uncle joined in, she snuggled closer into his chest and relaxed into sleep.

Having felt her go boneless, Charles looked down to assure himself that she was asleep. He looked at his mother. "We'll do it your way for now, Mama. She doesn't need any more disruptions."

"Right," Jessica said and leaned over to kiss Cassie's cheek. "I guess in a way it helps that that child killed herself. We don't have to put Cassie through the drama of a trial."

"Yeah, the best thing for her now is to just forget," Charles said. He frowned. "It bothers me though, that we can help her to forget, but the ones who we need to forget, won't."

Jessica knew that he was referring to the press. "I've been thinking about that, son. What do you think of dropping the Edwards off her name? Everyone knows her as Cassidy Edwards, but no one knows her as Cassidy Hamilton. I could do it before I enrolled her in school, and that way she could have a fresh start. Edwards is our family name, and I know it's hard to think about taking it from her," Jessica said when Charles remained quiet. "But we have to do what's best for her, Charles. We can't really think about how we feel right now."

Chapter 2

Twelve years later

Tall, thin and undeniably beautiful, Cassidy put away her last pair of thong underwear and pushed the drawer closed with her hip. She'd outgrown the awkward skinniness, the acne, the braces and the devastation of the loss of her parents. Her uncle and grandmother had done what they thought best, and had tried to erase her memories of that one instant in time that had so irrevocably changed her young life.

Now she was a young woman embarking on a new journey, and she couldn't wait to get started. She'd been adventurous and effervescent as a little girl, and the deaths of her parents had done little to change that. If anything, their deaths hade made her even more daring because that had taught her that anything could happen. She believed in taking her opportunities where she saw them, and going for it—with "it" being whatever challenge she felt was worth her time to take on.

Hugging her arms around herself, she slowly spun in a circle, taking in every detail of her new dormitory room. The room was non-descript with its two beds, two desks and plain walls, but it was hers! She'd done it! She'd actually gotten into Yale University's theater program!

"I did it, Granny," she whispered to her absent grandmother. "I'm at Yale. We worked so hard for this and I just know you're smiling. I can feel it."

Unable to control her excitement any longer, she did a couple of pirouettes across the room, her long brown arms perfectly straight. Humming "Fairies' March" loudly, she enjoyed herself to the fullest, deciding to worry about appearances later. No one was there, so, what the heck? Why not have a little fun?

"I say, rather tall for a fairy, aren't you? Or even a ballerina, for that matter."

Startled, Cassidy stopped mid-turn to smile with unabashed glee at whom she assumed were her roommate and her family. *Well, aren't they a pretty group*, she thought as she took in their wide smiles and blonde hair. She watched as they brought suitcases into the room. "Yeah, it's a bummer, but I am—all seventy inches of me. How do you do? I'm Cassidy Hamilton—you can call me Cassie—and what you've just witnessed is the end result of seven years of training, tragically cut short by disloyal bones that grew and grew without a thought as to how I'd feel about it!" she finished in mock disgruntlement and held out her hand as she walked across the room to greet the newcomers.

"The bloody betrayers!" The owner of the dry voice, a slim girl of about eighteen with twinkling green eyes smiled back and held out her hand. "I'm Esme Carleton and these are my family. Lord and Lady Carleton, and the ever-present, annoying big brother, Anthony."

"You're British. That is too cool!" Cassidy said as she shook hands with each family member. "I've always wanted to visit England, but London especially and the theater district even more so! My grandmother and I were supposed to take a trip two years ago for my sixteenth birthday, but..." Her voice trailed off as she got a good look at Esme's brother when he stepped forward to shake her hand. "I don't want to embarrass you, but good Lord, you are one good-looking man!" She shook his hand vigorously and then released it to playfully fan herself. "Whoo, all of a sudden it's hot in here! Anyone else a little warm?"

Turning to Esme, she said, "I hope you don't mind, but I've already chosen where I'd like to sleep and everything else. See, I got here really early, and I just started unpacking and before I knew it, I was all finished..." She let her voice trail off again as she noticed that none of the Carletons were responding and that their faces were all arrested in varying degrees of astonishment. "What?" she asked the group. "Do I have something in my nose?" She playfully rubbed at her nose.

Esme's laughter was filled with delight. "It's nothing major, mind you, but are you always like this?" When Cassidy only stared at her with a question in her eyes, Esme elaborated. "You're like a speeding locomotive without any brakes. And I'm afraid you've quite shaken the reserve for which we British are so famous. It's absolutely wonderful. Why, just look, you've stumped Tony and I can't remember the last time anyone was able to do that to him. Oh, I do like you!"

Cassidy looked at Tony, whose very gorgeous face was red with embarrassment. She'd done it again—just said whatever was on her mind without any thought to whom she was saying it to "Oh, I'm sorry for embarrassing you, Tony—can I call you that?" Barely waiting for his stiff nod, she continued, "but you have to know how drop dead gorgeous you are. All that wonderful thick hair, that strong jaw and those green, green eyes... Frankly, I can't imagine that you don't have a swelled head over it." Having deliberately stumped Tony again, she turned to Esme, who wasn't even trying to suppress her wild laughter. "And as for your question, Esme, yes, I'm afraid I am like this most of the time. I talk a lot—sometimes too much, I've been told—but I try hard not to offend anyone."

"Yes, I can see that," Esme said skeptically. "We're going to get along famously, you and I."

"I think so too," Cassie said with a smile. "Do you need help with the rest of your things?"

"If you wouldn't mind. Much of my things have been shipped over and haven't arrived yet, but you and I could get the last little bit from the car while my family stay here and discreetly go through your things to see if you're into drugs or anything else so wonderfully corrupting," Esme finished with a grin.

"Esme, dear, do behave," Lady Carleton chided in a mild voice that implied she was used to her daughter's outrageous behavior and was no longer impressed. "It's kind of you to offer to help, Cassidy. Are we too late to meet your family? We were thinking it would be lovely if we all went to supper together."

"I'm afraid I'm it for right now. My uncle Charles is here, but he's down at the registrar's office taking care of some last minute paper work."

"Are your parents not here, then?" Esme asked.

Cassidy winced. This was the part she hated most about meeting new people. Her explanation always made things awkward. "My parents died when I was six. My grandmother raised me and she died last year. So you're stuck with me, myself and I, but the three of us are starving and would love to go to dinner with you," she finished, trying to make a joke.

"Oh, I am sorry," Lord Carleton said.

"It's okay. I've been living on my own since I was 17 — oh, it wasn't so bad," Cassidy hurried to say when she saw the dismay on their faces. "I stayed in Granny's house. My uncle travels a lot, but after my grandmother died, I saw much more of him. Also, her friends sort of took care of me. There wasn't a day that went by that I didn't talk to, or have dinner with one of them." Trying to dispel the mood, she said, "And let me tell you, while they may go a long way toward being good for you, casseroles, stews and their requisite green salads certainly are not without their shortcomings!"

"Oh, don't be too hard on them," Esme said in a voice as dry as dust into the silence, "They're only trying to *health*."

Cassidy looked at her. Esme looked back, they both looked at everyone else who clearly didn't think anything was funny. Cassidy's lips twitched and then the girls were leaning into each other for support as they both fell into helpless fits of laughter.

"God, that was terrible!" Cassidy said with a huge smile. Esme was right: they were going to get along really well.

"I know, but I couldn't help it," Esme admitted as their laughter wound down. "So, you don't live with your uncle, then?" she asked, and flinched when she felt a pinch on her arm. "Ow!" She threw Lady Carleton an accusatory look as she rubbed the stinging spot. "Mum!"

Lady Carleton only looked at her in question.

"Why did you pinch me?" Esme asked.

Lady Carleton rolled her eyes. "It was meant to be a warning, you daft girl. As you can see," Lady Carlton said to Cassie, "our Esme is remarkably quick on her feet."

Cassidy, who had already been chuckling at their antics, laughed even harder. "It's okay, really. I don't mind sharing. In answer to your question, Esme, no, I don't live with my uncle.

He wanted me to, and I thought he was going to make me move in with him when my grandmother died, but then I convinced him to let me stay in my grandmother's house."

"Really? How did you manage that?" Esme asked.

"Well, I'm not really proud of it, but I whined, pouted, sulked and became just a big old horrible brat until he gave in."

As Cassidy and Esme laughed again, Anthony silently speculated just how hard it would be to resist a beauty like Cassidy when she was sulking... and immediately censored his thoughts. *Oh no, old man, don't you dare go down that road. The chit's entirely too young.* Shaking his head, he tried to pay attention to what was being said.

"You'll be having dinner with us tonight, Cassidy," Lord Carleton said. "Don't say no."

"I'm sure Uncle Charles has dinner plans for us, but I don't think he'll mind us all joining in together," Cassidy said.

"Let's ask him when he returns, shall we?"

Cassidy smiled back at Lord Carleton. "Sounds like a plan." She turned to Esme. "Ready to go get the rest of your stuff?" she asked the other girl.

"Yes, let's," Esme said as they walked to the door.

"Poor, little moppet," Lady Carleton said, once the girls had left.

"She's hardly little, Mum," Tony said wryly.

"Don't be difficult, Tony. You know what I mean. She's practically all alone in the world."

"Well, she seems to be handling it well," Tony replied as he wandered over to look out of the window. He watched as Esme and Cassidy exited the building, as carefree as only the really young can be. Cassidy was undeniably a stunner with her dark, intelligent eyes, smooth, dark skin and long, lovely body. As soon as he'd seen her, he'd felt uncomfortable. He was much too old for someone her age and yet, he'd felt that very familiar hot tightening in his stomach that signified lust. It had gotten even worse when she'd laughed and thrown her head back on that long, graceful neck of hers.

God help him, he found himself wondering if the lips of her mound were as lovely as the ones on her face, even as she'd been jabbering on and on about nothing and insulting him with that clever tongue of hers. Swelled head, indeed! He wondered how she'd react if she knew which one of his heads had really swelled! Too bad she was so damn young. If she weren't, he'd definitely pursue her. He sighed, knowing she could be trouble if he let her. It would be rude, but when he came to New York for business, he'd see Esme and not invite Cassidy along. He couldn't chance it.

"You won't forget now, will you Tony?" Lady Carleton asked.

"I'm sorry, Mum," Tony said as he turned from the window. "Forget what?"

"I said that whenever you're in New York City for business, you'll come and get the girls and take them out for a nice dinner or to the theater or something. Naturally, you'll visit Esme to check on her, but now that we know Cassidy's situation, you must never forget to include her in your plans. I'm sure she'll be perfectly lovely company."

"She'll be a bloody nuisance, is what she'll be," Tony growled in a low voice of disagreement.

"Anthony Carleton, why ever would you say such a thing?"

"You don't need a divining rod to see it, Mum. She and Esme together are going to be royal terrors. They're already getting on as if they were a bloody house afire."

"Yes, and it isn't that wonderful?" Lady Carleton asked. "I was worried for our Esme being so far away, and I still am, but now that she's met Cassidy and they get along so well, I feel a bit better. As for Cassidy, the poor girl probably needs a kindred spirit. It's lucky for all of us that Esme and she like each other. After all, both of them could have been stuck with someone completely unsuitable to their personalities. They've clearly got the same sort of senses of humor. So, you won't forget to include Cassidy will you, dear boy?"

Tony wanted to object, he really did, but one look at his mother's face told him that resistance would be futile. She had that "I must be obeyed" glint in her eyes. He sighed again. "No, Mum, I won't." Bugger it! Thirty-two years old and still hesitant to disappoint his mother!

Chapter 3

"I'll get it, Es," Cassidy yelled out to her roommate in response to the knock on their apartment door. They'd graduated to apartment living after two years of living in the dormitories. The apartment was small, but cozy, and decorated in the bright reds and blues that the girls preferred. Each girl had her own bedroom.

"I'm not expecting anyone. Are you?" Esme yelled from her room.

"No," Cassidy responded, bending over to pick up a large pillow that had caused her to trip. She tossed it on the futon as she approached the door. "Hey, maybe it's that cute guy I met a couple of days ago. Maybe he's come to take me away from the doldrums of college life," she finished dramatically with a chuckle as she pulled the door open. The laughter caught in her throat when she saw who was on the other side. *Oh Lord*, she thought frantically as she felt her stomach drop.

"Hello, Cass," Tony said with a grin. When she just stood there looking at him, he frowned and said, "Are you going to let me in or are you too disappointed that I'm not that cute bloke from a couple of days ago?" He chuckled when she hurried to step back and open the door wider.

Cassidy felt her stomach stop its descent only to clinch and heat up at the sound of his deep laughter. God, she could just eat him alive! She cleared her throat instead. "Hi, Tony." She gestured him inside. "Uh…I didn't expect to see you at all this trip." She closed the door behind him. She didn't know what to do with her hands so she stuffed them in the pockets of her cutoffs. She cleared her throat again. "Umm, is Es expecting you?"

"No, she isn't," Tony said as he took his coat off and hung it from one of four wooden hooks. Trying to ignore her nervousness, he walked further into the living room. He knew her edginess stemmed from her suddenly finding herself attracted to him a couple of months before. If asked, he could pinpoint the exact day and time it had happened. She didn't know that he found her just as attractive and he wanted to keep it that way. Otherwise, he'd forget her age, his age, all his ethics and bloody hell, probably even *his own name* as he laid her down and took what he wanted. He wouldn't let her up until he'd gotten his fill and from the way his cock reacted whenever she was around, that wouldn't be for a long time.

Tony sighed and put his briefcase down. These visits to see his sister were difficult to make since Cassidy was there and getting even more beautiful and fascinating as she got older. He waited for her to sit on the futon before taking his own seat in the lone chair. "One of my meetings ended earlier than I expected and I thought I'd pop over to see her one last time before heading back home."

"Oh, okay," Cassidy said and folded her legs beneath her in the chair so he wouldn't see the chipped polish on her toes. *Damn it, I knew I should have gotten a pedicure this morning!*

Tony dragged his eyes away from those long brown legs of hers. They seemed to go on forever and the miniscule pair of shorts did very little to stop them. He felt sweat trickle down his back as he thought about how perfect they'd feel wrapped tightly around his waist. He took out his handkerchief and wiped his brow. "It's awfully warm in here, Cass. Can you turn down the heat?"

Cassidy grimaced. "Sorry, Tony, but the radiator's on the fritz. We've called the landlord and he promised he'd take care of it, but he hasn't yet."

"How long has it been?"

"A couple of days. Hopefully, he'll come tomorrow. I could take your suit jacket if you want."

"Yes, thanks," Tony said as he stood and removed the jacket.

Cassidy stood as well, and walked over to him. She took the jacket from him, her mouth filling with water as his scent drifted from his body toward her. "You always smell so good, Tony," she whispered.

"Ah, thanks," he replied, feeling uncomfortable with her nearness. The heat she was generating made him take a step back. "I'll take that, Cass," he said and reached for the jacket. "You shouldn't be waiting on me." He took the jacket and made his escape back to the entryway.

Cassidy watched him, a smile dawning on her face. He wanted her! She could tell. *Well, it should certainly make things easier*, she thought as she took her seat again. She'd been trying for months to build up her courage to approach him with this new attraction she had to him. She didn't know if she was in love, but she did know that she woke up thinking about him, thought about him at least once during the day, and fell asleep with him on her mind. She thought she could spend every moment of the day with him if he allowed it. *Either I'm in love or I'm on the road to becoming a stalker*, she thought with a smirk.

"So, Cass," Tony said as he sat back down. "Es told me you missed dinner in the city the other night because you had a class. What are you taking so late at night?"

"It isn't that late. It starts at seven and it's twice a week. It's just a set design class. I couldn't fit it into my schedule during the day, so I took the night class."

"And just how late do you get out of this class?" Tony asked with a frown. "How do you get home safely?"

"Stop acting like a big brother, Tony," Cassidy chided softly as she looked straight at him. "Es is in the other room, not out here," she reminded him and leaned forward urgently before saying, "I'm not related to you in any way, shape or form, you know." Cassidy hoped he was picking up what she was putting down. Subtlety had never been her strong suit, but she'd try it with him.

Tony lifted a brow and almost smiled. So, she'd figured out he was attracted to her, had she? And now she was throwing down the gauntlet. He chuckled and shook his head. *Cheeky baggage.* Time to nip it in the bud. "No, Cass, you're not related, but you are my baby sister's best friend. You're like family and as long as the two of you are in each other's lives, I'm going to treat you as such. I'd never forgive myself if something happened that I could have prevented just by asking a simple question. I'd ask the same question of Esme. Now be a good girl, puss, and tell me how you get home safely when leaving your late night class?"

Cassidy slouched back against the futon again, frowning as she thought about what he'd said. He was as clear as a bell: he wasn't going to get involved with her because she was like family. Maybe she'd read him wrong, after all. She looked over at him when he cleared his throat. He still had that one sexy brow lifted as he waited for her answer. She studied him for a moment and decided to give it one more shot. She just couldn't be wrong about this. She could practically *feel* his attraction for her.

She tried to think of something to say that would trip him up. Nervously clearing her own throat, she took a huge gamble. "But I'm *not* Esme, Tony, and I'm not your sister, or your responsibility. I wonder…would you have a different response if I were…uh…well…if I were sitting in your lap?"

Tony had been sitting forward, and now he jerked back in stunned surprise, his mind helplessly conjuring up the image of her in his lap. His eyes narrowed and words to describe her went through his head. Outrageous, cheeky, wicked, sneaky, gorgeous, sexy, maddening, going-to-be-the-death-of-me, brilliant, beautiful, little witch! "You're way out of line, Cassidy," he said in repressive tones.

Cassidy studied him some more, and making up her mind, she said, "No." She paused, and mortification keeping her from looking at him, said to her lap, "I'm not. I think you want to be with me as much as I want to be with you." The last came out in a rush because she knew if she didn't hurry and get it said, she'd never say it. As it was, the only thing keeping her in the room with him was her desire for him.

Tony's breath came out in an angry hiss. "Stop this, Cassidy. Immediately. I don't play games with little girls."

"I'm not a little girl —" Cassie tried to say.

"You are in my book," Tony told her as he tried to ignore the hurt he saw in her eyes. "Now, do tell me how you get home at night after your class."

Cassie was thrown off guard by the switch in topics. "I manage," she mumbled around a pout.

"Cass," Tony drew her name out in warning. Damn it, was

there nothing about her that wasn't sexy? Even when she sulked, she was erotically appealing.

Cassidy was too upset and blamed him enough that she didn't want to give into him. "What difference does it make? The reality is that I'm not your family, so I give you permission not to worry," she finished and was surprised that she had to struggle not to cry from crushing disappointment.

"Cass," Tony said her name again, softly this time. He waited for her to look up at him and felt his stomach tighten at the dejected look on her face. "Please just tell me how you get home at night. I'll worry if you don't."

Cassidy sulked a little more before answering. "We do have campus security, you know. And besides, I'm not the only one who takes a late class. There are always plenty of people out."

"All right, then," Tony said softly. He wanted to say more, come clean about his attraction, but knew it would be best if she thought there were no possibilities of the two of them being together. He sighed. He certainly wished there was. What more could he ask for? She was intelligent, funny, clever, beautiful and sexy. It was too bad she wasn't at least five to ten years older. He should be so lucky. He sighed again, feeling almost as miserable as she looked.

"So, Cassie, who was at the—Tony? What on earth are you doing here?" Esme asked when she walked into the living room.

Tony stood and accepted her hug. "I had a meeting to end early, so I thought I'd drop in on you. I won't be back here again for months."

Tony ran the family business and had finally convinced their board of directors to do more business in the States. As a consequence, he found himself in New York every couple of months.

"Care to go out to dinner with your big brother?" He turned to Cassidy. "You too, Cass, especially since you didn't make it the other night."

"Oh, that would be fabulous, Tony!" Esme said excitedly. "Now we don't have to look forward to boxed macaroni and cheese for dinner. Come on, Cassie. Let's get changed."

"No," Cassidy said. "You two go on without me. I think I'll just stay in and study for an exam I have on Monday."

"Oh," Esme said in disappointment. "Can't it wait?"

"No, it's okay," she said and rose. "I'm not doing so well in the class and the extra studying will do me some good."

"Oh, you're a straight A student and you know it, Cassie!" Esme chastised in surprise. "Don't you want to come out with us?"

"You know that normally I would, Es," Cassidy said, misery choking each word. She tried not to bolt to her bedroom. She was humiliated, but more than that, it really hurt to know that she didn't have a snowball's chance in hell with Tony. "I would just rather stay in tonight." She walked around them and toward her bedroom. At her door she said, "You guys have fun tonight. Safe trip back, Tony." She disappeared inside.

Tony frowned as he watched her go. *The chit really looked upset*, he thought in surprise. He was tempted to go after her and explain, but decided against it for the same reason as before. It was better not to let her know.

Cassidy lay on her bed, staring at the ceiling and thinking about her reaction to Tony's rejection. Without a doubt, it was strong and over the top, and it surprised the hell out of her. She hadn't known that rejection could be so devastating. It wasn't like she hadn't ever experienced it before; it was just that she'd never felt it so strongly before. This pain was so deep it was almost visceral.

She rolled over onto her side and clutched her pillow in her arms. "What am I going to do now?" she wondered aloud. She was wholly unfamiliar with this, and felt despair creeping in. "I'm in love with him," she murmured. "Somehow, I just know that I am. But how can it be? I mean, I know him, but I don't *know him*, know him. At best, I see him six or seven times a year, and that's only when Esme's around." She looked up at the ceiling again. "But it's got to be love. Who else but a fool in love would embarrass herself like I did tonight? His lap?" she whispered in disbelief. "My God, I can't believe I said that!" Moaning in humiliation, she covered her face with her hands.

Her eyes went to the frame on her bedside table. She reached out and picked it up, studying the old picture of the pretty brown-skinned woman and handsome dark-skinned man. "I wonder if the two of you knew right away. Maybe you did, and maybe that's where I get it from, huh?" Kissing each image in turn, she lay back on the bed and hugged the picture to her chest.

She sighed. "God! What am I going to do about it? Especially since he's already made it clear that he wouldn't touch me with a ten-foot pole?"

A loud knock on the front door made her jump and she frowned impatiently as she climbed from bed. "I'm coming!" she yelled in response to the knocking as she approached the door. "Yes? Who is it?"

"It's your favorite uncle."

"Uncle Cha-cha?" Cassie asked in surprise and excitement as she rushed to unlock the door. Opening the door, she launched herself into his arms, suddenly loving him so much and so gratefully that she felt it would overwhelm her. "Uncle Cha-cha," she said with relief as she hugged him tight. "I'm so glad you're here!"

"Okay," Charles Edwards said in confusion at such an eager greeting. He shut the door behind them. "To what do I owe such enthusiasm, Sweet C?"

"I'm just glad you're here, that's all," Cassie answered and held on tighter. She greedily inhaled his familiar, comforting scent. "I really missed you."

"I missed you, too, Cassie," Charles said as he released her, and tried to step back so he could look into her face.

Cassie's hold tightened. "No, not yet. Just a little longer," she said, taking comfort in his love. It was a definite balm to her bruised heart.

Worried now, Charles wrapped her in his arms. "What's the matter, baby?"

"Nothing, everything," Cassie murmured. "I'll be fine in a minute. I just need you to hold me for a bit."

"All right," Charles agreed as he felt her desperation. "I'm here for you."

"Oh, Uncle Charles," Cassie said and smiled because his response was so typical of the man he was. "You're so good to me. You're the best uncle in the whole world," she teased before kissing his cheek. She stepped back to look at him.

Charles frowned, and used his handkerchief to wipe tears from her face. "I thought I felt tears. What's going on, Cassidy Marie?"

Cassie took the proffered handkerchief and finished cleaning her face. She shrugged. "Oh, nothing. I've just had my heart broken, that's all. Would you like some coffee?"

The last had been said over her shoulder, and Charles caught up to her on her way to the galley-styled kitchen. He was confused. "Oh, is that all," he quipped. He took off his coat and laid it across one of four stools they'd placed along the waist-high counter. He watched her move around the kitchen getting the makings for coffee. "I don't recall your mentioning anything about being in love when I was here last month, or during the numerous telephone conversations we've had since," he teased, but looked at her sternly.

"I'm serious, Uncle Charles," Cassie said. "My heart is broken."

"Since when?" he asked doubtfully.

"Since about half an hour ago..." she trailed off when he smiled at her. "Well, it's true!" she insisted when his smile only got bigger. "Quit that, Uncle! I know it sounds silly, but it is true! My heart is broken, and Tony Carleton did the breaking right here in this apartment, not more than thirty minutes ago."

All vestiges of humor left Charles' face at that. "You'd better be talking about a fellow student because I know you're not talking about the only Tony Carleton that I know of. You're not talking about the Tony Carleton who's your roommate's brother. You can't possibly be talking about the Tony Carleton who's the president and CEO of Carleton International. I know you can't be referring to the Tony Carleton who is much too old to even be looking at you, let alone breaking your heart." He paused and took a deep breath because he could feel a shout coming on. "Now, Cassie...sweetheart. Be a good girl, and tell your uncle— who promised your sainted grandmother on her deathbed that he would keep you safe, and who would gladly slay dragons for you, if necessary—that that's *not* the Tony Carleton you're talking about."

Uh-oh, Cassie thought with a grimace. Once, when she was eleven, her uncle had had to ask her if the neighborhood bully had been telling him the truth when he'd said she'd kicked him between the legs and told him that she was making it her business to be his very own nutcracker. Charles had had a hopeful, yet pained, look on his face—like that of a puppy looking for a treat and hoping against hope that he didn't get a kick in the face instead. *Man*. She'd really *hated* having to tell him yes.

And now, he had that same look on his face again.

She closed her eyes to shut him out for a moment. Such naked hope was almost painful to look at. She opened her eyes again and tried a bolstering smile. Better to make it quick. "Uncle? Have you ever heard of that song, *Age Ain't Nothing but a Number*? It makes a good point—"

His aggrieved sigh was strong enough to send a sail boat flying, and she lifted her mug to her mouth, now trying to hide a smile that wanted to laugh.

"Oh, for the love of God, Cassidy Marie," Charles said mildly and took a sip from his own coffee. "You never make anything easy, do you?"

"I can't help who I fall in love with, Uncle Charles," she protested.

Charles sighed. He knew from her face that she was serious and really thought she was in love. Thought, hell—knowing Cassidy, it was fact. If she said she was in love, then she was in love. "Well, tell me what Tony says about it."

"Oh, he doesn't know that I'm in love with him."

"Then what do you mean he broke your heart?"

"Because he did. He just as good as told me that there could be nothing between us."

"So he doesn't feel the same way you do, huh?" Charles asked.

"No, it's not that. I know he's attracted to me, but he doesn't want to do anything about it because I'm Esme's friend."

"That's what he said?"

"Basically, yes. That, and that I'm a child," she muttered, all but seeing red as she thought of that particular comment.

Charles shrugged, trying to hide his relief. "Then maybe it's for the best. After all, you can't force the man."

Cassie chuckled. He was so obvious, and so protective. She had always been able to count on her uncle Cha-cha, always— even before the deaths of her parents. She loved him immensely. She studied him, wondering for the millionth time why he hadn't married. He was such a *good* man, one of the finest people she knew. And if that weren't enough, he was also good looking, quite literally fitting the bill for tall, dark and handsome. At forty-five, he'd been all over the world as a travel writer, was well educated, kind, and urbane. He was also the closest family she had, so she worried about him. "Why haven't you married Della, Uncle Charles?" Cassie referred to his long-time girlfriend.

Startled by the question, Charles frowned. "Why? What brought that on?"

Cassie shrugged. "I don't know. All this talk about me and my love life made me think about yours, I guess. You've been with Della for a long time, yet you guys aren't married. Why not? You can't mean to be a bachelor forever, you know," she teased.

"It might interest you to know, little miss, that I'm not the one holding out on marriage." He laughed when her mouth fell open in disbelief. "Yes, as hard as it is to believe, not everybody thinks that I'm the great catch that you think I am. And no," he said firmly when he saw she was going to say something, "I'm not going to explain. It's none of your business. Della loves me, and I love her. That's all you need to know. Let's get back to you and Tony."

"But—"

"No buts, Cassidy Marie. Take my advice and leave the man alone. I don't want to see you get hurt."

Cassie swallowed the questions she had about Della and said, "Don't worry about me, Uncle Cha-cha. You know me, if something is worth fighting for, then I fight for it. Win or lose, I have to go for it."

Chapter 4

Cassidy took another look around her now-empty living room. Two years living in the place had seemed to fly by, and now she and Esme had graduated and were moving out. She looked over at Tony, studying him with hooded, lust-filled eyes as he taped down one of the moving boxes. God, but he was one of the sexiest men she'd ever seen. For two years she'd been trying to get in his pants, or more accurately, get him to get in her pants. And for two years he'd been rejecting her—sometimes cruelly so.

But she'd never stopped trying. She would have if she hadn't seen and felt his eyes on her almost every time they were within vicinity of one another. He was attracted to her and she'd seen lust in his eyes more than once before he'd quickly masked it. He'd almost had her fooled that night two years before when she'd approached him, but then he'd slipped up on his next visit and she'd caught him staring at her mouth. And the battle to win Tony was on again.

She'd wondered why he was fighting it. After all, she was perfectly willing to lie down and spread herself wide open for him, both physically and emotionally.

Her attraction to him had just sneaked up on her. She'd always thought he was a gorgeous man, but she'd also always thought of him as her best friend's brother. But shortly after her twentieth birthday she'd opened the door and he'd stood there in a dark gray suit with pencil-thin stripes holding a leather brief case, and smelling delicious and subtly expensive. Lust had hit her so hard that she'd been unable to speak for a full minute.

From that day forward, she'd thought of no one else but him.

She'd had a boyfriend that she'd been seeing for more than six months and she'd broken things off because she'd only wanted Tony. And a year ago, after so many rejections from him, she'd wondered aloud to Esme if it was because she was black and he white.

Esme had laughed. *Uproariously.* "Oh, please! Dear big brother has possibly shagged every ethnicity of woman one could imagine."

Cassie certainly hadn't found anything funny. "Well, what's his problem, then? Is it because I'm American and he's British?"

Esme had looked at her in stunned amazement. "Wait, hold on a tic," she'd said urgently and made a show of looking at the wall calendar. "Oh, no, it is the twentieth century. For a minute there, I thought it was the 1700s and you bloody upstart colonials were whining over the tea tax and wanting to start a war, in which case, there's no way in hell my brother would get involved with you!"

"Be serious, Es," Cassidy had implored impatiently.

Esme had snorted. "Well, I will if you will," she'd chided in that crisp, British accent of hers. "Of course Tony doesn't care that you're an American. I dare say that's the last thing he'd be concerned about. It's your age, you silly wanker. Doubtless, he's uncomfortable with the age difference. At last count there were fourteen years between you. Add to that the fact that you're my best mate and he's known you since your were eighteen, and I can guarantee that he'll never come near you.

"Ever since I can remember, Tony has had this annoying habit of always doing the right thing. And in his mind, dating you would be the absolute wrong thing." Esme had shaken her white blonde head in pity before saying, "No, dear girl. I'm afraid you'll forever be sopping wet if you wait for Tony to quench his thirst on you."

"We'll see about that," Was the only thing Cassidy had said.

"Going to fight him for it, are you?" Esme had asked.

Now Cassidy didn't look so sure of herself. "Yes, but I don't know how," she'd admitted. *Why did he have to be so difficult?* "It would be different if there were some outside opposition, but it's Tony himself."

"Just keep throwing yourself at him, as you've been doing,"

Esme had suggested and had snorted again as Cassidy tried to look innocent and confused. *"Oh, please.* Don't think I haven't noticed how you *accidentally* brush up against him whenever he's here. And what about the time you came out of your room practically naked and tried to act surprised by his visit? A visit we'd both known about for an entire week."

Cassidy had snickered, still feeling her embarrassment over the situation. "I wasn't practically naked—"

"No? If bikini bottoms and two hands for covering aren't practically naked, then—"

"I was on my way to the pool—"

"Then," Esme had repeated over her protests, "I'd like to know what dictionary you're using! And then for you to drop your hands and run and throw your arms around his neck in greeting—" Breaking off, Esme had shaken her head in disbelief. "I dare say the poor dear didn't know whether to hug you or maul you!"

"You don't think it was too much, do you?" Cassidy had asked. She still couldn't believe she'd had the guts to do it. "I mean, do you think he thinks I'm a slut?"

"No, I'm sure not. If he did, he'd tell Mum and Dad that I shouldn't be allowed to room with you. Besides, he has his needs and you have yours. We're all adults here."

"True."

"Speaking of which, have you actually had sex with Roger, yet?"

After being rejected so often by Tony, Cassidy had decided to try to get on with her life. She'd started dating Roger several months before. "If you mean the actual act, then no."

"Then what is all that noise I've heard coming from your room?"

Shocked, Cassie had had to open and close her mouth several times before she could think coherently. "Oh, my God, Es! Have you been listening?"

"I've hardly had to actively listen. You two make so much noise, I could be partially deaf, and still hear you."

Cassie had closed her eyes in mortification. "God, I'm so sorry!"

Esme had waved away her apology. "Don't be. So, it's just

been oral, then?"

"Yeah. I'm just not ready to have actual intercourse, at least not with Roger."

"You're saying that you are with Tony?"

"Yes. I feel bad about this, but sometime when Roger's, you know...going down on me... I'm thinking about Tony doing it."

"Good God, you've got it bad, Cassie!"

"That's just what I've been trying to tell you! I'm in love with him," Cassie said in exasperation.

"Are you sure?"

"To borrow one of your favorite terms: Quite."

"Cass!"

Cassidy looked over at Tony with a secret smile of memories from a year ago. She could tell he'd called her name more than once, and she looked down at the box she was taping up. "I'm sorry, Tony, darling. I was daydreaming. Did you need something?"

Yes. You spread eagle with my face buried where we'd both enjoy it, Tony longed to say as he stared at her pretty face. "I've told you before, Cass; don't call me 'darling,'" he reprimanded.

She tried to look contrite, but he knew it was all an act as she said, "Yes, Tony...baby." The last word was whispered as she looked down again, but he heard it anyway.

Tony narrowed his eyes at her and decided to ignore the endearment. God was surely playing a joke on him. Cassidy had only gotten more intelligent, more beautiful and sexier over the years. She just happened to be fourteen years younger than he and his sister's best friend to boot. Yes, it was a fucking laugh riot! Not only had he had to see her at least six times a year when he was in the States on business and visited Esme, but now she was coming back to England with them and staying in the family home. Indefinitely. Ha, ha, very funny.

For at least the thousandth time since he'd been there, his eyes traveled over her body, which was encased in a thin, white, sleeveless T-shirt sans bra, and one of those bloody mini skirts all the young girls liked to wear. Hers was particularly short and it played havoc with his body, showing off her yards of legs as it did. As he stood looking at her, her nipples slowly hardened until they were pressing against her shirt, he heard her breath catch and watched as she licked her full lips. He moaned low in his throat. God, she was killing him!

Cassie pressed her legs tightly together and moaned softly. "*Tony*?" The bare whisper was both questioning and pleading.

It went through him like a jolt of lightening. A hard breath shuddered through his lips, and he could swear he smelled her arousal. He resisted the plea he saw when she raised those dark eyes to look at him and licked her lips again. He needed to teach her a lesson, he decided. She didn't know how dangerous a game she was playing. Quickly making up his mind to show her, he looked around to make sure neither his parents or sister were back from the rental van, and he surged across the room and took hold of her before he could change his mind. Trapping her against the wall, he looked into her eyes. "You're playing with fire, Cass," he warned her softly and distractedly as he let his eyes wander her face. "You know that, don't you?"

Cassie was more than a little surprised and felt a little thrill when he cornered her. She leaned her head against the wall so she could look at him and wondered if he could feel her heartbeat hammering against her chest. Her eyes widened as she took in what he was saying. A bit nervous now, she licked her lips. Meekly, with down-swept lashes, she whispered, "Yes, Tony."

Chapter 5

Tony swore softly when all his hand encountered when he touched her was skin. Damn it! Even an honest man didn't stand a chance.

"Naughty girl," he chided. "Was this little shirt and half skirt for my benefit?"

"Yes, Tony. Just for you." Cassidy nodded and struggled to breathe. Her breaths were coming fast and labored. She pressed her naked thighs tighter together, loving the feel of skin against skin.

"You won't wear it for anyone else, will you, love," Tony demanded as he gently pinched her nipple through her shirt. He watched her eyes widened again in surprise and then slowly close. His breath blew on her lips as he pressed closer.

Breath hitching from the fierce sensation, Cassidy moaned low in her throat. "Nnnn…" she licked her lips and tried again… "No, Tony, I won't. I promise I won't."

"Have you saved yourself for me, then? Are you all mine?" he whispered, and pressed kisses to the sides of her mouth, while his fingers now played with both of her nipples.

"I'm all yours, Tony, yes," Cassidy moaned and her eyes slowly closed when his mouth closed over her nipple through her shirt. "And yes, I did save myself for you. Well, mostly…" she trailed off.

Stunned, Tony looked up at her. Was she saying she was still a virgin? She couldn't be. This was the same girl who'd so brazenly hugged him wearing nothing but bikini bottoms! He cleared his throat. "Uh, mostly?"

Still caught up, Cassidy nodded. "Yes. I've

never…um…technically, I'm still a virgin."

Holy fuck, Tony thought and tried with all his might to suppress the pure male satisfaction he felt. It didn't work. An arrogant, "I'm-the-man" grin spread across his face. *I suppose beating my chest with my fists is completely out of the question*, he thought as he raised her shirt up to feast on her breasts. He clamped his teeth on her nipple, plying it with his tongue, and ignoring her shocked, pleasured cry. When she clutched his knee between her legs and mindlessly rubbed her cleft against it, he opened his mouth wider, sucking her nipple and more of her breast into his mouth.

"Ah! Tony, that feels so good! More…please!" Cassie was frantic.

Tony raised his head to look down at her. "Do you like that, love?" Raising her skirt up, he pushed his jeans-covered, ever-hardening penis between her legs, watching as she gasped, moaned and widened her stance to accommodate him.

"Ah, y-y-yes, Tony, I do!"

Growling low in his throat, Tony bent his head and took her mouth with his own. Immediately pulling her tongue into his mouth, he sucked it hard as he slipped his hands under her thighs and lifted her legs until they were wrapped around his upper thighs. Capturing her moan in his mouth, he kissed her ravenously, moaning his own pleasure before releasing her mouth. "How wet are you for me? Open," he commanded.

Shocked again, Cassidy could only stare at him for a moment. "Oh, God, I can't," she said, not knowing *how* she knew what he wanted, but knowing nonetheless. Her fingers dug into his shoulders as she slammed herself up and down against him.

"Yes, you can," Tony insisted. "Open yourself for me."

Whimpering, Cassidy released one of his shoulders to fit her hand between her legs. With difficulty, she pushed her wet, slippery thong aside. Her fingers brushed her clit and she whimpered again. "Hurry, Tony, please," she begged him.

Tony gave her his hand and she took his fingers, inserting one inside her grasping cleft. "Tony!"

"Good girl," Tony said, taking her mouth with his again as her vaginal muscles clasped his finger and she furiously rode it. The wet slick membranes milking his finger made him want to be balls deep inside of her.

Excitement and arousal making her breath come faster and harder, Cassidy screamed in his mouth as the pressure built within her. Throwing her head back against the wall, she let out a long moan when his thumb started rubbing her clitoris. "Yessss, Tony. Please don't stop." Gripping his arms with her nails, she bit her lip before saying, "I want you, Tony. Please...."

Tony felt his cock harden more as he watched her start to succumb. Her response to his touch was enough to make him lose sight of his original plan and he reached down to open his zipper.

Cassidy shamelessly rutted herself on his finger as she reached for orgasm. "Yes, yes, yes..." she whispered urgently. "Oh God, Tony, please... I need more."

"Damn!" She heard him whisper and then his fingers were gone. Cassidy opened her eyes to look at him in shock and bewilderment.

"Sorry, love," he said apologetically. "The family's coming."

"I don't care, Tony! *Please*." She was almost in tears.

"Shush, puss," Tony said softly as he caressed her and then regretfully lifted her off him. "It will be all right. Run to the loo and fix yourself up."

Legs shaky, Cassidy still clutched his arms. "But, Tony," she said plaintively. "It's not fair," she whispered, finally hearing what he'd heard — Esme's voice. She guessed they could count themselves lucky that Esme talked particularly loud and that the elevator was down the hall and around the corner. But she didn't. "God!" she moaned, grabbing his hand and pushing it up her skirt again where he cupped her. "I'm so close Tony! All I need is a little more time." She trapped his hand between her thighs and rubbed against it.

Angry with himself for touching her in the first place, Tony helplessly caressed her one last time, removed his hand and shook her impatiently. "It's not going to happen, Cass — not now and not ever. This was a mistake. Now do as I say and go to the loo to collect yourself!"

But Cassidy didn't move as she took deep breaths to calm herself. She folded her arms and straightened her stance with a mutinous expression on her face. "What do you mean, it's never going to happen? Explain yourself."

"There's nothing to explain. You're twenty-two and I'm thirty-six. I shouldn't have touched you. Now go to the washroom if you want to avoid being embarrassed in front of my family." When she still remained, he reluctantly said, "We'll speak of this later. Now go!" Possessively slipping his hand up her skirt and palming her butt, he pushed her towards the bathroom.

"You bet your ass we'll speak of it later," Cassie warned just before she surprised him and cupped his still hardened penis. "And I'm not the only one who should worry about embarrassment. And while you're doing that, imagine me in the shower finishing myself off. My fingers aren't as thick as yours, so it won't be as filling, but they'll get the job done!" Satisfied from the stunned expression on his face that she'd given him something to think about, she walked angrily to the bathroom. Two could play this game.

Watching her leave, Tony's mind filled with an image of her naked and in the shower. A vivid image of her leaning on the tiled wall with her firm ass jiggling as she rode her fingers popped into his mind and it was all he could do to restrain himself from breaking the bathroom door down to have at her. The chit would be his downfall; he knew it without a doubt. After a few seconds, he looked expectantly toward the door, waiting for his family's arrival. Finally hearing footsteps again, he quickly bent down to pick up the last box and turned just as his sister came through the door.

"Room for more?" He nodded his head toward the box.

"Just," Esme said. "I've just introduced Mum to the new tenant down the hall. She's a British export, like myself. Isn't it lucky her flat is right down the hall from this one, so it saved us time for introductions?" she finished with a knowing smirk, causing Tony to think she was aware of what had happened between Cassidy and he.

His suspicions were confirmed when she cocked her head towards the bathroom as if she were listening to something and said in a voice full of mock concern, "Oh dear, is Cassie having *another* shower? I swear that girl is forever getting…wet."

Tony longed to take her over his knee as he'd done when she

was a child. Instead, he raised a brow in question and said, "Yes, well that's her problem, isn't it? I'm afraid I haven't the remedy for her symptoms." He allowed his own smirk to appear when he saw that Esme got his meaning quite clearly.

"Whatever are the two of you on about?" asked Lady Carleton. "We have to hurry. Dad's waiting in the car."

"Nothing, Mum," Esme said. "I think Tony has the last box and we're all set. Once Cassie finishes in the loo, we can hit the road."

"'Hit the road,' indeed. I do wish you'd cease and desist with the American colloquialisms, darling. They are one of the many things I regret about your attending university here. You did pick up such dreadful language."

"I hope I'm not listed among those things you regret about Esme attending school here, Lady C.," Cassidy said with a smile as she exited the bathroom, clutching something in her hand.

"Darling girl, of course not," Lady Carleton took Cassidy's free hand and smiled at her. "You were one of the bright spots of this whole ordeal. I'm so proud of you and Es, both of you graduating at the top of your class. How marvelous!"

Cassidy kissed her cheek. "Thanks, Lady C. and thanks for making me feel like a part of your family."

"Nonsense! You are a part of the family and have been ever since we met you that first day in the dormitory."

"I'll just take this down and wait in the lorry," Tony said to the room at large and ignored the liquid brown eyes he could feel burning a hole through the back of his shirt.

"Wait, Tony!" Cassidy called. "There's one more thing I found in the bathroom. I don't want to leave anything behind."

Tony stopped and turned. "Well?"

"Catch!" Cassidy said with a mischievous smile on her face.

Tony watched in horror as something small and white came flying through the air. He hoped that it wasn't what he knew it was! His horrified gaze searched for his mother, and he silently thanked God that she was occupied in the kitchen. Leaning against the door for balance and holding the box with one arm on his thigh, he reached out and snatched the material out of the air. His nose told him he was correct before his eyes actually confirmed it. Her thong! The little wretch had tossed him her knickers, which were newly wet and carried her musky scent of arousal. Tamping the urge to raise the crotch to his face and lap at it like a hungry dog, he looked over at her in reprimand. It had all taken a matter of seconds.

Hands clasped behind her back, Cassidy shrugged innocently, but he could see the lascivious intent in her eyes quite clearly. "Just put them anywhere. Since the boxes are all closed, maybe they'll fit in your pocket. I'll get them from you later."

"What are they, dear?" Lady Carleton asked as she walked out of the kitchen.

"Oh, just my...socks," Cassidy said, and hoped her blush wasn't too intense. Throwing her thong had been a reckless idea to begin with, but it just hadn't seemed so at the time. *Well, in for a penny, in for a pound,* she told herself, and cleared her throat before saying, "They've gotten a bit wet and I don't want to put them on after showering and all. I decided that I'd much rather go bare."

Tony's ears only focused on that last word and in his mind's eye he saw her naked mound just as clearly as his disbelieving eyes had seen the thong. His eyes went immediately to that special area and traveled back up to her face with a questioning look in them. Her slight nod had his breath coming in pants and his eyes promised her retribution. Dear God, the little wench was certainly getting her own back for the lesson he'd tried to teach her.

"Mum, maybe we should look around to make sure we haven't left anything else as innocuous as Cassie's socks," Esme said with an astute smirk that only Tony could see as he was facing everyone in the room. "Perhaps we could check the bedrooms?"

"Good idea," Lady Carleton agreed.

"You don't mind holding those...socks for me, do you Tony?"

Ignoring her for the moment, Tony stuffed the thong in his pocket, dropped the box and waited for his mother and sister to leave the room. Once the last back had turned the corner, he looked over at Cassidy. "Come here," he said in a low voice.

Cassidy's eyes widened, but anticipation had her obeying him. "Yes, Tony?" she whispered when she was standing directly in front of him.

"You're playing with fire, you know that, don't you?"

"Yes, Tony, you already said, but I wouldn't mind getting burned," she admitted, peeking up at him through her lashes. "Not if it's by you."

"Behave, Cass." His voice was practically begging her. "I told you that a relationship between us is impossible."

"Well, I don't agree," she said sincerely. "We're both consenting adults and can do whatever we want, as long as it's legal."

Tony sighed. Now was not the time to argue with her about a relationship; there was a more pressing concern. "You need to put on your knickers. I'm going to go down and fetch—"

"Why should I? I like being naked for *you* and thinking about you thinking about me makes me feel all shivery inside," she said and her eyes widened when the thought did make her shiver.

No longer able to control himself, Tony slipped his hands beneath her skirt and encountering naked flesh, caressed and patted her butt as he pulled her closer. *Jesus*, he thought as his eyes fell closed and he caressed her some more, *the teacher has been taught*. "I need you to behave," he whispered against her lips.

Cassidy's breath shuddered between her lips and she closed her eyes when he pressed a kiss to her mouth. "I don't want to—"

"You're going to put on knickers because I want you to—"

"But I don't want—"

He pressed his finger to her mouth to shut her up and felt his eyes nearly cross when she sucked it in. "Listen to me, you wicked chit. We don't have time to argue. I will not have you parading around in that little swath of material with a naked arse beneath! We have to go to the shipping office and fly across the bloody Atlantic and you will not be half-naked while doing so! Is that understood?"

Eyes lowered to hide the secret thrill at the knowledge that he was jealous. She nodded. "All right. I'll put something on. I'll need my small bag, though."

"Good," he said as he turned away to pick up the box. "Now I'll go down and get your bag. Don't get into any trouble while

I'm gone," he warned over his shoulder.

"All right."

Cassidy slowly turned away from the door, biting her lip in joy and anticipation. She couldn't wait to be in England, where she'd be able to see him much more frequently. She quickly altered her expression when she saw Esme looking at her knowingly with a smile on her face. "What?"

"See here, you sneaky, sex-starved scamp!" Esme whispered with a wide grin. "You be careful. Wet socks, indeed!"

"I'm as careful as I'm going to get," Cassidy said and felt like she'd burst from bottled-up anticipation.

"*Be careful,*" Esme emphasized with a pinch on her arm. "Tony doesn't like to be pushed. You do too much of it and he'll never come round to your way of thinking."

"He wants me. I know he does."

"I never said he didn't want you. But wanting something and allowing one's self to have it are two different things. It's his conscience that you need worry about."

Cassie frowned as Esme's words began to penetrate her happy fog. "Worrying is—"

"Worry? What's there to worry about?" Lady Carleton asked as she came out of Esme's bedroom.

"Cassie's worrying needlessly and I've just told her so," Esme said smoothly. "Mum, please tell this foolish girl how thrilled you and Daddy are that she's coming to stay with us. She keeps going on and on about how she doesn't want to be a burden."

"Of course you're welcome, Cassie," Lady Carleton chided her. "I wouldn't have you stay any other place while you take that summer acting class with Sir Desmond. Lord Carleton and I are proud of you for earning such a coveted space. Even we know that thousands apply for a few meager available spots. We'd be offended if you didn't stay with us!"

"Thanks, again, Lady C. It will just be until I find my own place near the theater district."

"You'll stay as long as you need. Our home is your home, as is everything in it."

"Yes, ma'am!" Cassidy said and bit her tongue to keep herself from asking if that 'everything in it' included Tony as well when he came to visit. Whispering in Esme's ear, she said, "Thanks for keeping your parents occupied so I could have some time alone with Tony. It turned out better than I could have hoped!"

Esme gave her usual response: she smirked.

Chapter 6

In her element and vibrating energy, Cassidy stood on the stage in the small London theater where her acting class took place. She was playing the role of Katherina from *The Taming of the Shrew*, and in this particular scene, she was sparring with her husband to be, Petruchio. She loved the role, and as she waited for the actor playing Petruchio to finish his lines, she put herself in the role of the character even more.

Thinking that she'd be royally pissed if her father was marrying her off just so her younger sister, who was more agreeable and more beautiful, could get married, Cassie advanced upon her classmate playing Petruchio, and just as he finished his line about them getting married on Sunday, she bared her teeth and spat at him that she'd see him hanged on Sunday first.

"Bravo, ladies and gentlemen, bravo. Let's leave it there. We'll finish it next class."

Cassidy looked out from the stage towards the seats of the audience to smile at the graying, dignified Sir Desmond and the rest of her classmates. God, she felt so alive, as she always did when she was acting. There had been very few things in her life that had come close to making her feel the way she did when she was on stage.

"Good job, Cassie. I'll be Petruchio to your Katherina any time."

She turned and smiled at her classmate. "Thanks, Peter. I like working with you, too." Exhilarated, she skipped down the stairs that took her from the stage to audience. As she passed her instructor, she smiled. "Thanks for letting me play her, Sir Desmond," she said, stopping before his chair. "It was such a thrill."

"You're welcome, Cassidy," he said with a smile. "It was thrilling watching you. Will you see me before you leave, please?"

"Sure," Cassidy agreed, wondering what he wanted as she continued up the aisle to where her belongings were. Gathering her things, she went back up towards the front to where Sir Desmond stood with a man she didn't recognize. They were on stage.

"Yes, she's perfect." Cassidy heard the stranger say with excitement as she got closer to the stage. The man watched her so closely that Cassidy began to feel like she was on display.

"As I told you she would be," Sir Desmond said, as he too watched her approach. "She's one of my best students."

Cassidy climbed the stairs, studying the stranger who was short, round and balding. "Hello, I'm Cassidy Hamilton, and you are?" she asked as she stuck her hand out to the stranger.

"Oh, how very American you are," the man gushed as he eagerly shook her hand. "Marvelous, just marvelous!"

Cassie turned her eyes to Sir Desmond, lifting her brow in question.

"Cassidy, my dear, this is Ian Hotchkiss," Sir Desmond told her. "He's the director for a soap opera that's filmed here in London."

"Oh," Cassidy said with a questioning smile as she released his hand. "It's nice to meet you."

"Oh, I assure you, the pleasure is all mine."

"Ian has a proposition for you," Sir Desmond told her. "I'm sure he'll tell you what it is as soon as he's able to control his embarrassing enthusiasm. Shall we sit?"

"She'll have to audition, of course," Hotchkiss said as they walked to a group of chairs at the back of the stage.

As Cassidy sat down in one of the chairs, heart pounding furiously with nerves, she thought she was beginning to get the picture.

❖ ❖ ❖

"Okay, Cassie," Esme began when she sat down next to Cassie in one of two deck chairs they usually met at for lunch in St. James Park. "Why the big happy grin? What's happened since I last saw you this morning?"

Cassidy continued to stare at the lake that snaked through the park. She simply couldn't believe what had happened in class. She lifted her eyes westward to the stunning view of Buckingham Palace that rose pale and majestic from the lush greenery. She grinned as excitement peeled through her. "There was a director in class today," she told Esme.

"Yeah, and?" Esme said impatiently as she bit into an apple.

"*And*, he was there when we all got to class this morning, and he stayed throughout."

"Yeah? What's his name? Is he some famous Hollywood type? Is that what's got you looking like the cat who swallowed the cream?"

"His name is Ian Hotchkiss, and he's not from Hollywood," Cassie said, shifting in her seat. The lunch crowd was growing by the second. She understood why. St. James Park was beautiful in full bloom in summer.

Esme frowned in concentration. "Seems to me I've heard that name before. What's he done?"

"Oh, just some local stuff. A few commercials, a couple of music videos…a soap opera, you know. Like I said," Cassie tried to sound nonchalant as she shrugged, "local stuff." The news was practically bursting to get out of her, but she enjoyed teasing Esme too much to let it.

Esme stopped concentrating on her apple long enough to narrow her eyes at Cassie. "That's how it's going to be, is it?" she asked mildly. "We're to play Twenty Questions until I've no choice but to scratch your bloody eyes out?"

Cassie laughed. "No, I won't torture you that long," she finished and fluttered her lashes playfully.

Esme's lips twitched in response, but she held on to her frustration. "Bloody hell," she said with a reluctant smile. "I do hate it when you're in a teasing mood."

"Okay," Cassie said with calm, "but only because you insist. The director, this Ian Hotchkiss, asked me to audition for a role on his soap opera."

"Why, that's fantastic news, Cassie! Which one is it?"

"I know it's good news, and I'm shamefully proud of myself, but I don't know if I'll do it. You know I want to act on the stage."

It seemed that she'd dreamt of it as long as she'd been alive. And while she knew this audition for television would make many other aspiring actresses ecstatic, it wasn't what she really wanted.

Esme was nodding her head impatiently. "Yes, yes, I know, but it's still a huge break for you, Cassie. Now tell me the name of the blasted show, will you?"

"Oh, right. Have you ever heard of a show called *The Proud and the Profane*?"

Esme's mouth fell open in amazement. "Heard of it? It's only one of the most popular shows in Britain. It's definitely the most watched soap opera in the country! You're telling me that you're to audition for that show?"

"Well, I haven't decided if I will yet, but that's the one I've been asked to audition for, yes."

"What do you mean you haven't decided?"

Cassie shrugged. "Just what I said. I haven't decided if I'll audition. I want the stage, Esme. I've wanted it since I was four."

"I know that, Cassie, but you'd be crazy not to go for this. It's an opportunity of a lifetime for an unknown actress."

"You sound like my agent," Cassie admitted. She'd hired an agent once she'd arrived in London. She'd gone to him because he had offices in both London and the States. "He says if nothing else, I should consider it a juicy tidbit for my résumé."

"Exactly, and you should listen to him, Cassie. It is his industry, after all. He knows what he's talking about."

"I know," Cassie said with a sigh. "But —"

"But nothing, Cassie. It's an opportunity. Take it. I'm sure that that's what Sir Desmond said, isn't it?"

"Yes, so did Uncle Charles."

"Well, then stop being so glum, will you? And besides, it's only an audition. What can it hurt?"

"Nothing, but I know I'd get the role, Es. I just know I would. The director was too happy and certain of me for me not to get it. I don't want to get derailed, that's all."

Esme frowned. "Derailed? How?"

Cassie thought about it. "Television and movie acting aren't taken as seriously as acting on the stage."

"But you have done the stage, Cassie. You did it all throughout university, and you told me yourself that you did community theater growing up."

Cassie sighed. "College theater is not the same as the London stage or Broadway, or the Chicago stage."

"I know it isn't, but you still have the experience, and you'll take this role and use it to your advantage. You really can't lose here, Cassie. When do you audition?"

"Next week, but the character wouldn't start on the show until August."

"Well, it's settled, then. You'll audition, you'll get the role, and you'll keep it until something else that you really want comes along. Perhaps this will be the start of something big. You've got to have faith, Cassie," Esme said and gave her a big smile. "Now, what will it be after lunch today? St. James's Palace, or Westminster?" she asked, referring to two of the three historic palaces that bordered the ornamental park.

Cassie chuckled and shook her head. "Don't change the subject. You just want me to audition so you can meet some of your favorite soap opera actors."

"Bloody right," Esme said with a nod. "I intend to use you ruthlessly, and without shame. Did you ever doubt it?"

Cassie snorted. "Not even for a second. And I think I'd like to check out St. James's today, but only after we take a nice stroll through the park."

Esme groaned and looked down at her sandal-shod feet. "I'm not wearing the appropriate footwear, Cassie. These aren't exactly trainers, are they? Why you insist on hiking through St. James's every day is beyond my comprehension."

Cassie shrugged. "I like nature. Today, I'd like to walk over to Duck Island and see the different birds. Besides, the gardens are so beautiful and peaceful."

"You won't be able to drag me about like this once *P&P* makes you a star," Esme teased. "Imagine! My best mate on *P&P!*" she said as if the import of it had just hit her.

Cassie only laughed and threw an arm around Esme's shoulders.

Tony sat back in his chair and watched as his company's board of director's filed out of the long, spacious conference room. The meetings were becoming tedious, but unfortunately he had to put up with them. The old guard called meetings more than ever since he'd taken over the company after his father's retirement. He knew that they were concerned because of his age. Not a single one of them was younger than sixty, and most of them had been on the board or involved with the company in some way for decades.

The Carletons owned and operated one of the world's largest corporations. Diversification had been the key to the company's 150-year longevity. Tony's great-great-great grandfather had started out building luxury carriages for London's royalty and aristocrats, garnering the family a hereditary baron title on the way; his great-great grandfather had diversified and had started manufacturing bicycles and the next generation had grown the company further by manufacturing parts for automobiles. Tony's grandfather had gotten into all sorts of products including ladies' hosiery. Lord Carlton had taken it even further and now Tony headed a company that produced everything from bicycles to biscuits to children's games to various paper products.

The board didn't want to loose the reins, and he was sick of it. They questioned almost every decision he made, and called him in to account for his rationale every chance they got. He supposed that one of the biggest problems was that they'd known him since he'd been able to wipe his nose by himself. Many of them still saw him as nothing more than Richard Carleton's whelp. They thought that he should be an extension of Richard. And he was to some extent.

He was also his own man with his own ideas, he thought as he stared at one of many Art Deco paintings that made the room look like it was straight out of the 1930s. They were just waiting for him to slip up and create a fiscal mess, and because of his age and their image of people his age; they waited for him to create some scandal as well. The reality of the situation was that there had never really been an irresponsible bone in Tony's body. Oh, he'd had his youthful mistakes, as everyone did, and he still made them. However, as the son of respected members of the British peerage and one of the wealthiest families in the country, he'd always been acutely aware of his position and his responsibility towards it.

He'd never been caught drunk and disorderly at a party or a club. Not that he hadn't gone to clubs or parties; he'd just never been caught behaving in a manner that was less than circumspect. But while many of the wealthy or famous, or the children of the wealthy or famous, were in the newspapers or on the telly for their behavior — good or bad — he always eschewed notoriety. He just wanted to do what he was meant to do, grow the company and feel good about it.

Tony had had his share of fun, and still did occasionally. But mostly, it was just about the work these days. He'd always known that he'd take over the family business. Barely a week had gone by when his father didn't mention it in some way. He supposed he was lucky that he liked the work, because he certainly hadn't been groomed to do anything else. His presidency had always been a foregone conclusion. It was only that no one had expected him to acquire it so early.

However, his father, who had been running the company for more than two decades, had simply grown tired of it. And as he'd stated on more than one occasion, he'd taken his head out of ledgers long enough to realize that Tony was more than capable of running it. So he'd retired a whole decade earlier than he'd always planned. There was resentment over his ascendancy, and Tony didn't fault anyone for feeling it. But he didn't intend to apologize for having his position, either. He'd paid his dues and was more than suitable for the job.

"Whatcha, Tony?"

Tony looked up with a smile on his face, already knowing who'd interrupted him. He only knew one person who would greet him like that. "Shawn!" he said as he rose to greet his old friend. He'd known Shawn McCauley since they were boys at school together.

"And how's it going, your lordship?" Shawn teased as he vigorously shook Tony's hand. "It's been an age since I saw you last."

Tony clapped him on his back with an apologetic look. "What can I say, Shawn? I've had work to keep me busy."

"Well, don't go thinking you're the only one who has his work," Shawn chastised. "I've had my share of busy days and nights, but I always make room for friends. You, on the other hand, hide here in this stone and rubble and never return a call."

Tony studied his old friend. He was a tall, thin man with pale skin, brown eyes, brown hair and a face only a mother would love. And right now, that face had a decidedly accusatory look on it. "And how's television news production treating you these days, Shawn?"

"Oh, bugger the business end of things, mate! I've come to get you and force you to sit and have lunch with me. Numerous phone calls and appeals to your loyalty as an old friend haven't done the trick, so I thought a personal appearance was in order."

Tony grimaced. "Lunch, you say?" he hedged.

"Aye, lunch. And don't you go trying to get out of it."

Tony sighed. He really didn't have the time to take more than a few minutes for lunch. He thought about the work that was waiting for him and the latest skirmish with his board. "All right, then, Shawn. I'll have lunch with you."

Shawn smiled. "Good man. Let's go, then," he commanded.

"Wait a tic while I stop by my office, will you?" Tony began to gather papers from the table.

Shawn grabbed his arm. "None of that. We leave now. I know how this works. You'll go to your office, something will come up and I'll be stuck cooling my heels until I'm forced to leave and go back to work. In that scenario, I will have had nothing to eat and no time spent with my best mate. My way," he continued as he shuffled him out the door, down the hall and to the bank of elevators, "I get to fill my belly while I pick your brain about your life."

"I haven't got my wallet, Shawn," Tony protested.

"It's okay. It will be my treat." Shawn stepped into the elevator. "Now in the lift with you," he demanded when Tony only stood there.

Tony shook his head and walked in. "May as well give in gracefully," he murmured. "Otherwise, I can probably expect this same behavior from you tomorrow."

Shawn beamed approvingly. "See what eight years at school together will get you? A man who knows you as well as he knows himself."

Tony could only laugh, feeling more carefree than he had in weeks.

Chapter 7

"Hello, Tony, darling."

Tony groaned deeply into the telephone receiver. "God, Mother, it's a bit earl—"

"Oh, dear," Lady Carleton said, "you're calling me 'Mother' and your voice has gone quite polite. I believe I must have upset you somehow."

"You're a dreadful actress, Mother," Tony said in resignation. "Stop trying to sound remorseful for something we know you're not the least bit sorry for and tell me why you've rung me at this ungodly hour."

"A bit cheeky, aren't we, Anthony?"

Tony sighed and gave up. "Tell me something," he began conversationally as the sheets beside him rustled. "Why is it you can be so formal with me and call me 'Anthony', so I know you're perturbed and dutifully act the remorseful supplicant, whereas when I try it with you, you blissfully ignore the hint and get even cheekier?"

"Why? Because I'm the mum, darling. You're not allowed to even think that I'm being cheeky. I did change your nappies, after all."

"Oh, God, Mum. Before I wade even deeper into the muck and mire, please just tell me why you've rung me."

"Of course, darling. I aim to please. Your father, the girls and I are off to Wimbledon today and we have a ticket for you. Don't say no, Tony," she said hurriedly as she anticipated his answer. "We've hardly seen you these past few weeks since we've returned from the States more than a month ago. You've not come to dinner even once and you're always too busy to see us."

"No exaggerating, Mum. We've had lunch together at least three times."

"A hastily eaten sandwich taken with tepid tea in between your business meetings does not a proper luncheon make, Anthony," she finished.

Tony could almost see the reprimand on her face. "I know, Mum and I am sorry, but since Dad retired, I haven't exactly had time to do much of anything."

"Oh, that's a pathetic excuse, and you know it. I saw you at least twice weekly every week until recently. Is something wrong?"

Tony had always hated the fact that his mother was so damned astute and intuitive. It had been a curse when he'd been a child intent upon getting away with mischief and it was positively deadly since he'd grown into adulthood. Yes, there was something wrong. And she was called Cassidy Hamilton. He hadn't been able to get the chit out of his mind, nor his dreams, so he did the next best thing. He practiced avoidance. That meant only seeing his parents when they came to The City and hardly ever seeing his sister because usually where there was Esme, there was Cass.

"Tony, dear. Please come today. You're welcome to bring someone if you'd like. We've got an extra ticket and it's even for Centre. We'll be right near the action and those wonderful American sisters who won the French Doubles this year are scheduled to play. Don't say no, darling, please. I miss seeing my son."

Tony could tell she was sincere, but didn't want to give in too easily. "Centre tickets, Mum?" He tried to stall.

"It was all your father's doing," she said dismissively. "Will you come, darling? As I said, you could certainly bring someone if your family aren't enough."

Tony looked speculatively over at his current bed partner. Amanda was only the latest in a fairly lengthy line of women he'd had sex with since returning from America with Cassie in tow. However, as hard as he tried, he simply could not forget Cassie and the sex they'd almost had in her flat that last day. He looked down in frustration at his cock as it tented the sheet —

hell; he was getting rock hard just thinking about it. "Knock it off, you bloody rotter," he muttered in disgust to his penis.

"I beg your pardon," Lady Carleton said stiffly.

"Uh, nothing Mum. Just talking to myself." He looked at Amanda again. No, she hadn't been able to drive Cassie out of his mind, but she'd make a perfect shield against her today. Perhaps Cassie would give up on him if he showed interest in someone else. "Okay, Mum. You've talked me into it. I'll meet you and the family at Wimbledon. I'll have a friend with me so bring that extra ticket, please."

"She isn't a skank, is she dear?" Lady Carleton asked politely.

Pure shock kept Tony quiet.

"You do know what a skank is don't you, darling? A skank is someone who will sleep with you because he or she is after your wealth, fame and material goods. Apparently good sex is not of paramount importance. If it happens that the sex is good, that's only a side benefit. A skank really—"

"Mum!" Tony hurried to stop her, having finally found his voice. Hearing his mother say such a word in that oh-so-proper, upper crust British voice of hers confused the hell out of him. "I know what the term means. I'm shocked that you do. You're a peer of realm, for God's sake!"

"Oh, don't be such a stick in the mud, Tony. The girls taught it to me. The word is quite rude and ugly, but that is precisely why I believe it is a perfect description for some of the women in your life and I want to educate you, dear. After all, you may not be famous, but your name has been bandied about in the papers before and you are wealthy in your own right. You must be made aware, darling."

"Yes, Mum," Tony agreed just to get off the subject. "I'll see you at the entrance," he said quickly before breaking the connection. He looked at Amanda again and pinched the bridge of his nose in weariness. No doubt about it, she was a skank of the first water and his mum would spot it right off.

In her sitting room in Mayfair, Lady Carleton hung up and smiled with relish, quite pleased to have stumped Tony. "Got to keep him on his toes," she murmured as she rose to get ready for the day.

"Stop fidgeting, Cassie. You're driving me absolutely mad!" Esme whispered as the family waited outside Wimbledon for Tony. "You look smashing, as you always do. Don't let Tony do this to you. He's nothing but a wanker and there are millions like him in the world."

"I'll thank you not to talk about my future lover/husband like that, Es," Cassidy tried to say jokingly, but was too nervous to pull it off. She sighed and gave it up. "It's just that I haven't seen him in so long and I just knew we'd get to know each other better once I moved here."

Esme shrugged one elegant shoulder. "It's pretty obvious, isn't it? You've scared him and he's running for his life by avoiding you. It's a common survival tactic that cowards use. Don't let it bother you."

"Well, I know he said that nothing more could happen between us, but I just thought it would be as difficult for him to stay away from me as it is for me to stay away from him."

"It probably is, but he's doing it," Esme said.

"He's just lucky that I haven't had the time to run him to ground. With my class, auditions and the tours your parents have taken me on, I've been kept pretty busy."

"Yes, I know. He's just —" Esme broke off when Cassidy's eyes suddenly lost their excited glow. "What is it?" she asked as she turned to look in the direction in which Cassidy was looking. "Why that effing asshole!" she said in outrage as Tony walked up with a willowy brunette.

"How could he?" Cassidy asked in a small hurt voice. "Oh, Es, she's beautiful and she's at least ten years older than I," she moaned.

Esme took her arm in an urgent grip. "Don't you dare," she whispered vehemently in Cassidy's ear. "Don't you dare let them — especially him — see how much this bothers you. You're an actress, damn it, so start acting! Get it together and hurry because they'll be over here as soon as they're done talking to Mum and Dad."

Esme watched as Cassidy took a deep breath and composed herself. "That a girl. Just remember, he's running scared and this is simply another tactic."

"Right," Cassidy said with a confidence she didn't quite feel.

"She's a tactic, a very beautiful, perfectly aged one, but still a tactic." She watched with narrowed eyes as Tony walked over with his lady friend. She pasted on a bright smile.

"Keep her occupied for a few seconds, will you, Es?" she whispered quickly. "Tony! It's so good to see you. I've missed you terribly," she said as she wrapped her arms around his neck and leaned in to kiss him on the cheek. "And I'm dying for you to finish what you started the last time I saw you. Still have my thong?" she whispered just before she licked the inside of his ear and moved to step back out of his arms.

Tony shivered involuntarily, but had enough wits about him to hold her arms to keep her in front of him. "You behave yourself today, Cass. I mean it," he warned when a defiant look appeared on her face.

Thoroughly pissed, Cassidy whispered back, "Whatever, Tony. Since you've brought your tactic over here to run interference," she indicated Amanda with a nod of her head, "all bets are off." She broke away, but not before slamming him with one last look.

Tony watched her introduce herself to Amanda and tried to get his emotions under control. Hell. The chit actually looked hurt and disappointed. *What right did she have*? he thought as he tried to suppress the guilt she so successfully made him feel. He'd never made her any promises. In fact, he'd told her that there couldn't be anything between them. If she chose to ignore him, that was her problem. He had every right to escort whomever he wanted to Wimbledon. "And I dare anyone to say otherwise," he mumbled, angry that he felt a desperate need to go over and apologize to her.

"I do. I dare," Esme said as she gave him a hug. "Hello, brother dear." She kissed him on the cheek and released him.

Seeing the look in her eyes, Tony groaned. "Not you too, brat. I ask you: what have I done wrong?"

"You know what you've done wrong and I never thought you cowardly," she said in mild disgust as she walked over to join Cassidy.

He watched the two of them link arms and they both flounced off after his parents, but not before treating him to dirty looks. "Brats."

Cassidy walked out of the ladies' room with her head down in contemplation. She sighed. It was quite clear to her now: she absolutely did not understand men. Tony wanted her; she wanted him. Neither one of them was married, so why couldn't they be together? It wasn't just lust. They got along really well, could discuss everything from the mediocre to world events, and they respected each other. But bigger than all of that, they had a strong connection that even he couldn't break with his stubbornness. She really didn't understand why age should be a big deal.

Still looking down, she studied her outfit. When she'd picked out the white, sleeveless, summer weight, knee-length dress and matching sun hat, she'd had two things in mind. She'd wanted to show Tony that though she was only twenty-two, she was still very much a woman and she'd wanted to look sexy to him at the same time. She'd been going for sleekly elegant and she believed she'd accomplished it. She'd tied a black silk scarf around the large hat to add a splash of color and had topped the outfit off with matching black and white sandals, *Breakfast at Tiffany's* styled, large, black sunglasses and an envelope clutch purse. Sighing, she slipped the glasses back on her face, thinking it had all been wasted on Tony.

Tony studied Cassie as she walked toward him. Even looking forlorn, she clearly outshone every woman there. And he wasn't the only one to notice; even now, people were staring at her. The hat and big sunglasses added to her glamorous mystique and made her look like the movie star he knew she was destined to be. "If you don't hurry, Cass, you'll miss seeing one of your country mate's play," he said as she came abreast of him.

Surprised by his appearance, Cassidy slid her sunglasses down on her nose to look at him (unaware that the move was unbearably sexy and made him suck in a breath), and shrugged her shoulders. "It doesn't matter. I came here to see you and you won't even talk to me."

Tony let himself groan mentally. He didn't know why those eyes of hers had such an effect on him. He'd felt them on him since they'd taken their seats earlier, and just knew that they were accusing him of something, and damned if they didn't want to make him squirm with guilt. So much so that he'd followed her out to talk to her. "I've done nothing wrong, Cass, and you know it. I told you from the beginning that there could be nothing between us because of the age difference."

She was nodding her head in agreement before he even finished his sentence. "Yes. Yes, you did," she said calmly in contrast to his defensive words. "But you also brought me into seconds of orgasm, as well. Additionally, you stare at me like you want to eat me alive and you've shown a certain possessiveness for me that men usually only show to women they consider theirs."

Completely taken aback, Tony didn't immediately have a comeback.

He remained quiet for so long that Cassie said, "So you can see why I can't believe that you would do this to me—to us."

"That's just the problem, Cass, there isn't an 'us.'"

"Not yet, no. But there could be and should be, and you know it just as well as I do. You're just scared. In fact," she said as something occurred to her right at that moment, "I don't think the age difference is the big problem here at all. You're just plain scared. You're afraid of the potential of us because you know it would be wonderful and earth shattering and all the things that make a person want to be with one person and one person only. You're using age as an excuse."

"That's not true, Cass," Tony said evenly as panic seared through him. "You're far too young for me."

Cassidy nodded her head again calmly and she *was* calm because her earlier revelation concerning his fear gave her a newfound confidence. She knew she was right. "Yes, Tony, if you say so. Will you kiss me, now?" She stepped closer.

"Stop this, Cass," Tony said and grabbed her arms to hold her still.

"Please," she begged sweetly and moved even closer—so close that their shoe tips touched and she felt his breath on her lips. "Did you know that you're the only one who calls me that? It makes me tremble to know that I'm your Cass. Yours and only yours," she said softly against his lips. "It's so deliciously intimate. It makes me feel almost as good as I'd feel with you inside me slowly taking me until both of us want to die from the need and the wanting."

Tony ate the rest of her sentence, completely taking her mouth with his. Despite the urgency she made him feel, he was gentle at first, removing her sunglasses and cradling her face in his hands and sliding his tongue against hers.

She moaned softly and shivered against him when he licked the roof of her mouth. The completely new sensation made her fall into him and she handed him her purse so she could lace her arms around his neck, leaving her hands to dangle. When he did it again...and again, she lost all sense of equilibrium and felt a pressing need to hold on tighter to him. Folding her arms around his neck now, she gripped an elbow in each hand and tried not to embarrass them both by coming right there.

Tony tightened his arms around her waist when he felt her shiver uncontrollably and kept up his assault on her mouth. His hunger for her took total control of him and he slurped at her mouth, intermittently licking the roof and the inside of her top lip. She was incredibly sensitive to that, he discovered when she cried softly into his mouth.

"Tony? Tony...p...please," Cassidy whimpered between licks and laps. "St...st...stop...I can't take it much longer. I'm going... going to...oh...oh...oh...ohhhhh..."

Tony realized that Cassidy was actually coming and covered her mouth with his again as he maneuvered them into a hidden corner and sheltered her body with his against the wall. Keeping his eyes open, he continued to bathe the inside of her mouth with his tongue to help her reach that final peak.

Entirely caught up in the pleasure, Cassidy had long since become unaware of her surroundings. Her hands gripped the front of his shirt and Tony watched as her body grew stiff and her eyes opened. "Oh, Tohhhny..." she moaned one last time before collapsing onto his chest. Her hat slid off of her head.

"Shh," Tony murmured soothingly as he cradled her in his arms. He'd heard the surprised bafflement in her voice. "It's all right, love," he whispered and kissed the top of her head. These actions were completely at odds with what he was feeling physically. He was in pain. He was so consumed with lust that his stomach muscles shook from the strain. His dick was so hard that he had to forcefully tamp down the urge to push her dress up, press her against the wall and rut inside her like an animal. The kiss itself had turned him on, but her uninhibited response to it had set off a raging inferno inside him.

"Bloody hell, woman," he pronounced mildly when she remained quiet and still for what seemed forever, "if you've fallen asleep, I believe I shall strangle you."

Cassidy snorted out a laugh and kept her head buried in his chest. She gave a languid sigh and finally lifted her head to look at him. She tried to straighten, but her knees were still wobbly, so she continued to lean into him, feeling punch drunk. Her eyes held embarrassment and amazement. "I'm sorry," she said sheepishly with a shy smile. "That's never happened to me before. I mean I've never, *ever* climaxed from just a kiss. But then again, I've never been kissed like that before. It was wonderful!"

"Dear God," he said softly, "if this is how you react to a kiss, what will you do when my cock is buried deep within you?"

Cassidy shivered helplessly and closed her eyes. "What do you think? I'm sure I'll erupt like a volcano. If you want," she said, looking down to smooth the wrinkles in his shirt. "We could put my theory to a test and put you out of your misery. Not here," she said quickly when she raised her head and saw he was about to object. "I mean later at your flat or a hotel."

Tony came back down to earth with a thud. What in hell was he doing? This was completely irresponsible of him. Giving his baby sister's best friend an orgasm in public and at Wimbledon, no less! He had to get away from her. "I'm sorry, Cass, but we have to stop this. There will be no hotel, nor will we go to my flat."

Cassidy only looked at him before she pushed away from him. She bent down to pick up her hat. "Fine," she said calmly before positioning the hat in a rakish tilt on her head. "I can't make you accept us." She held out her hand. "My purse, please."

Baffled, Tony looked at her and then realized he was holding her purse. He handed it over, briefly wondering when he'd gotten it.

"Now the glasses. Thank you," she said and placed them on her nose. "Now," she said standing as straight as a soldier, "I'm going to the ladies' room to wash. And this time, there will be no panties for you," she said crisply before walking away.

Tony watched her leave, knowing he should feel happy that she seemed to be accepting things. But for the life of him, he couldn't. At best, he could only feel regret. Gone was the sulky girl from Chicago who had practically stamped her foot in anger when he told her there'd be no relationship. In her place was a woman whom he found even more attractive.

Later that night when he reached in his pocket for the key to his flat, his fingers encountered soft silk. Frowning, he pulled it out and grinned helplessly when he saw white silk bikini panties. Her scent permeated the material and filled the air. Tony knew it shouldn't, but the sight of her knickers cheered him and he whistled as he unlocked his door, wondering when in the hell she'd put them there.

Chapter 8

Tony sat at the Carleton dinner table and let the conversation swirl around him while he contemplated his situation with Cassie. He hadn't seen very much of her in the weeks since Wimbledon, but this was a celebratory dinner, for she had won the role on *The Proud and the Profane*. He admitted to himself that he was glad to see her. Though he'd been out to his parents' home in Mayfair's exclusive Berkeley Square several times, he'd only seen her a couple of those times.

Each time, he found it increasingly difficult not to beg her to consider going out with him. He always managed to suppress the urge, however, because he remembered their age difference. Though Cass had been correct when she'd accused him of being afraid of what they could become, she had been incorrect in assuming that the age difference was just an excuse on his part.

As sure as he was that they could have a wonderful relationship, he was just as sure that he didn't want to take advantage of her and her youth. He'd been lusting after her since she was eighteen and the time he'd spent with her on his trips to the States had not only made the lust stronger, but had also helped him to fall for her. Yes, he could easily see himself spending the rest of his life with her. However, he could not make himself steal her youth in that way. The business side of his life was filled with wealthy, old men with wives young enough to be their daughters and they sucked the youth and vitality right out of those wives. And those same wives often grew tired of their husbands and cheated with men their own age.

No, he wasn't old enough to be Cass's father, but he was quite a bit older than she, and he refused to steal her youth away from her or put her in a position where she felt trapped with an old man. He would love a relationship with her, but he couldn't chance it.

"Cassie?" Lady Carleton called from one end of the long dining table. "Tonight is supposed to be your special night, yet you look so forlorn. What's the matter, dear?"

"Oh, I was just thinking about what taking this new acting gig will mean for me," Cassidy said with a small smile. "I'm really grateful to be given a shot, but I am a bit nervous and wary. I mean, I'll be the new girl on an established television show and the role they've given me is so stereotypical, that I'm afraid I'll get trapped."

"Oh, come on, Cassie," Esme chastised. "It's a plum role, despite the fact that your character is so completely opposite of who you are."

"I know, I know," Cassidy said. "But my God, my character is so repugnant. She's a beautiful, loud-mouthed, empty-headed, greedy American model whose primary goal is to snag a rich husband. She spots a British tycoon, decides she wants him and spends the next twelve episodes plotting to get him, despite the fact that he has a wife and three children. A wife, by the way, who is letting my character stay in her house and who is wheel-chair bound because she stepped into London traffic to save an old lady."

Lips twitching madly, Lady Carleton said, "Yes, well, P&P has never been known for subtlety."

"Or taste?" Cassidy asked with a teasing smile.

"Here, now, child," Lord Carleton began. "It's just one acting job. It's a way to get your foot in the door—in a big way. *The Proud and the Profane* is one of the most popular shows in Britain, after all, and the writing is pretty good."

Cassidy didn't want to belabor the point. She knew she was quite lucky to have gotten the role, but how to explain that it embarrassed her to have to play such a part? Her grandmother wouldn't like it, of that she was certain.

"What is it, Cassie?" Esme asked.

"Well, I was just thinking about my grandmother. I don't

think she'd like me playing this part. She always said that I represented our family when I went out into the world. She told me to remember that what I did in private was my business, but what I did in public became everyone's business."

Tony stared at Cassie. He couldn't stand to see her look so unhappy when she should be jumping up and down with excitement. "Your grandmother sounds like she was an astute woman," he said, causing her to look at him for the first time. "So astute, in fact, that I'm sure she understood that acting is just that — acting; it isn't real. The role doesn't represent who you are, only what your abilities are. I'm sure that your grandmother would be very proud that you've gotten such a big part so quickly in your career. I know I am."

Cassidy smiled shyly and gratefully at him, and ducked her head. "Thank you," she said. "You're right. Typical actress behavior though, right?" Her smile was self-deprecating as she rolled her eyes. "I just have to be dramatic. It's just that my grandmother was such a wonderful woman that I never want to do anything that would make her ashamed of me."

"What of your parents?" Tony asked, unable to check his curiosity. "What were they like?"

"Oh, they were great. I remember my mother always singing and laughing and my dad making jokes and reading a lot. They both taught. My mom was eight years older than my dad, you know," she finished with a look straight at Tony.

"Never say so," Lady Carleton said in surprise. "How wonderful for her."

"Yes," Cassidy affirmed. "They were married twelve years before they died."

"Well, how lucky for them that they could have so much time together before they passed on," Lord Carleton said.

Over dessert a while later, Lady Carleton looked up to see Cassidy still looking pensive. "Cass? You've gone quiet again. Are you all right?"

Cassidy sighed and looked at Tony. After Wimbledon, she'd determined that she'd stop chasing him and she'd been very good at keeping away from him. She'd done her damnedest to leave him alone when he came over to his family's home. But tonight just made her love him all the more. She decided that she just had to give it another try. Making her second sigh sound particularly forlorn, she said, "You'll probably think I sound selfish, with all the good luck I've been having, but my life isn't quite the way I want it yet. I don't feel that it will be until I get this one last thing that I want."

"One last thing? What is it?"

"Well, I'm in love—really, truly in love."

This was said with another sad sigh. She quickly ducked her head when Tony suddenly raised his gaze to look at her.

"But that's wonderful," Lady Carleton said.

"Well, yes, it should be. I feel good about it, but I get the distinct impression that he doesn't want me to be. He's avoiding me."

"I'm sorry to say it, darling, but perhaps your young man doesn't feel as deeply for you as you do for him."

"Well, I know he's attracted to me, but he's fighting that attraction. He feels that I'm too young for him and he's making things difficult." She ignored Esme's stifled snort of laughter and continued, "He's being stubborn. We have a great rapport, we're on the same wavelength on so many issues and our attraction burns really strong and fierce. I just know that we'd have a great relationship if he'd only give us a chance. I've been here for two months and he's done nothing to take advantage of that fact."

"Oh, so you knew him before moving here, then?"

"Is he English?" This came from Lord Carleton whose face was mottled with embarrassment while his eyes showed helpless curiosity.

"Oh, yes, he's a very proper Englishman. It's one of the things I absolutely adore about him, that and his intelligence, witty sense of humor and gorgeous physical appearance."

Again, Cassidy ignored Esme's snort, which managed to sound both disbelieving and snide. She also ignored Tony's determined gaze that warned her to knock it off.

"What do you think, Lady C.? Do you think age should matter?"

"Oh, no, not really. I'm not one for pedophilia of course, but I do feel that it's hard enough to find love and when one does, the little things shouldn't matter all that much."

"That's just how I feel," Cassidy said passionately. "But he won't listen to reason."

"Well, just how much older is he than you, child?" Lord Carleton asked.

"A measly fourteen years; that's all," Cassidy said and sniffled as if holding back tears. "I didn't know love could hurt so much."

"Oh, I am sorry," Lady Carleton said. "Perhaps your young man will come round to your way of thinking."

"Yes," Lord Carleton agreed. "If he's as smart as you say he is, he'll at least give it a chance. Do we know him? Who is he?"

"Tony," Cassidy said.

Not yet making the connection, Lady Carleton took a sip of coffee before saying, "What about Tony, dear?"

"I'm in love with him."

Lady Carleton's head jerked up to look from Tony to Cassidy, from Cassidy to Tony and back again to repeat the process. "Surely you're joking?"

"No," Cassidy said with a definite shake of her head. "I'm not. I'm in love with Tony."

Lady Carleton stared at Cassidy in stunned silence for a long moment. She blinked. "Why, whatever for, dear?"

Into the silence after that disloyal question came Esme's raucous laughter and from Tony in a disgusted voice, "Thanks loads, Mother, for that ringing endorsement," which only made Esme laugh harder, so hard that she ended up pushing her chair back a bit so she could hold her stomach while tears of hilarity streamed down her face.

"I didn't mean it like that, Tony," Lady Carleton began, before snapping, after a particularly loud guffaw from Esme, "Oh do be quiet, Esme!"

Lord Carleton tried hard to control his twitching lips, but a chuckle escaped anyway, which he masked with a cough when Tony shot him a hard look.

Cassidy let the room quiet before saying, "In answer to your question, Lady C., I'm in love with Tony because he's a wonderful man. He has a strong sense of duty, he's smart, he makes me laugh, he makes me think. And as I said, the attraction between us is explosive. I have the most wonderfully wicked thoughts about him and—"

"All right, that's enough!" Tony interrupted with a screech of his chair as he pushed it back to stand. Cassie was getting carried away and he had to stop her. As she'd spoken, her face had taken on a look of deep passion and her voice had gone soft and husky. He doubted she'd even realized it. Next she'd be entertaining the table with tales of their near-fuck against the wall. He walked around to her side of the table and pulled her chair out. "Come on!" Barely giving her time to stand, he grabbed her hand.

"But, Tony," Cassidy protested.

"No buts! Let's go! Please excuse us," he said over his shoulder as he dragged her from the room while everyone looked on in astonishment.

The silence left behind in the wake of their exit was deafening until Lady Carleton cleared her throat and said, "Well, I never! Tony's manners are atrocious—"

Esme couldn't help it; the comment surprised another guffaw out of her.

Lady Carleton shot her an exasperated look and continued, "And Cassidy! Can you imagine? The girl has lived here for two whole months and I never would have guessed."

She was contemplative for a moment before saying philosophically to her husband, "But it is quite marvelous, isn't it, darling? We do love Cassie. We'll have the wedding here, of course."

"Now, Anne, don't make any plans. It doesn't look like there will even be a relationship of any kind and you're already planning a wedding?" Lord Carleton asked.

Lady Carleton, whose fondest dream in life was to see her children eventually happily married, would not be swayed. She waved her hand dismissively. "Don't be obtuse, darling. Of course they'll be married. She's in love with him and it's clear that he's in love with her. Did you see his face? She's perfect for him, now that I think on it. My money's on Cassie and I wager they'll be married and quite soon at that."

Lord Carleton gave up. "You're probably right."

"And do you know what the best part about all of this is?" Lady Carleton asked him excitedly.

"That Tony will be happy and provide us with grandchildren?"

"Yes, well, that too," Lady Carleton said hurriedly, "but the really marvelous thing is that Cassie is not a skank! Having known her for so long, we can say that with absolute certainty, don't you think?"

Having no idea what a skank was, Lord Carleton merely reached for his cake. "Quite so, dear," he said blandly before taking another bite.

To which Esme burst into laughter again.

Chapter 9

Tony pulled Cassidy into the library and shut the door behind them. "Sit," he commanded with a frown.

Before she could think about it, Cassidy did, quickly sitting on a cream-colored leather sofa in the middle of the room. When she realized that she had, she frowned and began to stand again until she got a good look at his face.

"Don't even think about moving from that spot," he warned in a low dangerous voice as he paced away from her. He was forced to stop when he was confronted with one of the floor to ceiling bookcases that were built into the walls.

Swallowing hard, Cassidy sat back down. She'd never seen him quite so angry.

Tony looked at her and snorted in disbelief. "I don't believe it! For once, you're actually going to listen to me?"

Cassidy frowned. "Now, really, Tony. There's no need to be—"

"I'll bloody be what I want, if you don't mind!" Tony said. "Settle down and listen to me! That's better," he said when she very deliberately clamped her lips together. "Now," he said as he began to pace back and forth in front of her. "For the past several years you have done nothing but make my life a living hell."

He ignored her indignant gasp and kept going. "Especially when you got it into that beautiful head of yours that we were meant to be together. You've tortured me endlessly and it's got to stop. Are we clear?" He stopped in front of her to look sternly down at her.

"Hmmph," Cassidy said before folding her arms and turning

her head away.

"Refusing to answer? Well, no matter, it will save me the trouble of shutting you up again."

"You don't have to be mean about it," Cassie muttered in a defensive voice.

"What was that?" he asked and when she remained silent, "Still refusing to answer, are we? Good, because I'm not finished. Almost since I've known you, you've insisted upon bedeviling me at every turn."

"That isn't true," Cassidy objected as she turned towards him again. "And besides, I wouldn't have had to resort to…to…" she gave up trying to find a word and ducked her head to avoid his steely gaze so as not to feel like a naughty child as she finished with a resentful mumble, "to the things you forced me to resort to if you would just do what's right."

Tony exploded with disbelief and frustration as she laid the blame squarely at his feet. "Bloody hell, woman, if you had any common sense at all, you'd see that *I am* trying to do what's right!"

Thoroughly offended now, Cassidy gave an insulted sniff, folded her arms and turned away again. "Well, I never!" she said roundly, finding that the favorite phrase of her American Southern grandmother fit the situation perfectly.

"Oh, do give over, Cass," Tony said in complete frustration when a few moments passed and she still hadn't said anything else. He looked at her expectantly and sighed when she still didn't answer or look at him. He kneeled in front of her. "I've come to a decision, Cass, and hopefully, it will be something you can live with, because," he took her chin, turned her face towards him and said gently, "if you can't, then there's no hope for us. Understand, love?"

This got Cassidy's attention and she finally raised her eyes to look at him. She saw the tenderness in his green eyes and tried not to jump the gun. "No, Tony, I don't. What do I need to understand?"

"Keep in mind that I'm doing this for both our sakes, but mostly for yours," he cautioned her as he held her hands. "It will be good for both of us…eventually."

Cassidy frowned. "Eventually? What do you mean?"

"I mean that you are an extraordinary woman who made me fall in love and lust with her. But you are also too young for me."

"No, I'm not," Cassidy finally was able to get out after his declaration of love stunned her into silence. "There are only fourteen years between us. They don't mean anything!"

"I'm afraid they do, love, to me especially. No, listen to me," he said when he saw that she would object. "Before I snatch you up, I want you to be absolutely sure that I'm whom you want."

"Oh, but you are, Tony!" Her voice was in full-blown panic.

"Hush, darling," Tony said gently and softly kissed her lips. "I don't want you to miss out on life because you're with an old codger like me. I've lived my life the way I wanted, sowed my wild oats, so to speak, and I want you to be able to do the same. Therefore—"

Cassidy melted at hearing him call her 'darling' for the first time, so much so that she almost missed the rest of what he was saying. "You're not old, Tony!"

"Therefore," he said again, "I want you to take the next three years to make sure that you want to be with me and if you decide that you do, come and find me when you're twenty-five. I'll be waiting."

Cassie felt as if all the air had left her body. She stared at him for a moment, hoping that she'd heard incorrectly. His face said it all. "Oh that's an awful idea," she wailed because she knew he was determined and that there was probably no talking him out of it. "Please don't do this," she begged as she stood and moved away from him.

"Come on, buck up, old girl. It's only three years."

"But, Tony, that's such a long time. I don't want to wait that long!"

"To make this as easy on us as possible, this will mean that we can't see each other that much, even socially. I mean, I'll see you here at the house and sometimes when you're out with the family, but it shouldn't be that much because you'll soon be working a lot and you're getting your own flat."

Cassidy simply harrumphed in frustration. "It's not fair, Tony. It's just not fair and I don't want to do it."

"I'm afraid you'll have to, love. We'll both have to suffer through this. If I had any kind of honor, I'd hold out until you're thirty, but I really can't wait that long."

Cassidy said nothing. She couldn't believe that he would tell her he loved her in one breath and in the next tell her that they had to stay away from one another for three years. It seemed unnecessarily cruel.

"How can you do this to me...to...to us?" She vibrated with anger.

"I'm sorry, but it's for the best. You'll see," Tony murmured as he came up behind her. He stroked her back.

"No I won't," she said and stepped away from him. She turned around to look at him. "We don't have to do this and you know it. You're just being difficult." She tried to walk away, but he grabbed her arms and held her still.

"Difficult? You think I'm imposing these rules just to be *difficult*? Fucking hell, Cass, why would I do that when I want you so damned much that just the thought of you makes me hard?"

Cassidy pulled against his hold and sulked in indecision as she wiped her face.

Tony held her tighter still, determined to make her see reason. "Keep still, Cass and answer my question."

"I don't know why, but it doesn't have to be the way you want it to be."

"It does if you want us to have a relationship," Tony said implacably.

"I know what I want Tony and I resent your acting like I don't. Stop treating me like a child. I know my own mind!" She was so angry she could scream. He was making a decision that affected both of them equally, yet there was nothing she could do about it.

"I'm not saying that you don't, sweetheart. I only want you to have choices."

"I've made my choice. You just don't want to accept it," she said resentfully.

"I can't let you tie yourself down to me, not so early. If you do and change your mind later, I'll never be able to let you go. A separation now will be better than later."

At his words, all of the energy went out of Cassidy. "But what if...what if," she floundered and looked at him, miserable and pleading for understanding.

"What is it, darling? Just spit it out."

"What if you meet someone else and fall in love with her?" Cassidy asked nervously and quickly.

Tony laughed. "You're worried about *me?* Trust me, Cass, that will never happen."

"But how do you know? You came to Wimbledon with that Amanda woman. She's gorgeous and older than I am."

"Yes, Amanda is pretty, but she doesn't hold a candle to you. Besides that, your beauty isn't the only thing that draws me to you. I love you for you."

"Then if you have such faith in yourself, why can't you extend to me that same faith? I love *you*, Tony. I don't want anyone else. Why won't you believe me?"

"I do believe you. I just don't want you to rush into anything with me. You're so young and I don't want you to regret anything when you come to me."

"Honestly, Tony, the only thing I regret is your being so stubborn and highhanded!"

Tony shrugged. "I'm sorry you see it that way, but that's the way I feel."

Cassidy searched his face anxiously, hoping to see some sign of softening, but his eyes remained resolved. "So I guess you want me to date during this hiatus?"

Tony's eyes narrowed and he hesitated before saying, "Define date."

"The usual, Tony," Cassidy said impatiently. "D-a-t-e date. Meet a guy, go out with a guy—Date."

"If that's all, then yes, I expect you to date. I'll hate it, but how else can we be sure?"

"So no sex, then?"

Tony scowled at even the thought of another man's hands on her. "No, I don't want you to have sex, but obviously if you feel the need to, then you're not as serious about me as you think."

"Tony, I haven't wanted to have sex with any other man since you did what you did to me in my apartment in New Haven, and even before then," she said with impatience. "You know I'm still a virgin."

Tony couldn't help himself; he smiled. "I'm pleased to hear

that."

"Yes, well, I bet you didn't extend me the same courtesy, did you?" Her eyes burned with accusation.

Tony's wince was a sign of how uncomfortable he was with the question. "Now, Cass, you have to understand, I hadn't realized I loved you until recently and since then I haven't had one woman in my bed—except you of course, when I dream."

"Stop it, Tony," Cassidy said when he tried to kiss her. "We're not finished talking." She pushed his face away and turned her head, prompting him to nuzzle her neck.

"We are," he said between kisses. "You need to see the logic in this."

"I can't, and the obvious reason is because there isn't any."

"Well, you're not going to change my mind."

"Fine," Cassidy said as she pushed out of his arms and ignored the surprised look on his face. "Let's just get this little experiment started here and now." She walked toward the door.

Tony spread his arms wide in dismay. "Oh, come on, Cass, give us a kiss. Just one last kiss."

With her hand on the doorknob, Cassidy turned back to look at him. "No. After all, there's no point in starting something we're obviously not going to get to finish."

"Please, Cass," Tony said, making her pause in indecision. "This could possibly be the last time we see each other for a long while. Do you want us to leave each other on bad terms?"

"They're your terms," Cassidy said stubbornly with her hand still on the knob.

"I know, darling," Tony said from right behind her. He put his hands on her shoulders to turn her around. "But please don't be angry with me."

"Well, why shouldn't I be?" Cassidy asked with an angry glance of disbelief. "You're treating me like a child. I love you and you don't trust me enough to trust in that fact."

Tony winced when tears welled in her eyes. "Cass…sweetheart, don't cry." He was so tempted to tell her to hell with waiting, but deep down he knew that they had to do it this way.

"Oh, so now you get to tell me what to do with my emotions as well, huh? Well, I don't think so. I'm upset, Tony and when

I'm upset, I sometimes cry and you can't tell me that I can't!" Her voice rose higher and higher in direct proportion to those rising emotions.

"Oh, love, I'm sorry," Tony said as the tears fell in fat drops down her cheeks. He couldn't resist her pain and pulled her into his arms.

Cassidy pulled away. "Let go of me, Tony! I could have handled it if you had kept on denying your feelings about me to yourself, because I wouldn't have been sure. It would have been difficult. But it would have been bearable. But for you to tell me you're in love with me one minute and the next minute tell me we can't be together, why that's just unkind!" she finished.

Looking at it from her perspective, Tony saw with clarity how she could feel the way she felt. "Oh, Cass. I'm so sorry, love. Please, try to understand," he begged as he tried to draw her back into his arms.

"No!" Cassidy said fiercely and jerked away. Her eyes narrowed. "I'll give you your three years, Tony. But understand this, it's going to take me a long time to forgive you for this!" She flung the door open and stalked out after giving him one last fulminating glance over her shoulder.

"Oh, what did you do, you poor idiot child?"

Tony turned from watching Cassidy rush up the wide, Victorian staircase to look at his mother who'd come up behind him from the dining room. It was obvious from her frown that she'd seen the tears in Cassidy's eyes. He sighed. "Only what's right."

"And, what, pray tell, is that?" Lady Carleton asked. When Tony told her, she blanched. "Oh, why must you always be so responsible?" When Tony scowled at her, she said, "Well, I do hope you haven't blown it with her. She's exactly what you need."

Chapter 10

"So, what do you think of this place?" Cassie asked Charles and tried to hide her exasperation. He'd been in Spain when she'd told him that she'd gotten the acting role, and that she planned to move. He'd insisted on flying into London to see her and to help her find a place to live. Cassie always loved seeing him, but he was being overprotective again, and it was bugging her more than usual. They'd seen so many flats that she couldn't even remember the number, and always, he'd found something objectionable about them. Security was uppermost on his mind.

Charles did a turn around the empty living room. "Well, it's certainly big enough," he murmured, taking in the high-beamed ceiling of the spacious living area. "Tell me again why you think you need so much space?"

Cassie rolled her eyes. "It's only two bedrooms, Uncle Charles. I want the space because I like room." *I really don't need this*, she thought. *I've got enough to worry about with this television role, which I'm not at all sure I'll be any good at it.* Just thinking about it made her feel queasy.

"It's just that it's a huge expense, Cassie. You can afford it, I know, but for what you'd pay for it, you could have a mortgage."

"I don't want to own anything here, Uncle Charles, especially since London was just supposed to be a temporary stop in my plans. It's just a place to stay." *And besides*, she said to herself, *it would be stupid to buy a place when I'll be living with Tony eventually*. She quickly pushed the thought of Tony from her mind. Thinking of him only served to make her angry and depressed. *Him and his stupid plan*, she thought resentfully.

"Hmmm," Charles said.

Cassie hated that sound. It meant that he was thinking, and lately his thinking led to her being frustrated. God love him, he was only trying to protect her. That and his unquestionable love for her were the only things keeping her from telling him to mind his own business and that she'd live where she wanted to live. "Uncle Charles," she drew the words out to show her impatience.

"I still don't understand why you don't just stay with the Carletons. Lord Carleton told me they'd invited you to stay indefinitely. They have the room, Cassie."

"I'm not going to stay with them because I don't want to overstay my welcome. You know what Granny used to say about guests and fish. Besides, it wouldn't be right to stay with them when I can get my own place."

"But you're too young—"

"I'm not a child, Uncle Charles. This is what I want, and I'm going to do it. And you can't really object to this building. There's a doorman *and* a concierge. If you want me to be any safer, you'd have to lock me up somewhere, and keep the key yourself."

"Not a bad idea," Charles murmured with a smile. "I knew I should have talked Mama into sending you to the convent school all those years ago."

"Uncle Charles, you know you're here on sufferance, right?"

"All right, all right. This is the one you really like, huh?"

"Yes, it is. In fact it's the second time I've come to see it," she said and looked at her watch. "I invited Esme to meet us here before we head for lunch. We have a few minutes before she gets here, so let's hear your objections."

"Why? I can see you've already made up your mind?"

"Because if I don't hear them now, I'll have to hear them later," Cassie countered.

"Well, that was snippy."

Cassie knew it was, but couldn't help herself. She was on edge. She was starting a new job that she wasn't sure she wanted, and her personal life wasn't any great shakes, either, what with the two men in her life wanting to act like she didn't know her own mind. "Was it?" she asked.

Charles studied her. "What's going on Cassidy Marie? What's wrong?"

"Nothing's wrong," she insisted. "Everything is fine. Are you going to tell me what you think of the apartment, or not?"

"Watch the tone, young lady."

"Answer the question, please, Uncle Charles."

"All right, if that's the way you want it. It's too expensive."

"It's my money," Cassie said with a shrug.

"It's too big," Charles countered.

"It's my space."

"You'd have to live by yourself."

"It's my life."

"I'll say it again, Cassidy Marie, watch the tone. And you might want to keep that attitude in check while you're at it," Charles warned.

"Whatever, Uncle Charles. What are you going to do if I don't? I'm an adult. Why does everyone think they can tell me what to do?"

"I'm not trying to —"

"Yes, you are!"

A knock on the door sounded. "Uh…is this a bad time?"

Cassie turned around to face Esme, who was standing in the open doorway looking uncomfortable. Tony stood next to her. "Great, another man who thinks he knows what's best for me," she said with a curl to her lip, "that's all I need!" She whirled around and stomped off towards the back of the apartment, pushing through the swinging doors of the kitchen.

Esme rushed to follow her.

"Hello, Charles," Tony said as he walked forward with his hand outstretched. "It's good to see you again."

"Thank you," Charles said with a bit of reserve tinting his voice. He released Tony's hand as soon as it was possible to do so without seeming rude. "How are you, Tony? The last time we met was at the commencement."

"Yes, it was, and I'm fine, thanks."

Tony's mind was still on Cass and how good she looked in her unrelieved black — black Capris, black blouse, black sandals, black hair around her shoulders — so it took him a moment to realize that something was off with Charles. He frowned. He'd only met Cass's uncle a few times before, but he remembered him being a lot friendlier during those meetings. "Is something wrong, Charles?" he asked.

"As a matter of fact, yes," Charles said with a nod. "What have you done to my niece?"

"Sorry?"

"I think I made myself perfectly clear."

"No, I understood the question," Tony explained patiently. "What I don't understand is why you're asking it."

"Isn't it obvious? You come in, and she runs from the room."

"Yes, but I couldn't help but hear that the two of you were having a row before I even entered. Look, Charles, why didn't you ask your questions of Cass? Wouldn't that have been better?"

"I would have had I known that there was something going on between you two," Charles explained patiently. "As it is, I had no clue until a couple of seconds ago."

Tony stared at the man who looked so much like Cass that he could have been her father. "Rest assured, Charles, there's nothing going on between Cass and me."

"Are you sure? You couldn't tell it by me—not the way she reacted when she saw you."

"That's just it. She wants there to be, and I want there to be, but I think she's just too young. That's why she's angry."

"I thought you'd taken care of that two years ago when you turned her down."

"You knew about that?" Tony asked in surprise.

Charles gave a quick nod. "I showed up within an hour of your, according to her, 'breaking her heart.' She was so despondent, that even if she hadn't wanted to tell me, she was forced to. She badly needed comforting."

Tony felt regret. "I'm sorry," he said. "But surely, you understand why I did it."

"Yes, I do. In fact, I'm glad you turned her down. I happen to think you're too old for her. The problem is that Cassie doesn't, and she finds it difficult to give up on something she really wants."

"Tell me about it," Tony muttered. "I love your niece, Charles.

I'm in love with her, but I can't see myself being with her now when she's so young."

"I'd be the first to tell you that Cassie is spoiled because I'm the one that spoiled her," Charles said. "She's very much used to getting her way, so if you really don't want to be with her, you should probably just stay away from her, because she'll try at every turn to get you to change your mind."

"It's not that I don't want to be with her. I'm just willing to wait until she's a bit older," he explained when Charles looked at him in confusion. "Cass doesn't believe we should have to wait. She accused me of not trusting her to know what's best for herself, and it isn't that at all."

Furious with herself, Cassie closed her eyes and facing the sink, rested her hands on it and pushed against it. "Great, Cassie. You've just made a colossal fool of yourself."

"Oh, I don't know," Esme said crisply from behind her. "You always did look fantastic when you're in a temper. Flashing eyes, glowing cheeks—Tony's bound to have noticed."

"Oh, Es," Cassie said with a sigh and turned to face her friend.

"You have such a nasty temper, too. It's so marvelously catty, you know?"

Chuckling tiredly, Cassie covered her face with her hands. "Stop, Esme, you can't make me feel better. I've made a fool of myself in front of Tony, and now I have to face him. He already thinks that I'm young and immature, and that little display of temper just proved him right."

"Bollocks," Esme said mildly. "You're entitled to be angry, and he should see it. It won't make a bit of difference to him."

Cassie lowered her hands. "You really think so?" she asked uncertainly.

"Yes. And if it does, then he's not the man I thought he was, and he definitely doesn't deserve you."

Cassie stared at her while she thought about it. "You know what? You're right."

"Of course I am," Esme said. "It's time you stopped acting like Tony holds all the cards, as if you have to make yourself Tony-worthy, or something. You're holding a lot of cards yourself, and he has to deserve you as well."

"Again, I'm forced to agree with you," Cassie said playfully, and with a wry smile, "Hell, I'm a pretty good catch my damn self."

"Exactly. And you're smarter than he is. Who was the first to recognize that the two of you belong together?"

Delighted with her, Cassie laughed and played along. "I was, of course. He should be thanking me, the jerk!"

"Here, here!" Esme said and punched her fist in the air, making Cassie laugh again.

"What's he doing here, Es? I don't need him here with everything else that's going on. I really should be concentrating on getting ready for *P&P*."

"I didn't invite him. I told him that I was coming to see your new place, and he invited himself along. He said he wanted to make sure you were moving into a secure building."

Cassie rolled her eyes. "Geez, another one who wants to protect me. That's what my uncle and I were arguing about when you guys came in. He thinks that I should stay at your parents' place, and I think that he should mind his own business."

"Well, my parents did make it perfectly clear that you're welcome to stay."

Cassie shook her head. "And I appreciate it, but we've been through this. I've already stayed with your parents much too long. I was becoming a moocher."

"That isn't true, and you know it," Esme chastised. "And aside from that, everyone is concerned, especially with the latest news out of New Scotland Yard. They believe they've got a serial killer on their hands."

Cassie frowned. "I hadn't heard that."

"Yeah, it was just announced yesterday. It's really quite scary. There's someone going around raping and killing young girls in their early twenties."

"How old?"

"Early twenties—not a one has been older than twenty-five."

"Really?"

"Really," Esme confirmed. "And get this. They've all been black."

"Shut up!" Cassie said in disbelief. "Esme, you're just trying to scare me."

Esme frowned in offense. "I would never do a thing like that, Cassie, and you know it."

"I'm sorry." Cassie closed her eyes. "Oh, God. All I need is for my uncle to hear about this. He'll try to force me to go with him, or he'll give up his next assignment and try to stay here with me. Even worse, he might try to make me move back home."

Esme snorted. "One could hardly say you'd be any safer in the States, Cassie. But I've been thinking that perhaps you should consider moving back in with us—just until they catch this lunatic."

Cassie was shaking her head no before Esme had even finished. "No, Es. I'll be fine."

"You won't be afraid living here on your own?"

"I've done it before, remember? I lived on my own for practically an entire year after my grandmother died."

"Well, maybe you *should* tell your uncle. You don't want him hearing about it on his own, do you?"

"No, but if I'm lucky, he'll be on another continent when he does. He's leaving this evening. I should be able to keep him clear of all media until then, don't you think?"

Esme shrugged. "Maybe. But what about keeping him clear of Tony? He knows all about this serial killer, and he's far from happy about it."

"Shit," Cassie mumbled before rushing out of the room to prevent what she viewed as a disaster from occurring. Heels clicking on the hardwood floors, she came to a skittering halt in the living room when Tony and Charles both looked up from their conversation at the noise. She tried a smile, "Uh...hi...I...oomph—" She swallowed her words when Esme—apparently having gone completely blind in the few seconds since the kitchen—flew smack-dab into her from behind.

"Lovely! You might have warned me you were stopping like that."

The irritated, muffled voice came from behind her. Cassie ignored it and tried smiling again. "Hi, Tony. How are you? May I speak to you for a moment, please?"

Tony lifted a brow in question and decided he would enjoy

her apparent discomfort for a little while. It was obvious that whatever Cass had to say she didn't want her uncle to hear it. He leaned back against the wall and crossed his arms and legs. "Certainly. What about?" He smiled when she frowned and her eyes flashed a warning at him.

"In the kitchen, if you wouldn't mind," she said through gritted teeth.

Tony plastered a fake look of surprise on his face and straightened. "Certainly," he said again. He made a sweeping motion with his hand. "After you."

"Excuse us, please," Cassie said to Charles and Esme before turning and going back to the kitchen. The doors had barely swung behind Tony before she turned on him. "What did you say to my uncle?"

"Why do you need to know?" Tony asked with a lifted brow.

"Because I just want to know, that's why."

"If you must know, we were talking about you and our relationship, or our lack of one—oh, what now!" he asked in exasperation when she looked horrified. "What did I bloody do now?"

"You didn't!" she said in disbelief. "Please don't tell me you told my uncle about the plan you have for us to wait three years."

"And if I did?" Tony asked.

"Oh, never mind, that," Cassie said after a moment of thinking about it. "Just tell me you didn't tell him about that serial killer."

Tony straightened. This, finally, was why he'd come. "Ah, yes, the Midnight Strangler."

"The what?"

"The Midnight Strangler," Tony repeated. "That's what they're calling him. It's because of him that I came over here today. I think you should stay with my parents until they catch him."

"No."

Tony frowned. "It's just until they catch him."

"Is he breaking into homes to rape and kill women?"

"No, not so far, but I still don't like the idea of your being here alone."

Cassie stepped closer to him, deliberately brushing her body against his and wrapping her arms around his neck. "We could settle the whole thing by moving in together. You could rest your mind about my safety, and I'd feel better just because you'd be there."

Tony's hands went to her waist. "You know that that won't do, Cass."

Cassie shrugged and played with the hair on the nape of his neck. She'd already known what his answer would be. "Then you'll just have to deal with it, because I'm moving into my own place, and that's final."

Tony looked at the stubborn line of her mouth and the determination in her eyes and gave up. "You're maddening, you know that, don't you?" he asked her softly as he took his thumb across her bottom lip.

"Yes," Cassie said and kissed his thumb. "But you love me anyway."

"More fool I," Tony murmured as he lowered his head and took her mouth with his. He slid his lips across hers, sipping at her lips until she was opening her mouth for his tongue's entry. *I'll probably never get enough of her taste*, he thought as he sucked her tongue into his mouth, *thank God*.

Cassie held him tight, just glad to be in his arms again. She knew it would go no further than the kiss, but in that moment, it didn't matter. As the kiss wound down, she tightened her arms around his neck and did some sipping of her own. "Tell you what," she said between kisses, "I'll be extra careful, and try to never go out alone at night. I assume that that's when this Stangler person does what he does?"

"Yes, it's usually sometime around midnight. He's raped and killed four girls."

Cassie shook her head. "God, that's awful. I'll be careful, I promise."

Sighing, Tony kissed her forehead. "I guess I'll have to live with that."

Chapter 11

"You're an idiot, Tony."

Tony looked up in surprise at Esme and tried not to let exasperation show. He knew exactly why she was there. "Ah, if it isn't my darling baby sister," he said calmly. "To what do I owe this surprise visit to my place of work? As you appear to be quite allergic to the concept," he said, referring to her lack of a job, "it must be something gravely important."

"Ha, ha," Esme said as she plopped down onto the leather couch on the other side of the room. He always teased her about not having employment, thinking that the reason she didn't was because she was too flighty, spoiled and carefree. He'd probably laugh if she told him what she really wanted to do. No one in her family ever took her seriously anymore. Not since the horrible mistake she'd made at sixteen. She feared the incident would forever brand her as hopelessly irresponsible in her family's eyes.

Tony sighed at her seating choice. "Here to stay, are you?"

"Yes," she said around a pout. "At least until I've said all I need to say. Will you come sit with me, Tony? Please," she begged, knowing he usually couldn't resist her pleading. "I really need to talk to you."

Tony pushed his chair back and walked over to her. "Now," he said as he sat and accepted her kiss on his cheek. "I believe I know why you're here, but do get on with it."

Esme ignored his impatience. "Yes, I figured you would know, but I'll elucidate my reasons for being here anyway. It's Cassie. You're breaking her heart, Tony."

"Stay out of it, Es. I know what I'm doing."

"But don't you see that I can't stay out of it? She's my best friend and she's hurting. You're my big brother and you're miserable. I just have to try and do something."

"No, you don't. This is between Cass and me. I know it's difficult for her because it's difficult for me, but that doesn't mean it shouldn't be done."

"But Tony, why prolong the inevitable?" Esme asked plaintively. "You and Cassie are meant to be together, so what difference will waiting three years make?"

"Three years will make a hell of a difference. She will have had time to figure out if I'm really who she wants and to grow up some more."

"But don't you trust her, Tony? I mean, Cassie's one of the most mature people I know. She hasn't got an irresponsible bone in her body. You know as well as I do that because of the deaths in her family, she's had to grow up abnormally fast."

"Yes, I realize that and that's another reason why we should wait," Tony tried to explain. "Look, Es, Cass has hardly had a chance to act her age because of her responsibilities. Now is her chance to do that and she shouldn't have to be stuck with me while she does so."

"Well, I must say, you don't make it easy on a person when you get stubborn like this." Esme's indignation was all on her friend's behalf. "Cassie is absolutely miserable and all because you won't trust her to know what she wants. It's unfair, Tony, and you bloody well know it!"

Tony shut his eyes and asked God to grant him patience to deal with his drama queen of a little sister. "As I said, Esme," he began as he opened his eyes again. "It's between Cass and me. You've nothing to do with it."

"Of course I do! Didn't you hear me before? She's my best friend! And don't you dare think that I haven't noticed that I haven't seen much of you because you're trying to avoid Cassie. You're avoiding me in the process and you're not in love with me!"

Tony could see that he really had hurt her feelings. "I'm sorry, Es, I really am. I'll try to do better. I promise. Perhaps you and I can spend some time together at the weekend?"

Esme's face brightened. She really did miss him and though there was such a huge age gap between them, they were quite close. "Do you mean it? Can we go to the cinema and have dinner afterwards?"

"What about taking in a new play on the West End?"

Esme was shaking her head no before he even finished his sentence. "No, I'm afraid not. I'd feel too guilty for not having Cassie along. She absolutely lives and breathes the theater."

"How is she?" Desperate for news of her, Tony just had to ask.

"She's settled into her new flat and loves it, as you well know, since you helped her move in."

Tony nodded absently, his mind conjuring up an image of her face, as it constantly did. "And her new television show? When does she start that?"

"Oh, she's already started filming her role. We'll get to see her make her debut next week. She's quite excited about it. And you'll never believe it, but she's already started hearing from fans of the show."

"Before it's even started? How odd," Tony said, unable to hide his surprise.

"Yes, I thought so too, but Cassie said it probably comes from the interview she gave for that soap opera magazine. They took pictures and talked about the role she'll be playing."

"Has she gotten lots of fan mail, then?"

"Actually, there was only one and it wasn't exactly a fan letter. It was more like hate mail."

"Hate mail? Already?"

Esme rolled her eyes. "I forgot. You don't watch *P&P*. If you did, you'd know that the character Cassie's character will torture is one of the most beloved characters in all of British television. Why, just that magazine's mention of what Cassie's role will be prompted someone to write her a letter telling her that she must not value her life because if she did, she'd have stayed on American soil."

Tony frowned. "It really said that? Did Cass take it to the police?"

Esme burst out laughing. "No, of course not. Why would she? It was just some stupid fan going overboard. She'll get hundreds of that kind if she does her job right."

"Really? Well, that won't be easy for her. The poor darling."

Esme looked at him skeptically from the corner of her eye. "Yes, I've never seen anyone poorer," she said wryly. "She's smart, beautiful and has one of the best jobs on the planet. Quick, Tony! Run over and offer her your strong, manly arms for protection. Or even better, move into her flat with her, so you can protect the pathetic, helpless thing."

In reprisal, Tony yanked a hank of her hair, over her laughing protests. As he chuckled with her and they started discussing other things, the letter slipped his mind.

"I saw Tony today," Esme said as nonchalantly as she could while she helped set Cassidy's table for dinner.

Cassidy stiffened. "Really?" She put wineglasses down at each setting. "Um…how is he?"

"About as miserable as one man can be," Esme answered gleefully.

Cassidy whirled around to face her. "Really, Esme?" she asked excitedly, as she smiled and clasped her hands together in delight. "You're not just teasing me, are you?"

Esme laughed at her. "Really, Cassie! Didn't your parents ever teach you not to take pleasure in someone else's suffering? It just isn't done!"

"Oh, stop teasing me, Esme, and spill your guts! Did he look just horrible? No, of course not," Cassidy dismissed her own question impatiently. "He's far too handsome to ever look really horrible. But tell me, did he look as if he were pining for someone?"

"If by that, you mean you, then I'd have to say yes," Esme answered after rolling her eyes in disgust of Cassidy's assessment of Tony's looks. "He acted like he didn't want to talk about you at all at first, but then when I'd mention your name, a certain look would come over his face. It was an I'm-miserable-but-I'll-martyr-myself look."

"That's wonderful news, Esme! It's made my day and if you knew the kind of day I've had, you'd realize the significance of that statement."

"That bad, eh?" Esme asked.

"Worse!"

Seeing the worry in her friend's eyes, Esme took Cassidy's hand. "What is it, Cassie? What's happened? Sit down and tell me about it," she said as she pulled a chair out for Cassidy and then one for herself. "We have loads of time. Mum and Dad won't be arriving for at least twenty minutes."

Cassidy sat heavily in her chair. "I got more hate mail today." Esme's brow arched, but she said nothing, so Cassidy continued. "It was even more hateful and threatening than the last."

"What did it say exactly?" Esme asked.

"Basically that the letter is to serve as a warning. I should go back home to America or deal with the fallout. I'm not wanted here and I deserve to die if I stay. Little American girls should stay out of England."

"You're joking!" Esme was wide-eyed and stunned.

"No, unfortunately, I'm not. It's difficult because the letter also said that I should stay away from Jocelyn and leave her family alone. So, just when I start to fear for my own safety, they throw in the characters' names and I realize that they're referring to them and not me."

"Yes, but that's still scary. I mean, this person, whomever he is, sounds like a total loon. Did you show it to anyone?"

"Yes. I actually showed it to Cameron Taylor, the woman who plays Jocelyn."

"And what did she say?"

"She tried to laugh it off, but I could tell it made her just as uncomfortable as it made me. She said that it's a bit creepier than what she gets, but it's all a part of the acting business. I showed it to my agent, Paul, as well and he basically said the same thing."

"Well, where is the letter now?" Esme asked. "The reason I want to know is because I told Tony about the first letter and he asked if you'd gone to the police. At the time, I laughed at him, but now that you've gotten another...well," she said with an uncomfortable shrug, "perhaps Tony was right and we *should* go to the police."

"No, I don't think so," Cassidy said. "The letter just made me uncomfortable because this person seems to be confusing me with my character and the show hasn't even started yet!"

"All the more reason to stop in and have a chat with a bobby, if you ask me," Esme said with a firm nod.

"No, Esme, I don't want to blow this out of proportion by going to the police. Besides, I've already thrown the letter away, just as I did the first one. Also, I'm just assuming it's the same person because the style of writing is similar to the style in the first letter, but I don't know that for sure. I mean, the letters could be from two different people for all I know."

"Brilliant!" Esme said sarcastically. "That takes all the worry away — you may have two psychopaths writing to you instead of just the one. Let's throw a bloody party!"

Cassidy sighed impatiently. "I only meant that if there are actually two different people writing the letters, there's less to worry about because it would mean that one person isn't focusing all of his energy and hatred on me and it's more random."

"Scary, but I think I followed that and I see your point. But, you have to promise me that you'll take this more seriously if another letter with the same style of writing comes to you. Promise?"

"Maybe," Cassidy said.

The room was small and dingy — so small that the huge portrait of the young girl on the wall seemed to take up all the space, all the oxygen. It didn't matter, however. None of it mattered. Not to the man who kneeled before the portrait with tears and longing in his eyes. Nothing mattered but the girl. It had always been the girl. "It's already begun, my sweetling," he whispered to the portrait. He stared hard, her beauty bringing tears to his eyes.

"I told you that I'd take care of everything, and I will. I must practice on other girls first, however. I've gotten four of them already, but it's not quite the way I want it to be. Not to worry though, we'll fix things right and proper. You'll see," he said as he lit a candle. "I've only just begun."

Lifting his eyes to the portrait again, he let sorrow overtake him and began to cry. "I love you, but if they knew about it, no one would understand. They'd call it sick, but it's not." He sobbed now. "She has to suffer for what was done."

Chapter 12

"All I'm saying is that you need to be more patient, my boy."

"I'm as patient as Job," Tony quipped to his father and sat back in an armchair at their club. "They're just a bunch of cranky old men with too much time on their hands, so they interfere in other people's lives." Tony watched as his father's blue eyes came alive with interest. Richard Carleton chuckled and took a sip of his port.

"It's not quite that simple, Tony. I'll admit that many of the men on the board are set in their ways and find it difficult to adjust to change, but there's one thing you can't fault them for. They all care about Carleton International."

"They care about the profits the company makes for them," Tony corrected, "which is why I don't understand why they're giving me such a hard time about my latest project. I've given them numbers, portfolios, in short, I've given them proof that it would be a smart and lucrative investment."

"Yes, Tony, I've seen the numbers. But you're asking them to invest in a computer chip manufacturing company. To them, that just screams risky venture."

"There's always a certain amount of risk when you're trying to make a profit. You've got to spend money to make money, as the saying goes."

"Yes, well, to many of the board, the risk is too great."

"What do you think? Do *you* think it's too great of a risk?" Tony asked his father.

"No, on the contrary, I see it as an exciting opportunity. But the board isn't in the business of excitement, Tony. They're quite a conservative bunch, as you well know."

"Yes," Tony said and frowned.

"Tell me, who's giving you the most trouble?"

"Oh, it's the usual suspects, Tim Flannery, George Cunningham and Henry Fitzsimmons."

Richard laughed. "Yes, stodgy tightwads all three."

"Exactly, and my problem is those tightwads hold tremendous sway with the rest of the board. They're a stiff-necked bunch, and I don't know how to get around them."

"You've got to court them, Tony. Don't just hit them with numbers and facts, court them."

"What exactly are you saying, Dad?"

"I'm saying that you've got to be more persuasive. Get on the golf course with them, wine and dine them. Essentially, you've almost got to court them like you'd court a woman."

"Court them?" Tony asked doubtfully.

"Yes. For instance, did you know that Flannery is mad about golfing? He goes to Scotland at least a half a dozen times a year."

"Bloody hell, Dad. Scotland?"

"I don't mean that you have to take him to Scotland, but you could arrange a golf outing at one of the courses here." He sighed when Tony still frowned doubtfully. "You've got to do something, Tony, because not all of them have accepted you, and some are just looking for an excuse to get rid of you. I'm not saying you'll change all of their minds, but you need to have as many on your side as possible."

Tony looked at him. "Courting, eh?"

"Yes, courting. What have you got to lose?"

"Well, I guess it's worth a shot."

"And speaking of courting," Lord Carleton began before taking a sip of his port, "how are things between you and Cassidy?"

"I haven't seen her in weeks, Dad."

"Weeks, eh?" Lord Carleton said skeptically. "I didn't think you'd keep up this asinine plan of yours to wait three years, Tony."

Insulted, Tony leaned forward. "It isn't an asinine plan, Dad. It's perfectly logical. If you'd think about it for more than a minute, you'd realize it's logical as well."

"With your mother constantly in my ear, Tony, believe me I've had little else to think about. Your wanting to give her a chance to grow up some more is honorable. I will say that much. But I'll also say that never have I met a young woman who knows her own mind as confidently as your Cassidy does."

Tony snorted. "All right, then, Dad. If Esme brought someone my age home with her, and said she was in love with him, you wouldn't protest?"

"Well, our Esme's different, isn't she? She's not at all as mature as Cassie. Yes, I'd protest, loudly, but that's because she's Esme. The two girls are vastly different in terms of their maturity levels."

Tony thought about Esme and frowning, shook his head. "I don't think I agree with you on that one, Dad. Esme has grown quite a bit since she went to school in the States."

"I still wouldn't trust her to know what she was doing with an older man."

"Trust is not the issue here," he said around an exasperated sigh. He was really tired of explaining himself to people. "I trust Cass. I just don't…" he trailed off as he tried to put his thoughts into words.

"What? You just don't what? Trust yourself?"

"Ah, there you are, Cassie love."

Cassidy looked up from the script she was studying to find her agent coming towards her. He was a huge man of fifty-five with a barrel chest, blue eyes and brown hair. She loved his attitude, and his approach to life. He seemed to approach everything effusively. She smiled as he caught her in a bear hug. "Hi, Paul. Who have we here?" she asked when he'd released her. She nodded her head at the two people who had come into her dressing room with him.

"This is Andrew Garrett," Paul said as he tapped the shoulder of a thin, pale man of about fifty. "Andrew here has spent some time in the States. In your kind of town, Chicago."

"Oh, have you?" Cassie asked him, studying his lively gray eyes.

"Da Bears, da Bulls," Andrew said in answer, using a nasally Chicago accent.

Cassidy laughed. "Yes, I can see that you have."

"And this is Gerald St. John," Paul said, calling her attention to a young, heavy set black man with startling light brown eyes who was carrying a camera.

"Hi," Cassidy said and smiled at each of them in turn.

"Andrew is our new man in publicity. You remember I told you how Kenneth left without so much as a by your leave? And Gerald, of course, is the photographer. They're here to ask questions and take photos for the publicity push I planned."

Cassie frowned as she looked at her watch. "But Paul, I have to be back on set in about fifty minutes and I still have lines to learn. This isn't a good time."

"Ah, but it's perfect, darling," Paul contradicted. "The shots I need will be candid ones, so you can just go on as you are."

"What I think she means, Paul," Andrew said, his deep voice teasing, "is that she won't be able to concentrate with us here."

Cassie's smile was sheepish. "Well, I wouldn't quite put it that way, but..."

"Well, I would," Andrew said with a gentle smile. He turned to Paul. "Don't you think it best that we do this another time? She's got to learn her lines, and I won't be able to ask her any questions if she's memorizing."

"I could take a few shots," Gerald volunteered. "If that's all right? I'll be as unobtrusive as I possibly can." He looked inquiringly towards Cassie and then Paul.

"Oh, all right," Paul conceded begrudgingly.

Cassie smiled apologetically. "I'm sorry, Paul. But if you had warned me you were coming, I could have told you that now isn't a good time—not for an interview, anyway. Pictures are good, though," she said encouragingly.

"All right, then," Paul said again. "Andrew, you and I will clear out. Gerald you stay." He leaned in to kiss Cassie, once on each cheek. "Bye, ducks. We'll talk soon."

"All right, Paul. I'll see you later. Goodbye, Andrew, it was nice to have met you."

Andrew smiled. "You too, Cassidy. I'm sure I'll enjoy working with you."

"Thanks," Cassie said to their departing backs. She looked back at Gerald. "I hope you meant what you said about being unobtrusive. I really do need to learn these lines."

"No problem," Gerald assured her as he began to set up.

He was already forgotten as Cassie began reading the script again. In this particular scene, her character, Brooke Lynn, was trying to seduce a man who was old enough to be her father, Sir Wickham. Brooke's plan was to get him drunk and then have sex with him. The end goal, of course, was for her to get pregnant with his child.

Cassie chuckled to herself as she read along. The writing really was clever, and to her surprise, she found herself liking being the bad girl. She'd been on the show for a total of three weeks, and she liked it more than she could have ever dreamed she would. She wasn't on every show, and that was just fine with her. She found that she liked having the down time. Her fellow cast mates had welcomed her with open arms, and she'd already developed casual friendships with more than one of them off set.

Flipping the page, Cassie read some more and burst out laughing at the lines. Brooke Lynne, all confidence and sexuality, had grown tired of waiting for Wickham to come to his senses. With nothing but a trench coat to cover her nakedness, she'd gone to his office one late night when she'd known he'd be working. Anxious to know what was going to happen next, Cassie flipped the page. Pure delight highlighted her face as she threw her head back and laughed some more. "Oh, you're kidding me," she murmured and continued to read.

Across the room, Gerald was mesmerized as he kept snapping his photos. *Perfect*, he thought, and snapped her right in that moment with the look of delight on her face. *Her face is pure perfection. Too bad those eyes will never look twice at me.*

Unaware of his thoughts, Cassie continued to read, finding something to laugh about on almost every page. The irony was not lost on her. Her character was trying to seduce an older man, while in real life she was basically trying to do the same. *Maybe, I should try that office bit on Tony*, she thought and grinned. *It seems to be working for Brooke Lynn.*

The grin disappeared from her face as she thought about how

long it had been since she'd seen him and how she couldn't get him out of her head. She'd even tried going out on a date with someone else. It hadn't helped, as all she'd done was think of Tony. God, she missed him. She hadn't known she could miss anyone so much. Sometimes at night she woke up aching for him, and an intimacy that she'd never had with him. On those nights, she found herself reaching for the telephone to call him. But she never did. She'd made a promise, and as much as it pained her to keep it, she was going to. Tony would have to make the next move. He'd set the rules; he'd have to be the one to break them.

She'd determined that in her mind weeks before. She wouldn't have it said that she seduced him before he was ready. Or worse, she didn't want him lamenting their relationship if it should get started sooner than his stupid start date. She had no idea if he actually would lament it, but she wasn't willing to take that chance. So she didn't plan on seducing him, putting him in awkward positions, forcing him to be in her company, or anything else. No, if they slipped up, it would have to be his fault, not hers.

Cassie sighed. It was hard to keep her promise to herself. She was naturally a doer, someone who went after what she wanted. So she found it difficult to suppress her natural inclination to do something sneaky and get him into bed with her. She struggled with it every day. "Damn him," she murmured. *But he won't last long,* she thought. *He just can't, not if he's feeling even one tenth of what I'm feeling.*

Cassie flipped another page on the script, determined to get back to her lines. Soon, she was engrossed again and smiling and chuckling at what her character got up to, what they all got up to. As she read, she wondered if they'd consider letting her write a scene or two. She'd always loved to write, and had written a couple of plays in college. They'd been received well. Chuckling some more, she decided she'd ask the director.

Gerald smiled in relief when she began laughing again. The sadness that had shown in her eyes moments before had been hard to stomach, but he'd taken his pictures, and as he had, he'd thought that it was a shame that such a beautiful girl was so sad.

Cassie turned back to her dressing table to pick up a pen and froze in horrified surprise when she saw what was there. Just one look and she knew what it was. That single sheet of paper with thick, black ink had become so familiar—too familiar. She didn't want to touch it, but she made herself reach out and pick it up. She was now getting at least two letters a week from this particular writer. They all came to the studio, and they all threatened her in some way. She received other letters, and not all of them nice, but those had a different tone. The other letters didn't make her feel so hated.

She knew she'd promised Esme, but she'd yet to go to the police with the letters. She had a deep distrust of the police. It had been borne that fateful day all those years ago when her parents had been murdered. Nothing much had happened since to shake that distrust. She didn't talk to Esme about the letters anymore because she didn't want an argument.

She unfolded it, and began to read. *You will regret coming here before I'm finished with you. My reach is long, and wherever you go, I will get to you.*

Frowning, Cassie turned the letter over, looking for more text. It was the shortest letter she'd ever gotten from her hated non-fan. She wondered what it meant. As she thought about that, it dawned on her that something was off about the letter. At once, she realized that it wasn't in an envelope and that she didn't remember seeing it there on her dressing table when she'd come in earlier.

In a daze she raised her eyes to Gerald then jumped from her chair. "Why are you doing this to me?" she accused him. "What have I ever done to you? I don't even know you!"

Frowning, and backing away as she advanced, Gerald said, "What? What do you mean?"

"You know what I mean!" Cassie was shouting now as the implications of the letter being there without postage settled deep in her bones. "You've been all over this dressing room, snapping pictures and ogling! You must have put the letter here! It had to have been you!" Her accusation was really more of a plea. She wanted it to be Gerald. She didn't know him. At least if it were him, it couldn't be someone she knew, liked and worked with on a daily basis.

"Here, girl!" Gerald said angrily as he backed into something and almost fell. "What are you on about?"

"Cassidy? What's going on?"

Cassie turned towards the door where Cameron stood. A small crowd had gathered there, but she didn't care. She walked over and handed the letter to Cameron. "This is what's going on," she said angrily. "I found this on my dressing table, and he put it there. He had to have. There's no other explanation."

Everyone turned to Gerald. "It couldn't be Gerald, love," Cameron said. "Why, I've known him for years, and he'd never do anything so nasty as this." Several of the cast members nodded in agreement.

Uncertain now, Cassie sank into a chair. "Are you sure?" she asked Cameron.

Rubbing her shoulders in comfort, Cameron said, "Yes. I'm positive. Gerald's just a shutterbug, nothing more sinister than that."

Cassie looked at Gerald. "I guess that all I can do now is apologize. I'm sorry for accusing you, Gerald."

Gerald was still frowning. "Where would I have kept a letter without it getting all wrinkled? I'd like to know if you've got an answer to that, then?" He held his arms out to his sides, showing that his pockets were small.

"You could have had it in your vest pocket," Cassie said in a small voice.

"Yeah, well I didn't," Gerald fumed.

"Cassidy," Cameron chided. "Take my word for it. Gerald didn't leave the letter. Perhaps it's time you called in the police, love."

"I'm sorry, Gerald," Cassie said again, right before he stalked out. When the others had left as well, she closed the door, and rested her head in her hands in defeat, thinking again that it could have been anyone. As she fell into pity for herself, the fleeting thought came that maybe now it was time for her to go to the police. But fleeting was all it was as entrenched bias reared its ugly head and had her dismissing the idea of the police almost immediately.

"No police," she murmured and tore the letter up.

Chapter 13

Yawning, Cassie continued her walk down Portobello Road. She'd been up since five that morning so she could get to the market when it opened. For years, she'd heard rumors about the Portobello Road Market, and now she was enjoying the reality. She had to admit to herself that the rumors didn't even come close to the reality. She was enjoying herself immensely. It was Saturday morning, the weather was beautiful and she had nothing to do but shop. Life couldn't be any better in that particular moment.

Scents and sounds assaulted her as she moved along from shop to shop, from stall to stall. She really loved London—more than she'd expected to. The city was so alive and diverse. It had so much culture that oftentimes she was on sensory overload trying to take it in. It was a bit expensive, yes, but she found it well worth the cost. She knew she'd miss it when she went back home. She didn't even let herself think of the possibility of not going home anymore. She'd realized that it only hurt to pin her hopes on Tony. Their future together was not guaranteed. She'd learned to live with that fact, but also tried not to think about it.

For now, she strolled happily along in her big sunglasses, Chicago White Sox baseball cap and jeans and sneakers, or as the English called them, *trainers*. It was her attempt at a disguise. She hadn't been on *P&P* that long, but just the week before, she'd been recognized on the street by a few fans. She didn't know how she was supposed to feel about that, but she had a feeling that she wasn't expected to feel a slight sense of dismay. She was grateful to be recognized for the work, but she wasn't so thrilled to be recognized for just being on television.

It didn't make much sense, she knew, but there it was. And it was a dilemma. She loved the work, there was no doubt about that, but she wasn't too crazy about the consequences of the work. She wondered how the really big stars did it, day in and day out. She was a small fish, and the flash of it already got on her nerves. "I need to get on a stage," she mumbled. "Then I wouldn't have to worry about having much celebrity, minor or otherwise."

She still struggled with her decision to take the role on the soap opera. As much as she loved the show, she wanted to be on stage so much that she could taste it. Going to the West End to see plays had become almost a weekly pilgrimage for her. She felt that she was getting soft without that live interaction with the audience, and she knew that she'd have to get on a stage soon if she were to keep her edge. She'd have to talk to Paul about getting her more auditions.

Portobello Road Market was unlike anything she'd ever experienced before in her life. It had to stretch for at least a mile or more, and a shopper could buy everything from antiques to vintage clothing, to house wares, to fresh fruit and vegetables. She'd heard of flea markets, but had never had the opportunity to visit one, and besides, she suspected that Portobello went beyond flea markets. The market was so alive and colorful, she found it hard to take it all in.

Hands already full with packages, Cassidy stopped in front of Charles Vernon-Hunt Books, and decided to go in. The shop specialized in non-Western art reference books, and she felt for sure she'd be able to find her uncle something on African art inside. Putting all of her bags in one hand, she muscled her way into the shop. An hour later, she made her way out again, her burden made heavier by not just one, but two books.

She smiled in triumph and began to make her way toward the area where she believed her map said she'd find fresh fruit. As she hadn't bothered to grab anything for breakfast, she was starving. Mumbling as she tried to get a better grip on her bags, and look at her watch, she swore silently when she felt herself being pushed from behind, and thrown unceremoniously into someone in front of her. "Oomph," she mumbled and her hands came up to brace herself against a fall, even as her heart raced with fear. She felt hands grip her upper arms, and immediately thought of her crazed fan. She struggled against the hold and tried to hold onto her packages. "Let me go!" Panicking, she kicked out wildly, making contact with a shin. Satisfied with the grunt she got in response, she kicked out again. "Get your hands off of me!"

"Ouch! Here, now! Hold on, will you?"

Cassidy's panicked brain didn't immediately recognize the familiar voice and she struggled even more. "I said let me go!" Though she continued to fight, she was so terrified that her movements were somewhat sluggish and her voice was barely above a whisper.

"Cass! Cass! Stop this now," Tony said and released her arms to grab her shoulders.

His words penetrated the fog and Cassidy stopped struggling, looking up in surprise. "Tony? What are you doing here?" Relief swamped her and she would have fallen into him if he weren't gripping her shoulders. After the relief came wariness and she straightened, trying to pull herself together. "You startled me."

Tony studied her for a moment. "Is that all?" he asked.

"Yes. It's just that I was recognized for the first time by some fans recently and it kind of threw me for a loop. I don't think it's something I'll get used to."

Tony was still frowning. He'd felt more than nerves when she'd bumped into him; he'd felt fear. She was as taut as a wire under his hands. "Are you sure there's nothing else?"

"Yes, I'm sure," she said. As with Esme, she didn't want to discuss the letters with him. She knew he'd worry and want to protect her, but she didn't want him coming to her because he wanted to protect her. Neither did she want to argue with him about contacting the police. Scowling, she stared at him, more than a little surprised to see him—and actually wishing that she hadn't, but she couldn't prevent her eyes from taking him all in.

She started from the top with his thick, blonde hair. Next came the wide shoulders covered by a black T-shirt, and that was followed by a sweep down his long legs, encased in jeans that were so old that white showed at the stress points. She rarely saw him in anything less than a suit, but whatever he wore, he wore it well. She held back a sigh. Why did he have to look so darn good?

"Cass?" Tony gave her a gentle shake when she didn't answer his question right away. He bit back a groan that started deep in his stomach. Blast, why did she have to look so bloody amazing all the time? Even in a simple white T-shirt and jeans, she looked good. He looked at the cap. "Where's your hair?" he muttered.

"Underneath my cap. I didn't want to be—" she cut herself off, not wanting to sound like she was bragging. "Never mind. What are you doing here?" she asked him again as he began to relieve her of a few of her bags. "Thanks."

"You're welcome. I've been shopping for Mum." He took her elbow as he tried to move out of the way of the bustling crowd.

Cassie frowned. "I didn't miss her birthday, did I? I thought that wasn't until October."

"No, it isn't her birthday," he said and a line creased his forehead. "This is my pitiful attempt to get out of the doghouse as far as she's concerned."

"Doghouse? Why are you in the doghouse? What did you do?" Cassidy asked.

Tony was bumped from the side and behind and decided that it was time to get out of the crowd altogether. "Let's find a place to sit, all right?"

"All right," Cassie agreed. "I am a little hungry. I was just going to grab some fruit, but I could sit and eat. This is my first time here, so you'll need to make the choice."

"Right," Tony said as he thought. "I've not been to Portobello in ages. Can barely stand the damned place myself—"

"You can't stand it? Then why'd you come?"

He shrugged, his voice distracted as he tried to think of a place to eat. "An attempt to bring back good memories, I suppose. Ah, I have it. Let's go to Electric Brassiere. They have a simple, but good menu, and if we're lucky, we'll miss the crush."

"All right, then. Lead the way."

As they walked, each concentrated on their own thoughts. They couldn't know that they were each thinking of the other.

The bloody chit looks wonderful, Tony thought angrily. *Damn and blast it all*. He flicked his eyes momentarily heavenward.

You enjoy punishing me, is that it?

Cassie's thoughts were a lot simpler. *Stupid, principled jerk,* she thought. *To hell with waiting. I want him now. Couldn't you weaken his resolve just a little bit, God?*

"Here we are," Tony said and held the door open for her.

Once they were seated, Cassie took up their conversation again. "All right, Tony. Tell me why your mother's mad at you."

"She's not mad."

"Really? Then why are you out at Portobello Road Market on a Saturday trying to find her a peace offering? What on earth did you do?"

"It's what I haven't done, actually, that has her ticked," Tony said with a scowl.

"Oh, okay. And what haven't you done...actually?"

Already irritated, Tony lifted a brow at her sarcasm, satisfied when her eyes narrowed into slits and she frowned at him. The muttered words "pompous jackass" floated across the table at him and he grinned. "I heard that, you know," he told her.

Cassidy shrugged and said clearly, "Good. Now we can rest assured that you're not deaf as well as—"

"Cass." Her name was said in warning.

"Fine. Just tell me what you didn't do that's got your mother upset." She wanted to regret her decision to have lunch with him, but couldn't. It just felt too good to see him.

"If you must know, she's ticked that I haven't been courting you. She, too, believes that a waiting period is extraneous."

Cassidy couldn't help it: she beamed. "Your mother's not a stupid woman. It's gratifying to know that she's on my side."

"As far as I can tell, the whole bloody world's on your side. Esme's mad, Mum's mad and Dad never loses a chance to tell me that I'm making a mistake."

"Well, just tell them to mind their own business if it bothers you so much. You've made your decision, right? Who are they to try and change your mind?"

Tony stared at her. "What are you playing at, Cass?" he asked.

Wincing at the suspicion that she heard in his voice, Cassidy said, "I'm not 'playing at' anything, Tony. I mean it," she stated when he still looked skeptical. "I don't want guilt, tenacity or anything else to make you change your mind about your decision. I've got my pride, and if you decide that you want to come to me in less than your three years, then I want that to be because you want to, not because of anything else," she said and buried her face in the menu. "Even if I do think that the plan is asinine and completely without merit, or *romance*," she muttered.

"Cass." His voice held another warning.

"Oh, quit saying my name like that!" she demanded as she lowered the menu. "I'm trying to be mature about this whole thing. I'm dealing with it in my own way, and if that means questioning your reasoning, or calling you filthy names in my head, then let me do it!"

"I love you, Cass," was his simple, honest response, partially because he didn't know what else to say, but mostly because it had to be said as the emotion simply flooded him as he sat across from her watching her.

Cassie put her menu down, and looked at him. She sighed. "I know you do, Tony, and I love you. And I guess you're pretty miserable too, aren't you?"

Tony thought about how much of his time was spent thinking about her and smiled wryly. "You could say that, yeah."

It was instinctive for her to ask him why, if he were so miserable, did he impose such a rule. But she didn't go with instinct this time. What was the point? She'd just get the same answer he'd always given, and they'd get into an argument. She found that she didn't want to argue, or try to convince. She just wanted to enjoy her time with him. She nodded. "Well, that's good to know. All right, we won't talk about it anymore. Let's just enjoy our meal," she finished as the waitress came over. "I'll have the French toast with orange juice," she told her.

"And I'll have the Full Electric," Tony said, finding that he was starving. "I'll take my eggs scrambled, and I'll have orange juice as well."

"That's quite a lot of food you're getting there, Tony— sausages, bacon, eggs, tomato, baked beans, black pudding—by the way, what the heck is black pudding, anyway?"

Tony winced. "Learning that might make you a bit squeamish and put you off your food, I'm afraid."

"Please," she dismissed his claim. "Nothing, I mean

absolutely nothing, can come between food and me when I'm this hungry."

"All right, if you're sure. Black pudding is also known as blood pudding, and that's because it's made of animal's blood, usually a pig's, onions, pork fat and oatmeal. At least, that's the way I'm used to having it."

"Mmm," Cassie tried to say with enthusiasm, "sounds appetizing."

"You think so? Would you like to try some when it comes?"

"Not on your life," she said unblinkingly, making him laugh.

She smiled. "Let's see what you bought Lady C," she told him when he'd wound down. "I hope it's a suitable please-forgive-me gift," she teased as he handed over his package. Her smile turned into a puzzled frown when she saw what was in the bag. "What is it?"

"It's an antique copper pot. Mum collects them. She'll love it."

Looking at his foolish, boyish smile, Cassidy didn't really have the heart to wipe it off his face with bad news, so she tried diplomacy instead. "I'm sure she will. It's so shiny and uh...coppery. How long has she been collecting?"

Now it was Tony's turn to look puzzled. "Now that I think on it, she hasn't actually done so in years. She used to when I was a boy." He frowned and raised his eyes to hers. "You reckon I ought to get her something else, too?"

Cassie's heart melted. He looked so cute when he was befuddled. She found it adorable that he wanted to please his mother. If he didn't already own her heart, she'd be giving it to him right that second. She covered his hand with hers. "Maybe you should. I can help you if you'd like. We'll go after we finish breakfast."

"You wouldn't mind? I don't want to take up your entire day."

"You wouldn't be. All I'd planned to do is shop anyway."

"All right," Tony said and rubbed his hands together in satisfaction. "We'll go after breakfast. And then maybe, I'll treat you to the cinema next door. It's one of the most fascinating in London."

"That sounds good. I've heard of the Electric Cinema. It's the one with the sofas, right?"

"Right, leather two-seaters. Now, tell me. Were you at the Market looking for anything in particular, or did you just decide to pop in to see what's what?"

"Oh, no, this was a well-planned excursion—none of that popping in stuff. I've been here since the Market opened. I'm Christmas shopping."

"Christmas shopping? In August?"

"Yes," she affirmed. "It's perfectly logical to do my Christmas shopping now," she defended when he continued to stare at her like she'd grown another head. "I like to finish early."

"Yes, but there's *early*, and then there's maniacal, slash, anal-retentive early."

Her lips twitched with laughter but she stilled them. "Whatever, Tony," she said in dismissal. "I'll have you know that those bags hold your mother's, father's, Esme's, my grandmother's friends, and my uncle Charles's gifts. And I got it all months, *months*, before Christmas. Whose the maniac now?" she challenged.

"I'm afraid you still are, sweetheart," Tony told her seriously.

"Again, whatever, Tony," she said, swatting at the hand he'd used to cover hers. "I was even able to get gifts for some of my cast mates."

A smile on his face, Tony watched as she pretended to pout while she fixed her napkin in her lap. He'd really missed that face. "Speaking of your cast mates, how are things going on *P&P*?" He leaned forward, grinning because she smiled and glowed as she talked excitedly about her role.

He watched her laugh and wanted to tear her face apart, even as he snapped another picture. He'd been watching her all day. He'd known the moment she'd left her flat, and there was nothing he hadn't seen. He'd been amused when she'd panicked and struggled against Anthony Carleton. "Flopping around like a bleedin' fish out of water," he chuckled.

Her reaction had reminded him of the reaction she'd had when she'd found his letter in her dressing room. He'd stood apart from the small crowd in the doorway and watched the panic shine from her eyes, and he'd wanted to cheer. "There will be more before I've had my fill," he mumbled. "Beauty has to suffer, after all."

He frowned when Cassidy laughed again. Such happiness from her was offensive. "You have no right." As he snapped photo after photo, he determined that he'd see to it soon that she had nothing to laugh about for a long time. His mind clicking as quickly as his shutter, he smiled when he realized exactly what he'd do.

Chapter 14

Cassidy sat on the floor of her new flat with nothing on but a robe and a pair of panties. The anger and despair she felt had practically immobilized her. First the letters at work, and now this. What else would go wrong? She reached out to pick up the newspaper that had been delivered outside her door. The front-page headline screamed at her.

SOAP STAR CASSIDY'S PARENTS DIE IN
SORDID LOVE TRIANGLE

Cassidy angrily threw the paper across the room. The headlines from two other papers said almost the same thing. She'd read the accompanying articles and they'd all been wrong. "I'm so sorry, Mom and Dad. It didn't even occur to me that this would ever happen. It isn't true, but no one cares. They just want to sell their papers."

Her father had been a college English teacher and the articles erroneously claimed that he had killed her mother because of an affair he was having with one of his students. Her father had then gone on, the articles claimed, to kill the twenty-two year old student and himself. "It's all lies," Cassidy whispered fiercely. Reporters had started calling her unlisted number when the first paper broke the story the day before and it had been a continuing saga ever since. They'd even gotten her cell phone number somehow.

At first she'd decided to answer, thinking she could set the record straight, but the one reporter she'd spoken to had mocked her. Cassidy had turned on the news only to find that same reporter telling her viewing public Cassidy's side of the story, but managing — without really saying it — to make it obvious that she didn't believe a word that Cassidy had said.

After that, Cassidy had turned off the ringers on all phones and had stopped watching television. She was only grateful that she lived in a secure building and no one had managed to actually physically present him or herself at her door. "Just let one of them show up here," she whispered angrily, "I'll give them a story!" Despite her righteous anger, she was a bit afraid. She felt cornered and trapped, stalked and picked on. She was scared to leave her flat for fear of running into any of the reporters that she knew lurked outside the building. The doorman had called her that first day and told her how they were hanging around and all the unwanted attention reminded her of the reporters who had tried to get to her after her parents had died.

The reporters had come to her grandmother's house and had even followed her to the playground once. As a six-year-old, she'd been terrified. Now as an adult, the thought of reporters still bothered her more than it should and she huddled in a corner of her living room, bringing her knees closer to her body to curl over them and bury her face.

Cassidy heard the sound of footsteps approaching her door. Though the halls were thickly carpeted, the floors creaked in some places. She waited for the footsteps to continue moving past her door, but they stopped right outside. Suddenly, she was tired of being afraid and she let her anger take over. "I don't know how they got up here, but it's time for this to end right now," she mumbled as she rushed to the door, momentarily forgetting that she was not dressed. Her fingers nimbly flew over the locks and she pulled the door open, prepared to give the reporter a piece of her mind.

"Hello, sweetheart. Are you all right?"

"Tony!" His name came out on a relieved sob as Cassidy went into his arms. "Oh, Tony, I'm so glad you're here," she said into his neck.

Tony hugged her to him, concerned to feel her trembling. "It's all right, love," he said as he closed the door. "Tell me what's been going on." He pushed the hair out of her face to look in her eyes.

Cassidy nodded and tried to stop crying. "It's been awful, Tony and they're scaring me. They keep calling with their questions and their lies. None of it is true. Why are they lying? I don't understand it. It isn't true, Tony, it isn't," she finished, having let her fear and despair overtake her now that he was there.

"Hush, sweetheart. It will be all right," he soothed as he rubbed her back. He was worried. He'd never seen her this way. She was almost hysterical. He led her over to one of the two sofas in the living room and sat, pulling her down into his arms.

"They're lying, Tony," Cassidy said again as her tears soaked his neck. "My father didn't kill my mother, himself or that girl. He never would have, Tony! Never! He never would have left me behind. One of the papers said that my parents abandoned me. They're making them sound like awful people and they weren't. They weren't. They were good, kind people and they loved me. They wouldn't have left me if they could help it; they wouldn't have!"

The sobs wracked her body, feeding the anger that Tony already felt towards the tabloid newspapers for emotionally reducing her to that scared, uncertain six-year old she must have been at the time of the deaths. "Hush, love, you're going to make yourself sick," he said as lifted her chin. Using his handkerchief, he gently wiped her face. The misery in her eyes as she looked at him made him pull her to him again.

"I don't know what to do," Cassidy wailed as she clutched his shirt in both hands. The tension coiled in her body and she went rigid. "I don't want to remember. What am I going to do? What? They won't listen to me. They won't listen to the truth."

"I'll take care of it," Tony promised and held her tightly as his anger grew. He'd been out of town, so hadn't seen any mention of the scandal until today. He'd read the article and the first thing he'd thought to do was call her, but she hadn't answered her phone. He'd had a meeting, so hadn't been able to get over to her until now. His parents and Esme were on holiday in the south of France and he'd called them to see if they'd heard the news, but they hadn't. Cass had probably been all alone when she'd seen the paper and that angered him even more. She'd been blind-sided.

When she quieted, he asked, "Cass? Have you been out today or yesterday?"

"No," she mumbled softly and closed her eyes. "Too many reporters and I don't want people staring and feeling sorry for me."

"How did you get the newspapers, then?"

"One is delivered and someone left the others outside the door."

"When was the last time you slept?" The question was prompted by the dark circles that marred her skin.

"I can't really sleep. I've been having nightmares."

"Have you eaten anything?"

"I'm not hungry," she mumbled lifelessly.

"What about yesterday?"

"I'm not hungry," Cassidy repeated with a bit of irritation. "Food is the last thing on my mind."

The irritation cheered him somewhat. "Cass, you have to eat. I'll get us something. How about that?"

Cassidy quickly became more alert. "You won't leave, will you, Tony?"

"I'll just go to the kitchen and get us a little something, darling, I promise."

Cassidy released him and Tony straightened. He watched as she lay down on the sofa and settled into the cushions. Satisfied, he went to the kitchen. He looked in cupboards, unsure of what he was looking for, but opened the fridge and found a block of cheese, apples and grapes. He found a knife and a cheese board and sliced the cheese and two apples. Arranging everything artfully on a platter, he went back to Cassidy.

She was asleep. He placed the tray on a table and lifted her, for the first time noticing that she wore nothing but a light robe and panties. He straightened and tried to remember which of the two rooms she slept in. When she moaned and snuggled closer so that her nipples burrowed into his chest, he decided to take his chances and chose the room nearest him.

He rushed over to the bed and bent to pull the covers back. Placing her on the bed, he removed the robe so she'd be comfortable and hurried to throw the covers over her nakedness. He breathed a sigh of relief and left the room as she turned on her side and snuggled in.

Tony made himself comfortable on the sofa as he ate the fruit and cheese and thought about Cassidy. True to his word, he'd stayed away from her. Even with the dark circles and blood-shot red adorning her eyes she looked beautiful. It was killing him not seeing her, but he still thought that it would all work out for the best. The newspaper articles had given him an excuse to come and see her, and he was glad that she'd put him on her list of people to allow into the building. The doorman hadn't gotten an answer when he rang her flat, but he'd been clearly worried and told Tony that she hadn't left the building.

The soap opera was only broadcast in the United Kingdom, so he didn't think that the scandal would be of interest to the rest of the world. His family had told him that the story wasn't in any French newspapers, nor had it appeared on television there. Hopefully, it would die down rather quickly. He promised Cass he'd take care of things and he would. Shawn could help. Tony thought he might talk to him about an interview with Cass.

He didn't know the story behind her parents' deaths, so the newspaper story had come as quite a shock to him. Cassidy rarely broached the subject of their deaths and knowing that the topic was obviously a painful one for her, his family tried not to bring it up. He wondered now what exactly had happened. He'd read all of the articles and they all agreed on the same thing: Cass's dad had killed her mum and the young girl by shooting them, and then he'd shot himself. According to the stories, he'd left a note explaining that he loved them both, but if he couldn't have them both, then they all had to die.

Cass had found them when she'd come home from ballet lessons. He picked up one paper, which showed a young, lanky Cass looking out at the world with huge, stunned eyes. She looked so fragile as she stood there in a leotard and frilly tutu, clutching someone's hand—fragile and clearly devastated.

Tony swore. "Bloody jackals will even trade on a child's grief."

He rubbed his hands down his face. Cassidy insisted that it wasn't true. He believed her, but wondered how all three papers could be so obviously wrong. News shows on the television were all reporting the same thing as well. Tony yawned and looked at his watch. It was after eight. Cassidy had been sleeping for a couple of hours. He kicked off his shoes and stretched his frame out on the sofa. He'd just catch a few winks himself.

He couldn't have been asleep for more than an hour when a piercing scream jerked him out of his sleep, making him sit straight up. Disoriented, he looked around and the scream came again. Realizing it was Cassidy; he rushed into her room to find her thrashing about on the bed. "Let me go! I want my Mommy! Daddy, help me! Let me go! Let me go!"

Her voice sounded like a small child's and Tony knew that she had to be reliving the day she'd found the bodies all over again.

"Why won't you wake up, Mommy? Please. Daddy? Daddy? Daddy!"

She screamed again and it was so full of torment and fear that Tony found himself lost in pain with her.

"Oh, baby, I'm here," Tony said in pure sympathy as he pulled her up. "Wake up, darling. It's going to be all right. Wake up," he urged her.

Cassidy tensed and screamed her terror. "Help! Someone help me!"

"I'm here, sweetheart," Tony mumbled soothingly. Not knowing what else to do, he simply held her and murmured reassurances.

Whimpering, Cassie fell deeper into the nightmare. *Her parents were so still. She wanted to go to them, but the emergency worker wouldn't let her. Couldn't he see that her parents needed her? She just needed to wake them up, and everything would be fine. She watched as the other worker covered her mother's face until she couldn't see her anymore. Panic became all consuming.*

"This one's dead. A total loss."

The callous words penetrated Cassie's terror. Her screams of denial filled the room.

In the screams, Tony heard all of the horror and devastation that she must have felt as a child. Fighting the sympathy he felt for the woman and the child, he made his voice stern. "Cassidy! Wake up! Wake up now!" Her pain stole his breath. He shook her hard once. "Wake up, Cassidy!"

Hearing his voice, Cassidy fought the nightmare's hold and gasping for breath, finally began to wake. "Let me help her...please, let me help...she needs me. Please don't take them away from me," she pleaded.

"It's all right. I'm here," Tony whispered and stroked her. "Cass, it's Tony. I'm here, darling," he said again and repeated it over and over. When the tension left her body and she became pliant in his arms, he knew that the nightmare had lost its grip.

"I'm all right, really," she said softly, even as she held onto him and curled into him.

"I know you are," Tony assured her. "Just let me hold you."

Cassidy wiped the tears from her face on his shirt. She hadn't had the nightmare in years. Therapy and the passage of time had helped to keep it away, but the stories in the newspapers had brought it all back again. She'd known that they would and that's why she hadn't gone to bed since reading the first one. Then Tony had come and she'd felt safer with him there and had let her exhaustion overtake her. Her defenses were completely down.

"Oh, God, what a mess," she said fervently into his chest when her heart rate had slowed.

"Would you like some water?" Tony asked.

"Yes, please. Thank you. There's a glass in the bathroom," she said, wishing she didn't feel so bereft when he left her. She drank the water and put the empty glass on the bedside table.

"Do you have that nightmare often?" Tony asked once he'd settled back in bed with her.

"No. I haven't had it since I was a kid. I had therapy for years as a child because finding my mother had been so horrific." Her breath caught as she relived the images and she had to take a deep breath before continuing. "There was so much blood. My mother was so weirdly still—so very still," she said softly, as if in a daze. "I'd shaken her to wake her up, because I'd thought that she'd had an episode. She was diabetic, you see."

Tony felt the renewed tension. "No more talking tonight, Cass."

"It's all right. I want to tell you. I want you to know the truth. I was so happy that day. The ballet carpool had dropped me off and I'd skipped through the door to tell my parents about the day. I was so happy to be home because we were going to put on a play, Daddy and I. But they weren't there to greet me like they usually were. They always met me at the door."

Remembering just that little bit brought back such pain that she closed her eyes. She tried to capture her parents' faces in her head, the happy times, and couldn't. All she could see were their lifeless bodies. She hated those reporters for that alone.

She sighed and tried to get back to her train of thought. "I couldn't find them, so I went looking for them. I checked downstairs first, and I didn't find them. Then I heard sounds coming from upstairs, so I went upstairs. I found my mother on the bed. She was just lying there, so I called for an ambulance like they'd taught me to. I didn't see my father until later. He was on the other side of the bed and, and…" Cassidy took deep breaths, but she couldn't calm down as her last image of her father's face invaded her mind. *Blood. There was so much blood.*

Tony sat up, bringing her with him. "Cass? What is it?" He held her arms gently as her breathing became choppier and she began to hyperventilate.

"Ha-half—Oh God, I'm going t-t-to…sick!" she said through a suddenly dry mouth and scrambled off the bed for the connecting bathroom.

Tony followed her into the bathroom to find her kneeling and vomiting in the toilet bowl. She looked so fragile, holding onto the bowl with desperate arms and fingers as her body contracted while her stomach expelled its contents. "Oh, sweetheart," he said in sympathy as he bent to put his arm around her shoulders and hold her hair away from the bowl with his other hand. Soon the retching accomplished nothing but dry heaves and very soon after that, there was nothing at all. "It's all right now, baby," he said as he helped her stand.

Cassidy stood in his arms until her stomach calmed, and she could speak. Embarrassment had her pushing away from him. "Water," she said.

"Oh, of course," Tony said quickly and moved aside so she could bend over the sink to drink straight from the faucet. He held her hair again and watched as she drank water, swished it around in her mouth and spit it out. She did this several times and when she appeared to be finished, he asked, "Better now?"

Cassidy nodded, opened the cabinet and pulled out toothpaste and a toothbrush. When she finished with that chore, she looked at him. She was tired, and from the quick glance in the mirror, her eyes looked miserable. She had no idea what to say to Tony. He stood patiently, and she knew he would wait her out. What she wanted to do was tell him to go home, but she also wanted him to stay. She knew he wouldn't leave. And she was pathetically grateful for that, so she didn't see the point in asking him. She turned to go back into her bedroom; actually wanting the comfort of her bed. She was just so damned tired.

When she was settled in bed again, she finished telling her story. "I called emergency services and my grandmother. My grandmother arrived first and found me with my mother. I was singing to her, hoping to make her feel better. I still remember my grandmother's face clearly when she stepped into the room. I'd never seen such horror on anyone's face before, and I was confused.

"You see, as she stood in the doorway, she saw everything that I'd missed. My father was lying on the floor with the gun in his hand, and there was a girl lying on top of him bleeding to death. And then she saw me kneeling with my head on my mother's shoulder and trying in vain to wake her up. She'd been shot, too. I just hadn't grasped that because she was covered with a blanket."

"I'm so sorry, Cass," Tony said and tightened his arms around her. She was quiet for so long, that Tony thought she'd gone back to sleep and so was surprised when she began speaking again.

"The girl, the real killer, hadn't died from her gunshot wound. She lived and was taken to the hospital. The newspaper articles got it all wrong. My dad didn't kill anyone, least of all himself. He would never have done that. He was one of the gentlest people I knew, and he loved my mother and me. He'd never kill her and himself and leave me all alone. Never," she said vehemently. "But the police wanted to wrap things up so quickly that they went with the obvious. And the obvious was all wrong."

"Do you feel up to telling me what really happened?" Tony asked.

"Not really, but I will."

Chapter 15

"Before you start, let's get you dressed, shall we?" Tony asked.

Cassidy heard the tension in his voice and surprised herself by smiling. She hadn't even noticed her own nakedness. "All right, Tony. If you insist."

Tony rose and walked toward her armoire. "Where are your sleep clothes?"

"Just grab a big t-shirt from the second drawer, please."

Tony did and tossed it to her as he got back into bed.

"Her name was Theresa Campbell and she was mentally unstable," Cassie began in a quiet voice as she settled the shirt around her. She made herself comfortable again. "The newspapers only had a couple of things correct. It's true that my parents died from gunshot wounds, and it's also true that I found them. Everything else is false," she said. "My father didn't shoot Theresa and he wasn't having an affair with her. She had a crush on him and had sent him love letters all of the time. I remember my father showing them to my mother. He'd even gotten so concerned that he'd called her parents in and showed them to them.

"My father wasn't the first male teacher that she'd fallen in love with and harassed. The first one had been her math teacher when she was fourteen. She'd had to transfer schools because of it and the teacher had almost gotten fired."

Some things were very clear in her head from all of those years ago, and others were fuzzy. But she remembered quite clearly that her father had been worried about one of his students and her feelings for him. Her parents had argued about it because Theresa had sent a letter to their house. It had been one of the worst arguments Cassie had ever seen them have in her short six years.

Sighing, Cassie looked at Tony. "I'm sorry. I was getting ahead of myself. We didn't find any of this out until after they were dead. Anyway, as I said, Theresa Campbell had a crush on my dad. She wrote him letters, found ways to stay after class to be alone with him and had even found out where we lived and drove by the house a couple of times.

"My dad reported all of this to her parents and to the dean and he thought that would take care of the matter. It didn't. Theresa became angry that he would do that. She thought that they were meant to be together and that nothing should stop them, even him. She's the one who killed them all; not my dad. But when she woke up in the hospital, the story she gave was that my dad had done it all, and the police swallowed it whole."

When she fell silent, Tony prompted her with a squeeze. "But, darling, how can you know all of this?"

"It eventually came out. Uncle Charles and my grandmother made sure it did. They knew all about Theresa and the letters because my dad had told them. They took the letters to the police. And even then the police didn't want to believe it, so nothing was done at first. But my uncle kept at it until they were forced to re-evaluate things. Somehow, he'd convinced Theresa's sister to hand over Theresa's diary. She'd written it all down—everything from how much she loved my dad and how she'd make him realize he loved her to her plans to kill herself, him and my mother if he didn't acknowledge that love. She hated my mother and blamed her for my dad's resistance, but she also blamed my dad for what she called his willingness to be duped by my mother.

"She set everything up and made it look like my father had killed her and my mother and then had committed suicide. All of her plans were in the diary. She even wrote how she'd gotten the gun and what she'd planned to write in my father's so-called suicide note, which she'd typed."

Hearing about the suicide note had almost been as bad as realizing that her parents were dead. She'd felt that her father had left her, and had taken her mother away, all deliberately. Her six-year old brain had not been able to comprehend that.

Cassidy continued. "In her diary, she wrote how she'd kill my mother first, shoot my father next, and then put the gun in his hand and pull the trigger on herself. She wore gloves while shooting them and then she took them off and hid them before shooting herself by my father's hand. We think that she was unsuccessful in killing herself because she must have heard me come in, and she got startled."

"But didn't the police notice any of the inconsistencies between the girl's story and reality?" Tony asked.

"I'm sure they did, but they chose to ignore them."

"Did they ever find the gloves?"

"Oh, yes. They'd found those early on. They were in my mother's apron pocket. They just assumed that they were hers and she'd used them to clean, so they ignored them as evidence."

"And no one investigated Theresa?" Tony was astounded.

"Theresa was wealthy and white. My family was middle-class and black. Even in 1983 in Chicago, there were people who couldn't stomach the idea of a white girl being attracted to a black man. No, it had to be him—black monster that he was—who went after her. In their minds there was no way that someone with Theresa's background of privilege would fall for someone like my dad."

Cassidy's voice was bitter and she was aware of it. She sighed before continuing. "Theresa even had relatives here. Her mother is from a well-to-do British family. They came to Chicago and her grandmother spoke on television about how horrified she was that something like that could happen to a wonderfully innocent girl like Theresa," Cassidy finished grimly.

"Her statement made in that cultured British accent of hers combined with their wealth made the story put out by the police even more credible to people. Eventually they had to investigate Theresa, though, because my uncle just wouldn't let it go. And when they finally did, they arrested her. There was going to be a trial, but she hung herself in jail. There was nothing else we could do, but get on with our lives. And since my grandmother and uncle wanted me to have a normal childhood, my last name,

Edwards, was dropped so that I became Cassidy Hamilton. They even switched my school to protect me. "

Tony was quiet for long moments as he processed what she'd told him. "This is all so fantastical, Cass," he finally said. "How did your uncle prove that it was her diary? And where is the diary now?"

"The police have the original, but Uncle Charles made copies. Dad's school gave my uncle access to his desk and in it he found compositions that my dad hadn't had an opportunity to return to his students. Some of the papers were Theresa's and the handwriting matched the writing in the diary perfectly. Uncle Charles was also able to get papers from Theresa's other teachers, who didn't believe that my dad had done it. Everything matched."

"Well, for fuck's sake," Tony was incredulous. "How on earth did the British tabloids miss all of this? And what put them onto it in the first place?"

"Oh, I think I know what put them onto it. My publicist sent press releases to the Chicago papers about my getting a role on *The Proud and the Profane*. You know, "local girl makes good" — that sort of thing. Three Chicago papers ran it in their gossip columns and one briefly mentioned my parents' deaths when I was little, but they didn't go into detail. What I think is that one of the British papers has a writer based in Chicago who saw it and started digging. It's the only thing I can think of," she said with a shrug.

"But you just said that your name was changed when you were a girl, Cass," Tony said. "How did they trace it?"

Cassidy had completely missed that in her misery. "I don't know," she said slowly and fell silent. Now she had something else to worry about. God, would it never end?

Tony was silent as well as he thought it through. How did the story leak, and why didn't they tell the whole thing? It was as if something deliberate and malicious was going on against her. But why? "Cass, do you remember if there was a lot of coverage when Theresa killed herself?"

Cassie frowned. "I remember my grandmother and uncle complaining that the story had become less newsworthy now that the real truth had been revealed. I'm not sure if any of it made front-page coverage. Remember my uncle and my grandmother were trying to keep things from me. I did hear them say that a lot of it was buried deep inside the papers and television stations barely mentioned it. And I heard them talking about it when Uncle Charles forced the police to re-open the case. I imagine they closed it again with the real facts. Well, what they really said was that since Theresa had killed herself and that there hadn't been a trial, they could only speculate that Theresa was the murderer, but all circumstantial evidence seemed to point in her direction. When my grandmother died I found all the clippings and the information that Uncle Charles had gathered. I still have the articles with the true scenario and copies of the diary. Would you like to see them?"

"Not tonight, darling. You're too tired, but I'd like to see them someday."

"I'm glad you said that," Cassidy said around a yawn. "Because I don't think I could move from this spot."

"Well, don't go to sleep, yet," Tony said. "I think I have a way to fix things. How would you like to set the record straight and put this behind you once and for all?"

Cassidy raised her head up enough to look at him. "How?"

"I have a friend who produces one of the news shows. I could talk to him and see if he'd be interested in interviewing you about this. What do you think?"

Cassidy thought about it. On the one hand, it would just bring more publicity to a part of her life she wanted kept private, but on the other hand, going on television would get the truth out and maybe she wouldn't have to deal with it again. "Okay," she said slowly, "I'll do it."

"That's my girl," Tony said encouragingly as she lay back down. "But Shawn will probably want to see your articles and diary copies, and perhaps speak to the Chicago police. Can you handle that?"

"Yes."

"Good. I'll call him tomorrow."

"Thank you," Cassidy said.

"It's all right, love, you just get some rest."

"You won't leave me, will you, Tony?" Cassidy asked. "I know it's silly, but I just don't want to be alone right now."

"I don't see it as silly, and of course I'll stay," Tony said as he started to rise.

"Then where are you going?" Cassidy sat up.

"I'll just sleep on your sofa. Where is your extra linen?"

"But couldn't you just sleep in here with me? Please?" she added when he looked like he would deny her.

"I don't know, Cass."

"Please, Tony. Will you just hold me until I fall asleep, then?"

Against his better judgment, Tony caved in. "All right, then. Let me just take off my trousers." He climbed out of bed, removed his pants to reveal a pair of boxers beneath. He also removed his shirt before getting back into bed with her.

"Thank you," Cassidy said as his arms came around her when she settled her back against his chest.

Tony suppressed a groan when her behind cuddled against his penis. To keep his mind off what his dick could be doing at that very moment, he went over company figures in his head. Biscuits were doing well that year, as were ladies hosiery and lingerie. Bicycle sales, on the other hand, had seen better days. He fell asleep a little while later trying to think of creative ways to increase the sales of bicycles, tire rims and plastic cutlery.

Chapter 16

"Cass," Tony murmured softly in her ear, "Wake up love and give us a taste of those sweet lips—both sets of them." He'd awakened a couple of times during the night with an erection hard enough to crack ice and each time he'd resisted making love to her. This last time, he decided to go with what came naturally and deal with the consequences later. "Come on, love," he whispered as he pushed her hair aside and tongued her neck. Cassidy moaned, but otherwise gave no indication that she was awake.

Turning her over on her back, Tony kneeled and leaned over to study her. Her t-shirt had risen to her waist during the night and he grabbed the end of it and rolled it up above her breasts. A shaft of lamplight shone from the connecting bathroom. "So beautiful," he murmured before moaning aloud from pure pleasure. Her breasts were high and firm and her nipples pointed invitingly upward. They were begging for a sucking.

They knew what time it was, even if Cassidy wasn't yet fully aware. Unable to resist, he bent his head and treated them each to a gentle nibbling. Tearing his mouth and eyes away from her breasts with difficulty, he gloried over her taut torso, took particular lusty notice of the fact that her navel was an "innie" — his tongue could work marvels in there—and traveled down to what he'd come to think of as his own personal pleasure giver.

Her mound was covered, but he could well imagine the delicate brown lips opening up under his tongue and fingers to reveal the beautiful pink bud within. He could even smell her. She was a heady mix of vanilla, jasmine and herself—her own special blend. He longed to bend his head and lap it all up, but that would come later, after his perusal. His eyes followed the long thighs. He could just imagine they would feel magnificently powerful as they gripped his waist in ecstasy. Then his gaze sloped over her perfect knees and landed on the long length of brown beauties that were her legs. They were sawing restlessly against each other, as if they too were aware of what was to come and were impatiently waiting for it.

Tony raised his eyes to Cassidy's face. She was still asleep, but it wasn't peacefully. Her mouth was tense and her brow was wrinkled. Bending down, Tony traced her neck with his tongue. He stopped when he came to the hollow in her neck. Opening his mouth wide, he planted his lips there and sucked the skin gently between his front teeth.

"Oh, Tony," Cassidy said dreamily, but she was still sleeping. Her hands came up to hold his head in place.

"Wake up, Cass," Tony murmured against her skin and straddled her hips. "Take your shirt off."

Cassidy awoke on a moan and from the sheer force of the rioting going on inside her body. She tried to catch her breath. "Tony?"

"Help me get your shirt off, love," he said as he slid his hands up her sides and underneath the shirt, making Cassidy arch up from the sensation.

Cassidy raised her arms and decided not to question him. She was just glad he was doing what he was doing. When the shirt was off, she placed her hands back behind his head, which had now reached the swell of her breasts. "Ohhhh," she moaned and squirmed beneath him when his mouth latched onto a nipple. Her back made a perfect arc as she came off the bed.

Tony released the nipple to stroke underneath it with his tongue, swirling it back and forth on the sensitive skin. Using his fingers, he treated the other nipple to the same kind of stroking.

"Oh, God!" Cassidy groaned. She released his head to trail her hands down his naked chest to his boxers. Slipping her hands beneath the waistband, she reached in and palmed his balls, making Tony drop her nipple in sudden excitement.

"Not yet, Cass. Let me take care of you first," he said and pulled her hands free.

"But, Tony—"

"Trust me, darling. Not yet," Tony said firmly and holding both of her wrists in one hand, he raised her arms above her head. He sucked a nipple into his mouth again.

Cassidy's legs fell open and she began bucking her hips against him, the feel of him against her driving her madder with lust. "Tony, now, please," she said urgently.

Tony ignored her demands and made his way over her torso and down to her stomach. He dipped his tongue into her navel, swirling it around slowly and finally stiffening it to push it in and out in imitation of the sex act.

Cassidy screamed. Her entire body was a mass of rioting emotions and she didn't know how much longer she would last before she exploded. "Now, Tony," she begged. "Please, Tony, I want to feel you inside of me."

Tony scooted lower down on her body and pressed his face against the blue silk of her panties. Stretching his tongue against her, he licked her cleft from bottom to top with gusto, making her push up against his face. He closed his eyes in bliss. "Is this all for me? Is this mine?"

Cassidy heard the questions, but didn't quite comprehend them. She was too concentrated on how he was making her feel. "It's mine," she whispered before pushing herself against his mouth again.

Tony grinned at her confusion. "Is it? Can it be mine, as well?"

The vibrations of his voice rumbling against her sensitive skin through her panties sent a powerful bolt of lust straight through her and Cassidy pushed herself towards his mouth. "Yes, Tony, it's yours, too," she agreed, knowing she'd say anything to get him to bring her to orgasm. "Just *do* something with it. Please!"

Tony slowly pulled her panties down and Cassidy lifted her hips accommodatingly. He rolled the panties down her legs and over her feet before tossing them on the floor. Seeing that the cream that had already flowed into her panties had also spilled down her thighs as he'd taken the panties off, Tony licked his lips in anticipation.

Cassidy moaned and thrashed about, pushing her behind up and down, desperate for completion and satisfaction. Her hand wandered down to cover her vagina and he slapped it away.

"Oh, no, this is all mine."

"You're torturing me!"

Tony licked his way up one leg, savoring the taste of her juice as he did so. Reaching the apex of her thigh, he bit the tendon there gently, making her rear straight up.

"Oh God, Tony!"

Tony grinned as she whimpered and flopped back down. He gave her another slow lick from bottom to top as he made his way to her other thigh to begin the process of licking her juices up all over again. When he finally made his way back up again, Cassidy rejoiced.

"Yes, Tony, that's it! Don't stop!"

"Open her for me, love," Tony said softly as he took hold of her thighs, bent her legs and pushed them wide open so she was fully exposed to him.

As the air hit her in that most sensitive area, Cassidy arched off the bed once again.

"Open her for me," Tony said again, this time more urgently.

Knowing exactly what he wanted from their experience in her old apartment, Cassidy reached down and making a "V" with her middle and index fingers, placed her hand on the top of her mound and used the two fingers to slide her lips open.

Tony put the flat of his tongue between her fingers and began to stroke upward on her clitoris. Feeling his tongue slide between her fingers as he licked her drove Cassidy wild. She screamed.

Tony continued to stroke, making slurping sounds in his greed. Stroking turned into licking in circular motions and that into gentle nibbling. Gripping the sheets in her hand, Cassidy lost all sense of self and screamed some more.

When she moved her hand away to hold his head in place, Tony used his own fingers to rub the slick membranes of the shaft of her clit. He kept his tongue relaxed and continued to lick and stroke her, inserting a finger inside her at the same time. Crooking this finger, he found her G-spot. Cream flooded his finger as she cried, "Oh God, oh God, oh God, ohhhh God! More!"

He felt her body straining as she pushed toward orgasm. Willing to help her along, he used his free hand to rub her lower abdomen, sliding it backward and forward.

Cassidy flew apart as the orgasm took complete control of her body. As wave after wave of passion and piercing pleasure shook her, she sobbed his name and ground herself against his mouth. "Yes, Tony! Yes! Yes!" The pleasure became so intense that she tried to curl into herself. The only thing preventing her from doing so was Tony, who still had his head buried between her legs as he tried to lap up every bit of cream that gushed from her body.

"Stop, Tony," Cassidy moaned half-heartedly as she weakly pushed his shoulder with her foot. The orgasm had taken almost all of her energy. "I won't be wet enough for you."

Tony grinned and shook his head. She was irrepressible. He'd have to get used to her being so vocal about...everything. After one last lick, which made her twitch and moan, Tony popped his head from between her legs. He looked at her as she rolled to her side. "It's all right, Cass. I'll take care of it," he said with some effort. He rose and with difficulty tried to leave the room, his dick looking like a pole as it stuck through the slit in his boxers.

"*What*?" Cassidy found enough energy to sit up on the bed.

"We're not doing this, Cass," Tony said from the doorway without turning toward her.

"Oh, you are soooo getting on my nerves with that statement!" she said in frustration. "You get back here!" Cassidy said indignantly. "We're not finished!" When he ignored her and kept walking, she rose from the bed and looked for her shirt. "The nerve of that man," she muttered angrily as she put the shirt on, "trying to get away without actual intercourse. I don't think so!" she said right before the shirt fell below her hips. She marched out of the room to find him sitting on the sofa. He looked perfectly miserable, yet determined. *Here we go again*, Cassie thought with a roll of her eyes.

"Tony," she said cautiously and persuasively, as if approaching a dangerous animal.

Indeed, he looked like one—a very beautiful, hungry one—as he turned those gorgeous green eyes on her. "Don't come near me, Cass. We're not going to—"

"Well, I'd like to know why not!" Cassidy stormed as she marched towards him, throwing all caution to the wind. "The fact of the matter is you started it and I want you to finish it. Finish me. I want to *feel* you." She stood directly over him with her arms crossed, feeling her vagina start to weep and contract again as she stared at his long, thick erection.

Tony noticed where her attention was centered, watched her lick her lips and groaned in agony. "No, Cass. We have a plan to stick to."

"Forget the plan, Tony," she said softly, completely mesmerized by the organ sticking out of his shorts as she sat on the floor by his legs. Unaware she was even doing it, she stretched her hand toward his penis.

Tony threw his head back and growled through his teeth as her soft hand closed gently around his pride and joy. "Oh, fuck me!"

"I will, darling," Cassidy purred. "I will." She scooted so that she was kneeling between his legs. "Can this be mine too, Tony?" she asked softly as she leaned in and licked it from bottom to top like he'd done her. "Mmm. It tastes good. I'd always wondered..." she said in distraction.

Tony's only answer was a clinching of his hands in her hair as she went by instinct and gripped the base to hold his cock in place while she closed her other hand around it in a fist andslid it up and down in a slow torturous movement.

Cassidy was getting hotter herself as she teased him the way he'd teased her. She stopped right at the head before slowly sliding her loose fist down the shaft again. She moaned. He looked delicious and she wanted to taste him so badly again that saliva gathered in her mouth. But she wanted to tease him more first. "Is this too slow, Tony?" she asked in a sultry voice, knowing that when he'd licked her slowly, it had driven her mad. When the pre-ejaculation cum pooled and dripped from the head, however, she couldn't resist and licked it, giving his head a thorough cleaning.

"Cass! For the love of God!" Tony gritted out.

Cassidy looked up innocently at him. "I'm only doing what you did to me. You don't like it?" Her smile was thoroughly wicked. She moved her stroking hand a bit faster up and down on his penis several times before finally rewarding him by closing her fist firmly just as it rose up and over the sensitive head.

Tony's hips jerked off the sofa. "Oh. My. God!"

Bending her head, Cassidy held his dick steady and closed her mouth over it, trying hard not to be too overzealous in her enthusiasm. Gripping the bottom of it, she slid her mouth up and down over and over again while her hand did the same thing. When Tony's hands clinched in her hair again, she stroked his testicles with the fingers of her other hand. She picked up speed when his hips starting jutting faster and faster. Twirling her tongue around the rim of the head, she stroked right below his navel to heighten his pleasure.

Tony roared like a mad man as his orgasm ripped through him. Cassidy swallowed all he had to offer and continued to lick and taste him after his hips had stopped bucking. His head fell back against the sofa as she released him. The orgasm had been like none he'd ever had before and he still wanted more.

"Tony?"

He opened his eyes to find Cassidy staring at his still erect penis with a greedy look on her face. She'd taken off her shirt and was rubbing her nipples against his leg. The tension in the air was palpable.

"No, Cass," he tried to say firmly. "I won't take your virginity."

Her brow creased and she sighed, still not taking her eyes off of his penis. "You don't have to. I'll give it to you."

Tony groaned, knowing he was fast losing the battle. "Cass. Cass," he said again, this time more firmly so that her eyes latched onto his. He had to get her attention away from his erection. "I don't have a condom. We cannot make love."

He thought she'd given up, but then her face cleared. "But," she swallowed as like a moth to a flame, her eyes went back to his cock, which was getting bigger and bigger each time her nipples made contact. "But," she tried again, "could—," she licked her lips, "couldn't I just sit on your lap? I'll put on my panties. I just want to *feel* you. And we'll stick to our plan...after."

Cassidy had to force herself to drag her eyes away from his penis to look at his face when he didn't answer her. She saw all she needed in his eyes. "I'll be right back," she said as she stood.

"Don't you move!" She rushed into her room, coming back in record time in a pair of silk, black panties.

Tony put his penis back in his shorts. He saw the disappointment on her face and hastened to reassure her. "Don't worry. I haven't changed my mind. Just thought I'd double our rather dubious protection."

Cassidy approached him and straddled him with her knees bent on either side of his thighs. She moaned loudly when her mound came in contact with the hard ridge of his erection. She closed her eyes, bit her lip and bent her upper body back, bracing her hands on his knees. "Oh, yes, Tony," she bit out when he grabbed her hips and rocked her forward.

She felt so good against him and the pleasure was agonizing. The wet sultriness dripped from her panties and flooded the front of his shorts, the smell of it rising in the air. He pulled her torso forward. "Give us a taste, love," he demanded when she opened her eyes.

"Oh, God, Tony, it would be so much," Cassidy said, even as she cupped a hand beneath her breast and put a nipple between his lips. The pull of his teeth against her nipple sent a bolt straight to her core and Cassidy jerked in his lap once before falling forward to brace herself against his chest while she rode him faster and faster.

Tony didn't even try to control himself. Reaching between them, he pushed her panties aside and slipped two fingers inside of her.

Cassidy mewled her pleasure and moved in pace with his fingers.

Tony removed his fingers and brought them to his mouth. Still keeping her nipple in his mouth, he slipped a finger inside as well. This proved to be his undoing. He exploded in motion, his hips bucking up wildly as he removed his finger and let her nipple fall from his mouth. "Cass?"

"Hmm?"

His fingers were at the crotch of her panties. "Will you get pregnant if we...?"

"No, Tony," she said eagerly.

"Caaass," he said in warning.

"No, Tony, I swear. It's not the right time and I'm on the Pill."

That was all Tony needed to hear and he gently flipped her so that she was on her back on the couch and he was lying on top of her.

"Ohhhhhhh!" Cassidy moaned loud and long and pressed her nipples into his chest.

Tony groaned. She was trying to kill him. "Be still, Cass. I don't want to hurt you."

"You won't, Tony," she whispered and cupped his face to bring his mouth down for a kiss. "I promise, you won't. You can't possibly."

Tony rolled his eyes. He may have had zero experience with sleeping with virgins, but he bloody well knew that the first time usually hurt. "I'm warmed by your eagerness, sweetheart, but let me take this slow, all right?"

"All right, Tony," Cassidy said and lifted her hips for him when she felt him pulling her panties down. Bending her legs, she kicked them off when they reached her ankles.

Tony peeled his boxers down and settled between her legs, releasing a long, drawn-out moan when he finished. Taking his cock in his hand, he found her opening and burrowed inside, feeling just a tiny wall of resistance as he did so. "Oh, great Christ!" he shouted as she closed around him and held tight as if never intending to let go. He tried not to move, wanting her to get used to the feel of him.

Cassidy barely felt the barrier break as she savored feeling him inside of her. She lifted her knees, wiggled a bit. God, it was a tight fit. She hadn't expected it would feel so...so...full and so intimate. "Oh, Tony," she said softly, dreamily, with her eyes closed and a tiny smile. "You feel so right, so perfect." She wiggled some more, trying to feel more of him.

"Be. Still. Cass," Tony said through gritted teeth. "Please, darling." Sweat dripped from his skin as he struggled with himself not to plunder.

"Yes, Tony," Cassie agreed, still with her eyes closed. Silence and then a soft, "Why must I?"

"Because I want you to get used to me."

Her hands fluttered to his sides to softly caress. "But I already am, Tony," she assured him. "Truly, I-I-I...Ahhhh...ummm..." She was unable to finish her thought as he pushed inside her until he was to the hilt.

"How does that feel, Cass? You all right?" Tony asked with effort.

"Oh, yes. It feels wonderful. I feel wonderful."

Worried about the dream-like quality of her voice and the tears sliding from her eyes and into her hair, Tony frowned. "You sure, sweetheart? Am I hurting you?"

"Only a little, and only the right way," she answered. "Tony?"

"Hmm?" He bent to kiss her, licking her lips and sipping from her mouth.

"Will you move some more? And faster?"

Even if he'd wanted to ignore the request, Tony would have been unable to. It was as if her words had awakened a sleeping monster and he roared his pleasure as he began to ride her. "Hold on to me," he told her as he took her hands in his and lifted them above her head where he entwined his fingers with hers on the couch.

Cassidy was barely paying attention to him now, as she let the feelings take over her. She matched him move for move, her passion growing deeper and stronger with each stroke.

"Faster, Tony," she demanded against his mouth when he leaned down to kiss her again.

Tony fed her his tongue as his hands went to her hips to control their speed. When she put her arms around his neck and held on tight, he rewarded her with a more thorough kiss, swallowing her scream as they came in unison.

Chapter 17

"I love you, Tony," Cassidy said later as she nuzzled his neck.

"I love you, too, darling," Tony replied and kissed the top of her head. He was still inside her and had never felt so completely whole in his entire life. "Are you cold?" He'd felt her shiver.

Cassidy shook her head. "No, that was just an aftereffect of the lovemaking."

"You're sure you're all right, then?"

"Yes, Tony, I promise you, I'm fine."

"I felt like a beast when you started crying," he admitted. "And you seemed so out of it."

Cassidy laughed. "There was hardly any pain, trust me. The tears were from the beauty of it and from the certain knowledge that I had just undergone an irrevocable change. I'm sure all women feel that way when they give themselves to the man they love; they've got to. As for my seeming out of it, well..." she trailed off and shrugged a naked shoulder. "I was. I was experiencing something I'd never experienced before. You were inside of me, and everything was right."

Undone, Tony could do nothing but stare at her at first. She constantly surprised him. Bending his head, he gently took her lips with his own.

Cassidy smiled and kissed him back. "It was wonderful," she said when he lifted his head. "It still feels wonderful," she finished and allowed herself to shiver in delight again.

"Yes, it was rather glorious, wasn't it?" Tony asked, playfully arrogant now. "I was sure you'd wake the neighbors with all your shouting."

Cassidy leaned up to look at him. She kissed his chin. "Well, I *was* having a wonderfully good time. And so were you," she reminded him. "My ears are still ringing." She deepened her voice to tease him as she repeated what he'd said just as he was exploding inside her, "Oh, fuck, Cass! Christ, you're good at this! That's it darling; you've got it! You've got it! Oh, oh, oh! *You're maaaarvelous*!" she finished on a loud, deep moan as she let her voice slowly pitter out on the last word. She arched her brow at him expectantly.

Her accent had been perfect. "Wicked chit," Tony chided good-naturedly and then sheepishly, "All of that?"

"Yep," she said with undisguised glee as she bit her lip to prevent laughter at his embarrassment. "Hardly proper conversation for a reserved British gentleman, is it?"

"Well, no," Tony began in an aloof voice with a frown, "now that you mention it, it isn't. It is, however, proper conversation for a reserved British gentleman getting the best fuck of his life!"

Cassidy laughed as she snuggled back into his arms. "The best of your life, really?"

"Most definitely," Tony said in contentment as he settled back and pulled the throw from the back of the sofa to cover them. "Which reminds me, you're quite young to be so good at this. Where on earth did you learn to be so uninhibited? And why are you on the Pill?"

Now it was Cassidy's turn to look sheepish as she buried a shy smile in his neck. "I'm on the Pill because I was waiting for you and my grandmother taught me, actually."

Tony was strangely quiet for a moment and then he said in a stunned voice, "I'm sorry, I must not being hearing you correctly. I thought you said your grandmother taught you how to be so wild in bed."

"Well she didn't *teach me*, teach me," Cassidy said around her chuckles as she laughed at his shock. "I just learned from her that I shouldn't be ashamed of sexual feelings. It all started when I was thirteen," she began to explain when he still looked shell-shocked and confused. "She caught me making out on the back porch with Bernard Jackson. It was my first French kiss. A couple of other boys had kissed me before, but we were too scared and inexperienced to actually open our mouths. Anyway, Bernard had walked me home from a birthday party. And since we'd been liking each other *like since practically forever*," in a flash her voice changed to roughly that of a 13-year old girl's— giggly, high-pitched, all-knowing and impatient—and Cassidy squeezed Tony gently when he chuckled at her efforts.

"It really had only been for about three months, but at that age, three months seem like forever. Anyway, since we'd liked each other for so long, I knew he was probably going to try to kiss me. That's why I had him walk me to the back of the house. I didn't want my grandmother to catch us. But catch us she did. We were really going at it, too.

The kiss started out slow, but once he slipped his tongue between my lips, it didn't take me long to follow his lead and things were hot and heavy by the time Granny caught us."

"Was there heavy breathing?" Tony asked teasingly.

"Of course. Heavy breathing, slurping sounds, the whole bit. So Granny catches us and I can still hear her voice now, "Cassidy Marie Hamilton! I know you're not out here in front of God and everybody actin' fast and loose! Have you lost your mind?"

Tony burst out laughing. He was sure her grandmother had sounded just like that—American Southern and properly outraged. "What did you do?" he queried. "Sit up, darling," he told her as he himself sat up. He pulled her onto his lap so that she straddled his thighs.

Cassidy grimaced at the remembered embarrassment and made herself comfortable. "The only thing I could do. I jumped away from Bernard as if he were on fire and said in a guilt-ridden voice, 'Uh, uh, uh... Ma'am?' But of course she'd seen it with her own eyes and after she lit into Bernard and sent him fleeing towards home, she dragged me into the house. I was completely mortified and I just knew my social life was over and that Bernie, the smartest, cutest boy in the eighth grade, would never ever come near me again—not when I had a such a fierce grandmother who wasn't afraid to embarrass you in front of the whole, entire world."

She was so lost in the memory that Tony could actually see the worry and embarrassment on her face. "But of course you were wrong. Your social life continued on as always and Bernard

Jackson probably suited himself in metaphorical armor, so to speak, to face your grandmother because he was just that determined to court you."

Cassidy looked at him in surprise.

Tony shrugged. "It's what I would have done," he said in a matter of fact tone. "And I don't know a single red-blooded male who wouldn't have. Bernard Jackson may have been the cutest boy, but I'll bet you were the prettiest, sexiest girl he'd ever laid eyes on in his short thirteen years of life. His raging hormones were screaming for him to face the dragon, which was your grandmother, in order to get to his beauty, which of course, was you.

"This gorgeous face of yours and his hormones wouldn't have permitted him to do anything else. I can guarantee you that old Bernard wasn't the only one who wanted to do it, either. I'm sure you were the fantasy of more than one adolescent boy," he finished and looked in confusion at the sappy quality that her smile and eyes had taken on.

"Why, Tony," she said with surprised pleasure and kissed him sweetly on the lips. "Thank you. I actually believe you would have — girded your loins to court me, that is. You're so sweet. And you're close in your estimation of what Bernie did. For the next year and a half, he came to our house, despite my grandmother's bad attitude, and tried to charm her into letting him be my friend, at the very least. He tried to ease in that way, but Granny was wise to sneaky ways and she had no problem telling him so. She finally gave in though, and when I was fifteen, we officially became girlfriend and boyfriend. We broke up six months later, but hey, it was good while it lasted."

When she was quiet for a while, Tony said, "Cass?"

Cassidy lifted her head to look at him. "Hmm?"

"That was a charming story, but you still haven't explained how your grandmother is responsible for you being so uninhibited in bed."

Cassidy laughed in embarrassment. "Oh God, I haven't have I? I'm sorry. So my grandmother dragged me into the house, sat me down and explained about the birds and the bees. She then went on to tell me that I should not be ashamed of the feelings and the urges that I would have because they were perfectly natural and they would happen quite a bit in the upcoming years.

"She told me that she wouldn't lie and tell me horror stories about sex, just to keep me from doing it because that would be her fear talking. She said that sex, if performed properly, would give me intense pleasure. She also told me that she trusted me with the truth because I was smart enough not to do anything stupid. Then she asked me to not consider becoming sexually active until I was at least twenty-one because she believed that that age was mature enough to make the decision."

"And this is why you're so uninhibited?" Tony asked.

"Yes. My grandmother said that I shouldn't be ashamed of anything that I do with my body in private and I believed her. Everything is perfectly natural. I had friends who parents did lie to them and I felt lucky that I wasn't in their situation. I could go to my grandmother about anything and she would tell me the truth—no matter how difficult or embarrassing the question. I always appreciated that and loved her for trusting me enough to actually tell me. That's why I didn't really consider becoming sexually active until I was twenty-one. Though at one point, I was highly tempted."

"Really?" Tony asked.

"Really," Cassidy confirmed. "She'd asked me to and it was the least I could do. But when I was twenty, and you came to our door in that pinstriped suit, I was ready to throw my promise to Granny right out the window," she teased "So tell me about your first kiss," she said once they finished laughing.

Tony looked offended. "Sorry, a gentleman never kisses and tells."

Cassidy poked him in the side. "Oh, come on. I'm sure you were a little Casanova, so you must have been all of what? Ten when you first kissed a girl? It hardly counts now."

"I beg your pardon. Casanova, indeed. I was eleven," he finished in a dignified voice.

"Oh, then pardon me, your lordship" Cassidy tried to say over her laughter. "Tell me about your first kiss at the ripe old age of eleven."

Tony smiled and tweaked her nose. "Nothing to tell, really. Her name was Emma Matson and I was mad for her. One day after a football—that's soccer to you—game, which I'd won for the team, she said she had something to tell me and that I should come with her. And being the curious, horny, little wanker that I was, I followed her into the school. It was after hours, so there was hardly anyone about. She walked into an empty classroom and I followed her. I'd hardly stepped in before she slammed the door shut, shoved me up against the wall and kissed me.

"She pressed up against me so that I could feel her brand new little nibblets pushing into my chest and my body shot into overdrive. She pushed her tongue into my mouth and moved it around a bit and as I was a fast learner and liked the sensation very much, I pushed mine right back at her. Neither of us really had any idea what were doing, but we gave it a jolly good go.

"She took my hand and placed it on her booby while she palmed me through my shorts. I was shocked and I froze for just a second, mind you. But Emma obviously didn't have time for slow reactions and the next thing I knew, she had stepped back and was saying, "Smashing game, Tony." And then she was gone, leaving me standing there with a hard on tenting my shorts, drool spilling from my mouth and a loopy look in my eyes. I was confused, frustrated and a bit scared, but extremely happy."

"Why, that little harlot! Imagine her taking advantage of your innocence that way," Cassidy tried to say with indignation over her barely controlled laughter. She imagined a green-eyed, eleven-year-old Tony after his first kiss. He must have been adorable! "How old was she?"

Tony thought about it. "Well she was a level higher than I, so she must have been at least twelve."

"And an older woman to boot," Cassidy tisked. "How naughty!"

Tony laughed and wrapped the blanket around them again as she lay back down on his chest.

They were quiet for a while and then Tony felt her tense against him. "Cass. What's going through that head of yours now?" he asked her softly.

Cassidy tried to laugh it off. "You know me so well. I was just thinking about what you said earlier. I mean it was more than sex, right? You do feel that we were making love, don't you?"

Tony heard the worry in her voice. "Yes, of course we were making love, Cass."

Cassidy relaxed against him with a sigh. "I know that we're not supposed to get serious for another three years, but I don't want you to forget how much we love each other in that time and I believe that that can happen. You know the old saying, 'out of sight, out of mind.'"

"Yes and I've also heard the phrase, 'absence makes the heart grow fonder.' Trust me darling," he said with a reassuring squeeze. "That's what's going to happen with us. I only love you more each day."

Chapter 18

"I've missed you," she said softly. "A lot."

"I've missed you, too," Tony said. "But I see your beautiful face every Wednesday and Friday night on the telly."

Cassidy's head popped up and she looked at him with pleased surprise, her sorrow forgotten for the moment. "You watch *The Proud and the Profane*? Do you really?"

Tony frowned. "Why should you be so surprised that I watch your show?"

She shrugged. "I'm just surprised, that's all. Do you like it?"

"Hang on a minute, Cass. We'll discuss the show in a minute. Didn't you think I'd watch your show?"

"I guess I didn't think you would, no."

"Buy *why*, Cass?" Tony's tone was one of urgency.

"I didn't want to have any expectations. You've given my self-esteem quite a beating, you know. So, I tried not to expect anything from you, that way I can't get hurt any more than I already have been."

Tony didn't like hearing that at all. "Well, bloody buggering hell, Cass! You just get that thought out of your head right now!"

Cassie reared back to look at him. "What are you talking about?"

"I can't believe that you don't think you can depend on me, and worse, that you refuse to have any expectations of me! Are you deliberately trying to insult my sense of honor?"

Cassie could see that he was actually angry, and she got angry right with him. She folded her arms and raised her voice as well. "Well, what else was I supposed to do? I have to protect myself!"

"Oh, bollocks to that, Cass! Protect yourself! From me? When I'd cut off my arm before I deliberately hurt you? Because you didn't get your way just that once, you take it to the extreme and say you can't depend on me?" Tony was outraged.

So was Cassie. "Like I said, I have to protect myself. I wasn't trying to hurt you. It's called self-preservation."

"Well, you'll stop it at once! Do you understand?"

"Stop protecting myself?" Cassie asked him. She scoffed. "Not bloody likely," she finished resolutely, defiantly borrowing one of his favorite phrases and his accent.

Cheeky little git, Tony thought with reluctant humor as he studied her mutinous expression. He sighed. "Let's call a truce, shall we?"

Cassie studied him suspiciously, refusing to give in. "No."

Tony couldn't help it; he kissed her, laughing when she tried to jerk away. Having already anticipated her, he'd taken her arms in his hands. Now he gripped them tight, making her stay still. "Come on, Cass," he said persuasively as he kissed her neck. "Surely, it doesn't have to be this way. We shouldn't be arguing."

"I don't see why not," she maintained stubbornly.

"Do you mean to say," he continued between the kisses he pressed to the corners of her mouth, "that you refuse to talk sensibly to the man who's just made love to you? To the only man who will ever make love to you? You can't be reasonable with the man who's so in love with you that when he moved in you and you moved so sweetly beneath him that he knew he'd found heaven?"

Cassie knew what he was doing, but she didn't care. Her mouth slanted under his and she wrapped her arms around his neck. *I just love him so much*, she thought and didn't fight the emotional shudders that shook her body as he gathered her close.

Tony felt the shudders and held her even tighter as love swamped his senses. "Here now," he murmured into her hair. "It's all right."

Too overwhelmed with emotions to say anything at first, Cassie just tightened her arms around his neck and burrowed closer. "I love you so much, that it scares me. And sometimes I think that maybe you don't love me as much as I love you."

"Oh, God, love, don't ever think that. I love you so much that I can barely go a day without thinking about you. I can't bear to think that you've given up on me, Cass."

"I haven't given up on you, Tony. But you need to understand that it's been really difficult for me."

"I do understand. It's been difficult for me as well, but it's a sacrifice I'm willing to make because I love you so much." Even as he said it, he realized what a hypocrite he was, given that he'd just made love to her.

Cass said nothing, thinking along the same lines. She didn't think he was a hypocrite, but she did think that it was ironic that after what they'd done, he could still talk of sticking to his absurd plan. She decided to change the subject.

"Let's just talk about *P&P* now, okay?"

"Of course. I wouldn't miss the show, you know. I even bought one of those highly technical TiVo contraptions. That way, I get to see you no matter how late I get in from the office. By the way, sweetheart," he said and pursed his lips in thought. "You really should stop being such a nasty bitch to the children. How on earth do you expect poor Wickham to really fall for you if you're a perfect beast to his kiddies?"

Cassidy laughed — and was surprised that she still could — when she realized he was talking about her character on the show. She wrinkled her nose. "I know! Aren't I just the most awful bitch? Those children hate me!"

"Yes, as does half of England, I imagine."

"Now, you're right about that. I hardly get any fan mail, but I get tons of hate mail delivered to me at the studio."

That gave Tony pause. "Tons? Just how many are in that 'tons'?"

"At least a couple of dozen a week. I guess that means I'm doing my job," she finished lamely and shrugged her shoulders.

Tony could tell, however, that it bothered her. "It's that hard, eh?"

"Yeah," Cassidy sighed the word. "I wish it didn't bother me so much, but some of those people really hate me. I mean I've even been threatened — well, not me per say, but my character, Brooke, has."

"How many are like the first one you received?"

Cassidy shrugged again, but this time tried to avoid his eyes as she suddenly remembered that Esme had said he'd wanted to call the police. "I get all kinds. One lady wrote and said that if I didn't stop meddling in Jocelyn and Wickham's lives, she'd put a hex on me to turn my pretty face into a messy, pock-marked tragedy and she could do it too, because she has Gypsy blood running through her veins thanks to her father's side of the family."

Cassidy laughed and said between chuckles, "There was also the one from the lady who said that if she ever got to London, she'd run me down in the street with her truck, I mean *lorry*, and cripple me so I'd know what it feels like for Jocelyn to be trapped in that wheelchair."

Tony didn't laugh with her. "Cass," he demanded quietly.

She peeked up at him for a moment before saying, "And then there was the letter that said that I should be shipped back — post-haste — to America, where my sort of person is apparently allowed to thrive." She decided not to tell him that the letter threatened that she'd be made to suffer because beauty always suffered. "And I wanted to write back and say that I'd be back in America sooner than they knew," she finished softly and waited. She didn't dare look up at him, so she studied his chest as if it were the most interesting thing in the world.

Tony was about to demand an answer again, but stopped when he realized what she'd said. "Cass?" He lifted her chin so he could look in her eyes. "Look at me. What are you saying?"

"I was going to tell you — really I was," she protested when he looked skeptical. When he continued to look at her with suspicion, she muttered, "Okay, so maybe at first I wasn't," she said. "I wanted you to wonder — and worry a bit — about where I was."

"Cass!" Tony said chidingly.

"I know, I know, it was a horrible thought, but I was still angry at you for making us wait and I thought to punish you by not telling you, but then I changed my mind. I thought about how much you would worry and how I would feel if you left for months without telling me and I decided to be mature and tell you. I just haven't had the chance to until now," she muttered and embarrassment made her avoid looking in his eyes.

"So tell me now," he said softly.

"Well, my character will be written out of the show in the next week or so and when she is, I'll be going back home to work. My agent has been working really hard and because I have *P&P* under my belt, he was able to get me an audition for a role in a play in Chicago. If I get it, I'll be performing at one of the most prestigious theaters in the entire city and while it may not be the West End, some of Chicago's theaters are quite renowned."

"Well, that's wonderful news, isn't it? You're finally getting the break you've wanted for so long. Congratulations!"

"Thank you," Cassidy said. "It will only be for a few weeks; six, eight at the most, if I get the part. It's a short run. And besides, I'll be back in London for your parents' Christmas party in a couple of months. I'm going to keep my apartment and the producers of *P&P* said that my role on the show would be a recurring one. Also, you could come visit me from time to time…if you wanted," she trailed off hopefully.

"Cass, you know I'd want to and I just might. But you know as well as I do that your being away fits into the plan very nicely. Now I'll have a whole ocean and half of your bloody country separating me from you, so it will be easier to resist just popping over to see you. Can't just hop in a taxi and be there."

"Yes, I know," Cassidy said.

"And besides that, your not being on television here will probably stop the letters from that crazed non-fan. The letters," he said with a firm look, "that you've yet to tell me about."

"The last letter I just told you about was one of them. I think they were from the same person—they had the same writing style, anyway."

"And what have you done about it?"

"Nothing. What?" She asked when he simply stared at her as if she'd gone around the bend. "Since I'm going to Chicago, the letters will probably stop. Out of sight, out of mind. You said so yourself," she protested when he still just looked at her.

"Cass," Tony said patiently as he bent his neck so he could see into her eyes. "Why are you afraid to go to the police?"

"I'm not," she tried to deny, but one look from him stopped her. She sighed. "When I received the first letters, I just didn't want to make a big deal out of something that could turn out to be nothing. But now, I don't want the press to find out about it. I already know how relentless they can be. If the latest debacle that brought you over here wasn't enough to convince me, then all the other pieces they've run about me are. Even before the information about my parents was discovered, I'd already been in the papers at least a dozen times—and I'm not even that famous."

"Cassidy, you have to go to the police. It only makes sense that you do. If nothing else, they'll have it on record if it should happen again."

"But—"

"No buts. You'll be coming back here after Chicago, won't you? And as you've just said, you'll eventually join the soap opera again."

"I know, but—"

"Cass." The word was soft, but firm, as was the light shaking of the shoulders he gave her. "Damn the press. Your safety is more important than a few stories. Now, you'll go to the police, won't you? In fact, we'll go together and take the letters with us. I've been thinking about how the stories about your parents got placed. It really bothers me that we don't know how they found out without knowing your proper surname. I'd like to talk to the police about it. I don't like it that the story was planted."

Cassidy gave in with a nod. "Okay, but I don't have the letters anymore. I threw them away."

"Well, that could muck things up a bit," he murmured. "If I'm not mistaken, the police will need at least two letters as proof that you're being harassed."

"How do you know that?"

"The law isn't that old, and I remember it being in the news when it was enacted," Tony said as she settled against him again.

"Do you remember what the punishment would be if a stalker is caught?"

"Six months, I believe, and maybe a fine of some sort."

"That isn't much," Cassie said.

"I know, but I believe, if they knew who the person was, you could file a restraining order against them," he finished and frowned in contemplation again. "It's too bad you've thrown away the letters, but no matter, we'll go to the police anyway. Right?"

"Right."

"Good, that's settled. Now tell me. Where will you stay in Chicago?"

"At home—in my grandmother's house," she explained when he looked confused. "I haven't sold it. My grandmother left it to me in her will, along with a trust. The trust takes care of the property taxes."

"Just how much money do you have?" Tony asked, realizing that he knew very little about that part of her life. He'd assumed that there had been wills and insurance; he just didn't know the details.

"Well, not as much as you filthy rich Carletons, but with what my parents left me in their wills and with my grandmother's bequest, I'm pretty comfortable. They also put the money from the sale of my parents' house in a trust for me. So I'm comfortable enough that I don't have to work for a while if I don't want to."

"And how long is a while?"

"Well, if I'm really careful, about ten years. And now with the money I'm getting from *P&P* to add to the kitty, I'll be fine for quite a while after that and still be able to keep homes on both sides of the Atlantic. So, relax, I'm not after your money, I'm only after you," she said with a smile.

Tony barked out a laugh. "Trust me, Cass, that was never a concern."

"It wasn't?"

"No, it wasn't. You're too much of a hard worker and a go-getter to be a gold-digger. It's simply not in your personality," he said patiently when she just looked at him in silence. "Now, let's have a shower," he said and rose with her in his arms. He groaned when she took hold of his penis, lowered her body and slipped him inside of her. "Cass," he chided and stopped walking.

"Well, it is growing again and besides, you know you want to," she said and wriggled closer with a moan. She twined her arms around his neck and slowly started moving herself up and down.

Tony groaned again and walked until her back hit a wall. "You could be too tender for this, and I don't like the idea of not protecting you," he said between her hungry kisses as he carefully pushed himself deep within her.

"I'm not too tender, and I trust you, Tony," Cassidy said breathlessly as the tip of his penis hit her womb. "I know you wouldn't do anything that could harm me. You're always protecting me. I can't…ah…ah…get pregnant…oooh yes, just right there…" she said after one particularly effective shove from him. "…and…and I know you would never give me a disease. You've probably never even…even…had sex without a condom b-b-b-b-eeeeeeee, oh my God!" she screeched.

Tony smiled in satisfaction when she couldn't finish her sentence. She was right, damn her; he'd never had sex without a condom before today. He would have never let things progress this far if he had. "That's it, love, scream for me," he said as he pounded into her while her breath came in faster pants and her internal muscles constricted securely around him.

Cassidy held on tight to Tony as her back hit the wall repeatedly with the force of his thrusts. Oh, she would never get enough of him. The sound of their flesh slapping together made everything tighten and coil inside of her. She wanted to wait for him, but she couldn't and she leaned in to kiss him, just as she came with a hard, ruthless force, screaming her release into his mouth.

Tony was lost in delirium as he continued to push forcefully into her. He kissed her back, biting her lips and tongue as the animal in him took over. God, she made him crazy and he felt as if he'd never get enough. Wanting them to experience release together, he began licking the inside of her mouth.

He knew just where to lick and just how much pressure to apply so that it wasn't long before she exhibited all the signs of someone about to have an orgasm. He held himself back just long enough for her to catch up. When she did, he allowed the passion to wash over and through him like a riptide. He slammed into her one last time, emptying himself into her. Overcome with the power of it all, he bent his mouth to her neck where he bit and sucked a tendon between his teeth, making her erk and spasm against him one last time.

He felt her shudder and fall weakly against him, and berated himself for his rough treatment of her. Bloody hell, he'd gone and done it. *She was so delicately made*, he thought with a wince as her head fell limply to his shoulder. Hesitantly, he lifted a hand to stroke her hair. "Cass?" When she only murmured feebly, he felt even worse.

"Are you all right, love? I'm sorry for the rough treatment. It won't happen again."

Cassidy raised her head so she could look at him in surprise. "Why not? Don't be an idiot, Tony," she chided when she saw the concern. "I liked it," she said and grinned.

Tony threw his head back and laughed in sheer delight and relief. "You did, did you?" When she nodded her head, he hugged her close. "Bloody, lustful wench," he said fondly into her hair.

"And?" Cassidy lifted her head again to look at him. When he just looked confused, she clarified, "Good screamer. I'm a good screamer, too," she finished and laughed when the confusion on his face was replaced with a grin as he remembered what he'd ordered her to do when she was on the verge of climaxing. "You demand, I deliver!" she said laughingly as he carried her to the shower.

The girl moaned pathetically and curled on the dirty pavement in an effort to protect herself. The pain was unbearable, and as she looked into the man's eyes, she saw her own death. "Please," she managed to say through dry, cracked lips.

"Sorry, love," he said to her with a gentle, sorrowful smile. "But there's always a bit of collateral damage in situations like this, you know," he said and uncurled the length of leather. "It scares you, does it?" he asked her when she tried to crawl away from him. He grabbed her leg and flipped her over.

"I don't know if you'll understand this," he said as he looped the leather around her neck. "But there's always sacrifice before one gets the big prize," he explained patiently, not even noticing when she weakly scratched at the leather with her fingers. The choking sounds she made were weak and pitiful. He'd already beaten most of the life out of her.

"She has to pay, you see," he murmured. "She let that bloke into her flat like a common tart." The strap was given another more vicious yank as he thought about how he'd stood across the street and watched Tony Carleton enter the building, and he'd waited for hours for his reappearance, which never happened. "Stupid, filthy whore."

Coiling the strap, and putting it in his pocket, he walked around to the front of the girl's lifeless body. "Got to fix you just so," he said as he folded her arms across her chest. He noticed the bruises that were starting to form on her brown skin. This last attack had been impossibly brutal. "Couldn't help myself, could I?" he muttered resentfully. "She shouldn't have let him stay."

Reaching into the inside pocket of his jacket, he pulled out a note enclosed in plastic. He lifted her shoulder and slid the note underneath. It said the same thing all the others had said: Beauty must suffer. "She'll suffer more before I'm finished."

Chapter 19

Cassidy bit back a curse as she looked at the newspaper. She'd made another headline. The reporters had been really tenacious outside her apartment building the past weekend and one had even been smart enough to hang around her garage. Cassidy was sure that Tony was not going to be happy when he saw this particular picture and story.

The picture showed her closing her car door as she climbed inside. So really all one saw was her leg as she was pulling it into the car and about three quarters of her face, just as she was turning it to face forward. Cassidy grimaced as she looked at the shot of Tony. She guessed that since the photographer had been so focused on her, he'd missed a good shot of Tony.

The only thing one could see was the top of his blonde head as he bent to get in on the driver's side. It was obvious to Cassidy that the photographer had just missed Tony opening the passenger door for her and she thanked God for photographers who weren't quite on their game. If the photographer had arrived a few moments earlier, he would have caught Tony and her kissing.

Cassidy knew they'd dodged a bullet on that one. Still, the short article that accompanied the picture speculated on who Tony was and the reporter had even guessed it correctly — he just didn't know it. The article read:

SOAPSTAR CASSIDY FLEES LONDON FLAT
WITH MYSTERY MAN
Curious people want to know. Is that the handsome, rich and

very available Anthony Carleton escorting the lovely, talented Cassidy from her building? It very well could be, intelligent reader. For as reported here two weeks ago, Cassidy attended university with Esme Carleton, Anthony's younger sister. The two darlings even roomed together during the four years they walked the hallowed halls of that prestigious American university called Yale. So what do you think, fellow busy bodies? Could that be the handsome Anthony Carleton on the other side of the car? Stay tuned, loyal readers, we'll find out...

Cassidy groaned softly with dismay as she finished reading the article for the umpteenth time that day. One photo and a few lousy lines may have ruined a perfect start to what she knew could be a glorious relationship. Considering how intensely private he was, the article might just scare Tony away for good. The weekend had been so perfect.

She'd convinced him to stay the extra two days because they'd assumed his friend would want to interview her Monday and Tony had wanted to escort her to the television station. She'd also been able to convince him to wait until then to go to the police station. They'd gone first thing that morning before the interview, and just as she'd thought, there hadn't been much the police could do. She was told to save any other missives that she might get and bring them to the station right away. They really had had no comment regarding the press clippings.

Cassidy glanced at the paper again. At least she and Tony had had two and half days and three glorious nights together before life had intruded. He'd left her at the television station that Monday morning with a goodbye kiss and a promise to see her again before she left town. Now, though, with the article, it might be best if she stayed away from him. She knew that his board of directors—all very proper and quite older—still had problems with him being so young and running the company. If they found out that he was seeing her, someone embroiled in scandal, they would probably lose complete confidence in him. She had a lot of thinking to do.

She didn't want him getting unwanted publicity. She couldn't believe how interested some of the British press was in her and her life. She was only a minor celebrity at best. Cassidy shook her head. Even Tony's producer friend had been eager to get her on air. The interview had gone extremely well and had been a fair and balanced piece. It had aired live that very morning she'd interviewed and Cassidy had seen snippets of it on the news that Monday night. As well as the interview had gone, she couldn't help but wish that it hadn't had to happen at all.

"Are you still mooning over that article, Cassidy?" A deep voice chided.

Cassidy looked up to see her agent walking toward her. "I'm not mooning over it, Paul. Unlike you, I don't think that this is good press."

"Oh, come now, darling. *All* press is good press."

"Not from where I stand, it isn't."

"That's because you're not the agent. I am," he said cheerily. "Now," he said as he took her arm and hooked it at the elbow through his as she walked towards the door. "I'll bet that even that Midnight Strangler bloke is thrilled with the attention he's getting in the press. His latest made all the front pages. And I'm sure he's not complaining. Everyone loves free press my dear. Everyone. So, why don't you just tell dear old uncle Paul who the mystery man is — I could get loads of press from it."

She couldn't believe that he was comparing the two. She sighed, pinching the bridge of her nose between two fingers and trying to remember that she usually liked him. Now, however, he just annoyed her. "No, Paul. I told you; my private life is just that — private. Or at least I want to keep as much of it private as I can."

"But, Cassidy —"

"No buts, Paul. I mean it. I don't want you promising Andrew in publicity that you'll get his name from me. I don't want any more stories about it. Clear?"

Paul sulked for a moment. "Yes, duckie, unfortunately it is — abundantly so. But tell me something. If you're so opposed to press coverage and love your privacy so much, why on earth did you choose acting as your career?"

The question didn't surprise Cassidy. Tony had asked her the same thing that weekend and now she told Paul the same thing she'd told him. "Acting is just something I'm meant to do. I've known it since I was four-years old and my parents took me to see *Annie* live on stage. It was the most amazing thing to me. I was enthralled throughout the entire program and I wanted to be one of those children in the show so badly that I could taste it.

"I've been in acting ever since then. It started with community theater and I got my first local commercial when I was five, though I didn't enjoy those as much as live theater. I like the immediate reaction, but besides that, acting is just a part of me and it has been for a very long time. So, I didn't choose acting, it chose me."

"That still doesn't eliminate the fact that the press loves actors and their personal lives."

"Yes, but my intention is to do theater. Theater is my first love. Well, acting is my first love, but I would prefer to do it in a live theater setting. Don't get me wrong, I like movies and television and I enjoy working in front of the camera, but if I have to choose between them, I'll take live theater every time. And live theater actors aren't even one tenth as famous as movie and television actors. So as a consequence, the only press really interested in them is the theater critics and they're only interested in their acting ability, not their private lives."

"But you would take an acting job in movies or television, would you not?"

"You know I already have. I told you about that independent film I was in last summer. It was a very small part, but I enjoyed it. But as I told you when we first met, it depends on the role. I mean, I took the role on *P&P* because I saw how it could help my career, and the role is a meaty one. However, you know I thought about it long and hard before even taking the audition."

"Yes, I know about that movie *End to End*. I've seen it, remember? And it's due to be released next spring."

"Right," Cassie confirmed. "There were some production issues, but I hear it will be shown at the next Sundance."

"Oh, that's brilliant! That movie might just make you a star. You were positively radiant in it."

"Thanks, Paul," Cassie said and then she snorted. "Don't count on me becoming a star from it, though. Of a two-hour movie, I might have had a total of thirty minutes screen time. Don't bet on this one making my career. You'd lose."

"So what would you do, little darling, if your career only leads you to television and movies? Let's face it, you have a face and figure made for celluloid. Your singing voice, however, is horrible, so that leaves out musicals."

"Hey," Cassidy objected. "I don't need you to remind me that I have a tin ear! No one knows that better than I. Live theater is more than just musicals anyway. Straight plays do still exist, you know."

"Yes, but there aren't all that many plum roles out there. At least not any that could keep you in silks and satins."

"That doesn't matter. I just want to act. If it's a good role for little pay, I'll take it. The play in Chicago is a good example. It's a wonderful role, but I already know not to expect to make a fortune off of it if I get it. I act for the pure pleasure it brings me, the money is not a huge concern. Getting wealthy from acting would just be a side benefit."

Paul frowned in mock horror. "Don't ever let a producer hear you say that!"

Cassidy laughed. "Isn't that why I hired you? You do all the hard stuff: the publicity, the negotiating, etc. And I'll do my part: the glorious acting!"

"Exactly, my girl, and I'm glad you mentioned it. Publicity. You need to let me do the job you hired me to do. When something like this mystery lover thing falls in our laps, we must take advantage of it. Andrew could get so much mileage out of it. I could discreetly arrange for a photographer—Gerald, of course—to catch you and your mystery man out and about at several different venues. We'd always catch your face, so there'd be no doubt that it is you, but him, we'd always get from behind or other ways that hide his identity."

Cassidy was horrified. "No, Paul. I don't want that. My relationship is private. It isn't for public consumption."

"Come, on, ducks. It will be just a bit—" He stopped when her eyes narrowed to dangerous slits. Even on such short acquaintance, he knew what that look meant and he quit while he was ahead.

"I'm glad we understand each other," Cassidy said when he remained silent. "I really have to get back on the set."

"All right, but think about it."

Cassidy turned back to him, speculation clear in her eyes. "You didn't send that information about my parents to the papers, did you, Paul?"

Paul looked stunned. "I didn't even know about your parents until the news hit the papers, Cassidy. How could you ask such a thing? I thought we had a better relationship than that. I'm all for publicity, but I would never do anything to hurt you. I would hope that that was understood from the beginning."

Cassidy studied him for another long moment. "Okay," she finally said. "It's only that you're so insistent, even when I keep telling you no and how I feel about it, so I just thought…" She let her voice trail off at the look on his face.

"Yes, it's true, that I think publicity is important," Paul said stiffly, "but I'd like to think that I'd have more class than to try and humiliate my client."

"I'm sorry, Paul. The past couple of weeks have been hell for me and I've chosen to take it out on you. Forgive me?"

Paul softened at her smile. "Well, of course, if I must."

She gave him a quick hug. "Good, I'm glad. Now I really have to get back on the set. Behave while I'm gone."

"No worries there. I'm headed back to the office."

"Oh," Cassidy paused in surprise. He was always on the set checking on her. She'd teased him about being as diligent with his other clients, but he'd only said that she was his latest investment and he always checked up on new investments. "Okay. Did I mention how grateful I am to you for everything you've done? Especially the Chicago thing?"

"Only a million times. Now go," he said, "Get back to work!"

"Yes, sir, Captain Bly," Cassidy saluted smartly and left.

Paul watched her leave. "Well, at least you did well on the telly the other day," he called after her. "That publicity should last us at least for another day or so."

Cassidy only shook her head at his tenacity.

Chapter 20

"Lady C!" Cassidy said when she opened the door to her flat. "I'm so glad to see you."

"It's good to see you, too, dear," Lady Carleton said as she accepted Cassie's hug. "It's been ages!"

"Yes, it has." Cassidy shut the door behind her guest and took her coat. "I was so pleased when the concierge told me you were in the lobby," she said as she hung the coat in the closet by the door. She led Lady Carleton into the living room. "Would you like a tour? You haven't been here since I moved in. I'm almost finished decorating now."

"A tour would be lovely. I hope you don't mind my just dropping by like this, but I was out shopping and realized you were just around the corner. And once I got it in my head to come and see you, nothing could stop me—not even manners, I'm afraid."

"Well, I'd have been insulted if you hadn't come by," Cassie assured her. "Okay, so what do you think of the living room? I kept it strictly old-fashioned in here."

Lady Carleton looked at the mahogany furnishings, the two deep brown sofas and hardwood floors polished to a gleam. She smiled. "It's lovely, dear. I believe I have a painting that would go perfectly in here. That is, if you wouldn't mind having it?" she questioned. "Not everyone likes what I like."

"Oh, I'd love it," Cassidy said. "I trust your taste. I love how you've decorated the Berkeley Square house, and the one you guys have in the country."

"Wonderful, then let's consider it a housewarming gift, shall we? And thank you for the compliment."

"It's true," Cassie said with a shrug. "Let's head to the dining room, okay? I basically kept to the same style in here. You know, mahogany furnishings, little if any colors. Oh, but I forget, you've already seen the dining room."

Lady Carleton chuckled. "It's all right. I'll see it again."

"So, that was the tour," Cassie said a little later as she led Lady Carleton back into the living room. "What do you think? Do you like it?"

Lady Carleton looked into Cassie's eyes, smiled reassuringly and watched as a smile bloomed over her face. "You've done a wonderful job, darling," she said and gave her a quick hug. Lady Carleton was well aware that she'd become a surrogate mother to Cassidy. In fact, she'd actively cultivated that specific type of relationship with her. *The child needed a female figure in her life*, she thought now, *and I was lucky enough to meet her at the time that she did.*

"Thank you, Lady C! I was hoping you'd like it. Now," Cassie said as they broke apart. "How about some tea? I have your favorite — PG Tips."

Lady Carleton laughed, delighted with her. "You're an absolute love. I'd adore some tea."

"Great," Cassie beamed. "I even have some of those great biscuits you always serve with tea. Notice, I didn't call them cookies. You stay here, and I'll be right back."

"I'll just freshen up, shall I? And after, I'll come in to help you. I don't want you waiting on me, Cassie."

"All right, Lady C. Whatever you say. You know where the bathroom is." Cassie left for the kitchen.

Lady C took a sip from her tea. "Perfect."

"You know, I never really liked tea until I met Esme. My grandmother preferred coffee, so I never drank hot tea. I was really just used to iced tea."

"Frightful stuff, that," Lady C said with a shudder. "Now, darling. Tell me how things are going. How's work on *P&P*?"

"Great! You know, I enjoyed my work on the show more than I possibly thought I could. It's been a blast."

Lady Carleton smiled sadly. "Of course, all good things must come to an end, as they say."

"But it's not really an end. I'll be back. I have a recurring role on the show."

"Oh, that's right. Esme did mention that. Tell me," Lady Carleton said as she scooted forward with avaricious eyes. "What's the plan for Brooke? How will they make sure they're able to bring you back?"

Cassie chuckled. "Shame on you, Lady C. You know I can't divulge secrets about the show. But since it's you..." she teased.

"Yes, yes. Go on."

"You have to promise not to tell anyone, not even your closest friends."

"I promise."

"Well, they're going to shoot me lying in bed in a coma. That way they can have it both ways. When they don't need me, they can say I'm in a coma, but still show images of me lying in the bed. And when they do need me, and want me to come back, I'll have a miraculous recovery."

Lady Carleton sat back. "Clever, but not very original, is it?"

Cassie laughed again. "Hey, it's a tried and true method."

"Well, I'm thrilled to hear that you'll be back. It's been wonderful having you here, and we've missed you since you've moved out."

"I've missed you guys, too, but I didn't want to be a burden."

"You were never that, Cassidy, and you know it. We enjoyed having you there. I've been so worried since you moved out."

"Worried? About me?"

"Of course, Cassie. You're so young to be off on your own in the big city. And let's not forget that they have yet to catch that horrid Midnight Strangler character. He's killed nine girls, Cassidy. I worry about you living alone here."

Cassie patted the other woman's hand and tried not to get misty. She hadn't realized how much she'd missed having a maternal figure in her life until she'd met Lady Carleton. "I'm fine, Lady C, honest. I'm very careful. I never walk alone after dark, and I try to steer clear of the area where they've found most of the victims."

"Somehow, that just doesn't alleviate my fears much, Cassidy. Won't you reconsider moving back in with us when you come back from the States?"

"Oh, that's so sweet. I'm so glad you care enough to worry about me, and it's because of that that I will think about moving back in with you guys. But I did sign an agreement on the flat, you know."

"All right then. But you will stay with us when you come back for the Christmas party. There's no getting out of it. How long will you be in town when you come back?"

Cassie shrugged. "That's kind of hard to say. If I get the part in Chicago, I'll come back here and stay a week for your party. But if I don't get the part, it could be an indefinite stay. Heck, even if I do get the part, it could be an indefinite stay. The show is only having a short run."

"Well, either way, you'll stay with us. How is your uncle?"

Cassie made a tsking sound. "A total basket case, of course. When I came up with my brilliant plan not to tell him anything about the Midnight Strangler, I didn't bank on him making it a point to find British newspapers wherever he happens to be. So, it was just my luck that he found out about the mad killer just about the same time he found out that someone had leaked the story about my parents to the papers. He threatened to come and drag me home, by my hair if necessary—his words, not mine."

Lady Carleton winced. "Well, I can't say as I blame him," she said gently. "We're all so very worried. How did you get him to calm down?"

Cassie frowned. "I didn't, exactly. I don't think he'll ever be calm about it, but I told him that I have a commitment to the show, and besides, he knows that as much as he wants to, he can't really force me to do anything."

"Surely, you can't be mad at him, Cassie."

"No, I'm not. Not really. It's just that I wish he'd stop treating me like a child. I handled the whole ordeal with the newspapers just fine. Tony helped me."

Lady Carleton noticed how Cassie's eyes turned soft and dewy when she mentioned Tony. She frowned. "He did, did he? How, dear, besides getting you an interview on that news show?"

Cassie was too caught up in her memories to notice how Lady Carleton's tone had sharpened. "Oh, he stayed the whole weekend with—" She cut herself off and looked quickly over at Lady Carleton, hoping she hadn't noticed the slip. "Oh, crap," she moaned.

Lady Carleton looked right back at her. So that's where he gets it from, Cassie thought, as she stared at the one brow Lady Carleton had raised in query. Cassie tried a smile, all the while knowing that she looked guilty as hell. "Um...well, you see...uh"

Oh, crap, indeed, Lady Carleton thought with an inward sigh as Cassie stumbled through an explanation. It looks like I'll be going to the City to visit that son of mine—the wretched, wretched boy.

Thirty minutes later, Cassidy closed the door behind Lady Carleton, for the first time ever feeling glad to be out of her company. She leaned against the door and closed her eyes. "Oh, God," she moaned. "I'm so embarrassed!"

Tony read the note from one of his board members again, and snorted in disbelief. The note went on about how much he'd enjoyed the trip to the golf course in Scotland in late summer, and speculated on perhaps checking out the Hampton Court Palace Golf Club while the weather was still nice enough.

"And I suppose I'll have to pay for it," Tony muttered. "Greedy, stingy bastard makes more money than ninety percent of the population, and still wants something for free." Shaking his head in disgust, he tossed the note in the trash. He'd taken them golfing, out to dinner several times and out to lunch, and they were still holding out on him regarding acquiring the chip manufacturer.

He dialed the number of his contact there. "Hello, Sheila. How are you? I'm doing well, thanks. No, I'm sorry, I've got no answer for you...board's still dragging its feet, I'm afraid." He frowned and listened. "Yes, I understand you've got other offers, and if you feel you must go with one of them, then accept it," he said with a thin smile. "However, it's obvious that the offers have not been to your satisfaction, otherwise we wouldn't be having this conversation...yes, you'll hear from me. Goodbye,

Sheila."

He frowned when his telephone buzzed immediately after he hung up. "Yes, Jean? I thought I requested that I not be disturbed."

"You did sir, but this is an emergency—"

Tony looked up as his door was pushed open. Forcefully. "See here—Mother? What are you doing here?" He studied her. He recognized that look. He'd gotten it often enough as a child to be thoroughly familiar with it. She was furious. He did a mental shuffle, trying to think of what he could have possibly done to cause such fury. He came up blank.

Lady Carleton shut door behind her with a quiet click. "Anthony Bertram Carleton," she began in a low, enraged voice as she ate up the distance between the door and his desk. "I ought to take a horse whip to you! Oh, how could you, Anthony? Just how could you?" Too upset to stay in one place, she began to pace away from the desk and back again.

Her rage had brought Tony halfway out of his chair in self-defense. He had no idea what she was talking about. "How could I?" he asked. "How could I what?"

Lady Carleton whipped back around and came charging towards him again. "Oh, you know what, all right! Just what are you playing at, young man? Your father and I did our level best to teach you how to behave properly! Surely, you could have taken the time to pick up some bloody home training! Speaking of your father, I don't know how I'll tell him about this."

Oh, shit, Tony thought. *I've had it now. She never curses*. He watched his mother as she did another turn to the door, all the while mumbling to herself. *I do not have time for this*, he thought right before he cleared his throat. "Mum? I don't know what you're talking about. If you'd just tell me…"

"Oh, I'll tell you. I'll tell you, all right. You deflowered her, Anthony! How could you have?"

Tony winced. So Cass had spilled the beans, had she?

"And no, Cassidy didn't tell me," Lady Carleton snarled, correctly reading his mind. "She didn't have to. It was all over her face, like a bloody neon sign—*just as your guilt is written all over yours*. And you should feel guilty, young man. If this were another time, you'd be forced to marry the girl! Oh, I can only wish that it were that time! Then you'd be found out for the bounder you are, and you'd have to do the right thing by her, wouldn't you? Of course, you can't be bothered to now. You and your three-years nonsense!"

Tony had had enough. "Hold on, Mum." He came from around his desk and took her arm. "Let's sit, shall we?" He led her to the sofa. "Let me have your coat."

Lady Carleton sighed. She took her coat off and gave it to him, perfectly calm now. She had spent her spleen, and now she was ready to listen to him. She sat and watched him hang her coat on a hook behind the door.

"How did this happen, Tony?" she asked as soon as he sat down next to her.

Tony raised a brow. "Do you really want to know that, Mother?"

"No, of course not. But darling, why? You're the one who came up with the plan to wait three years. It seems unfair to her to have seduced her."

Tony almost snorted. *He seduce Cass?* Clearly his mother didn't know her the way he did. The seduction was mutual, but all he said was, "Why? Because I love her, Mum, and I couldn't resist being with her, the woman I love."

"Oh, that's sweet," Lady Carleton began gently. "But really, darling, you should have tried harder to resist," she finished crisply.

"I know that," Tony said in exasperation. "My intentions were good. I went over to her flat to take care of her after that horrible story in the newspapers. I knew she needed someone, and I wanted it to be me."

"Again, that's sweet, darling. But now what? Are you going to rescind your three-years rule?"

"No. I can't. I still don't think it's fair of me to tie her down right now."

"Then you'll have to keep your hands off of her, Tony. You'll only give her false hope that the two of you can be together sooner. It's cruel. And if you don't think you can keep your hands off of her...I hate to say this, but perhaps you're right. Perhaps you should stay away from her, which should be made all the easier for you since she's going home to Chicago for a while."

Frustrated again, because it wasn't as if he hadn't already thought of all that, Tony smirked. "I know that, Mum."

Lady Carleton patted his knee in sympathy. "I know you do, darling. Now, give us a proper greeting."

Laughing, Tony kissed her cheek and hugged her. "*I* should give you a proper greeting? I'm not the one who stormed in here like a worried mama from the nineteenth century trying to protect her daughter's virtue. *Deflowered*, Mum? *Bounder*?"

Lady Carleton laughed sheepishly. "Sorry, darling. Too many historical romances of late, I'm afraid."

Chapter 21

Cassidy smiled her thanks at Andrew when he gave her a glass of wine. Once Paul had set up the auditions for her, things had begun to move at warp speed. First the rewriting of the script for her character, and now she was at her farewell party given to her by the producers of *P&P*. She was trying to make the most of it. She was really going to miss everyone. "Hey, Andrew. Have I ever thanked you for being so helpful to me since you came on board?"

Andrew smiled. "Aw, shucks, little lady," he said in his best John Wayne accent. "It was nothin'. It was all in a day's work."

Cassidy laughed. "No, really, Andrew. I mean it. Everyone has been great, but you've been really helpful, especially when you helped me to handle that situation with the newspaper stories about my parents."

Andrew shrugged. "It's been a pleasure working with you, Cassidy. I've enjoyed it because you make my job easy. I'm looking forward to your coming back."

Cassidy squeezed his arm. "Thanks, Andrew. You're so sweet. Excuse me a moment, will you? I want to mingle."

Andrew blushed. As usual, his emotions went overboard when he was around Cassie.

Gerald laughed as he came up alongside him, making Andrew's blush intensify. "She's hard to resist, isn't she? Beauty and brains: it's a potent combination," Gerald commented teasingly as he followed Andrew's gaze to Cassie. "Getting a taste of that bird wouldn't be a hardship, eh, Andy?"

Andrew smirked. "No chance of that happening—not for

either one of us. We're not her type, I'm afraid."

"Maybe you're not, but I'm sure I certainly could be," Gerald said with a cocky grin.

Andrew simply continued to smirk. "I guess that means you've gotten over your little tiff with her regarding the letter?"

Gerald frowned into his drink before taking a sip. "It was just a mistake."

"Yes. I know that, but have you forgiven her?"

"She doesn't know that I haven't, and that's what counts. I don't have to forgive her to shag her, mate," Gerald finished derisively.

Andrew shook his head in a chiding manner at Gerald's disrespectful attitude. "Not good enough," he said and continued to watch Cassie move gracefully through the crowd. "Neither of us."

Cassie made her way from one side of the party to the other and thought about what her leaving meant. If she got the part in Chicago, it could mean a huge boost to her stage career. Ideally, she'd get other parts based on her performance in the play. So conceivably, she could be in Chicago for months, no matter how long this particular play lasted.

As she looked around at the friends she'd made, the thought of staying in Chicago made her a bit sad. Not wanting to think about it anymore, she slipped into the first group of people she came upon. "Hi, all," she said to some of her cast mates.

"Well! It's the goodbye-girl," Cameron Taylor quipped with a big smile. "Darling," she began as she fondly put her arm around Cassidy's waist and hugged her to her side. "Now that you're leaving, whoever will here be to torture my poor character until she's lost her mind?"

"Hopefully no one," Cassie said pitifully. "I don't want to be replaced, you know, only temporarily forgotten."

"That won't be easy, I'm afraid."

Cassie looked over at Terrance Chalmers and frowned playfully. "Just you remember, Sir Wickham, I'm not someone to be trifled with. Just because I'm in a coma, doesn't mean I can't still ruin your life. I just might be pregnant, you know!"

"Ah, yes, the pregnant-coma bit," Cameron said. "It's always a ratings booster."

Cassidy laughed with the rest of the group and discreetly let her eyes wander the crowd, feeling a more than a little jumpy. She'd gotten another letter from her crazed fan, as she'd come to think of him, and he'd made mention of this party. The only way he could have known about it was if he were one of the people in the crowd. It had not been publicized. The publicity would come after it was over.

She scanned the faces in the crowd, wondering if one of the people she'd grown so fond of could actually be sending her the letters. *It's so hard to believe*, she thought stubbornly, *it just can't be true. But how else did he know about the party? It's got to be someone I know*, she thought. When someone grabbed her from behind, she jumped so violently that she dropped her wine glass.

"Oh, dear. Are you all right, ducks?"

Cassie turned to Paul with a quick, nervous smile. "Yes, yes I'm fine. Butterfingers, that's all." She bent to pick up her glass. "Thank God, it was empty."

"That's our Cassidy," Terrance said. "She'll flub everything else, but never her lines."

Again, Cassie laughed with the rest of the group, still nervous when Paul led her away. "Yes, Paul. Did you need something?"

"No, not really. I just wanted to remind you that the press release with pictures will go out tomorrow to all the papers. We're also video taping, just in case it's a slow news day, and someone can use shots of the party in their broadcast."

"Yes, okay. Sounds good."

"Also, whatever fan mail you get while you're gone, I'll send it to you once a week in bulk."

Cassidy frowned in distaste, but she said, "All right." *Better to know what I'm up against than to not know.*

"And last but not least, Brent will be waiting for you across the pond. He'll make sure that all of your needs, whether they be publicity or contractual, are taken care of while you're at home."

Cassie tried to focus. "Well, you never know, Paul," she said with a jerky shrug. "I may not need him because I may not even get the part."

"Oh, you'll get it all right," Paul said unconcernedly. "That part was practically written for you."

"Was it?"

"Yes, Cassidy, yes. They don't know it yet, but they've have just gotten themselves a star in the making."

"Thanks, Paul. But considering that they're looking for someone who is, and I quote: 'overweight and on the plain side,' they may not agree with you."

"So, you'll wear padding to the audition, and you'll hide that mug of yours under cake powder makeup," Paul said with a shrug. "Darling, I got the audition for you. My job is done. The rest is up to you. I can't be expected to do everything for you."

Cassie laughed. "Yes, I know, Paul. I'm very grateful, too."

"Good," he said with a satisfied slap of his hands. "Now are you ready for the audition? Have you learned your lines?"

"Yes, I have every scene in that play memorized down to the last period. I want this role, Paul. I really want it."

"Then you shall have it."

Cassie took his hand in gratitude, smiling when he gallantly bent over it and lifted it to his mouth for a kiss.

Paul frowned when she flinched when a camera flashed. He studied her silently for a moment. "Are you *sure* you're all right?"

"Yeah," she said with a smile. "I'm just tired and I'm also nervous about the audition. I'll be good as new after I've had a long night's sleep."

"And when will you get that, with the Carletons throwing you a party directly after this one?"

"It's okay. It will be small, just the family."

"That's good, then. Don't let them keep you up too late. Speaking of your foster family, here comes one of them now."

Cassie turned to see Esme approaching and relief rushed through her. Finally, someone she knew she could trust unequivocally. "Esme, hi!" Cassie didn't hear the desperation in her voice, nor did she realize it was also in the hug she gave her friend.

Esme recognized it in both and frowned in confusion. "What's the matter?" she asked Cassie when she'd released her.

"Nothing," Cassidy replied. "I'm just glad to see you, that's all."

"If you ladies will excuse me, I need to speak to Gerald," Paul said.

"Bye, Paul."

"Right, then," Esme said in a no-nonsense voice once they were alone. "What the hell is going on, Cassie? And does it have anything to do with your not wanting Tony to come to your going away dinner? Mum told me."

"I'm so freaking jumpy, Esme, I don't know what to do with myself," Cassidy admitted with frustration. "Just about every little noise makes me want to jump out of my skin."

"Why? What's happened?"

"I got another letter yesterday. This one was the worst of the lot."

"Another letter? What do you mean *another* letter?" Esme's voice was full of suspicion. "I thought they'd stopped."

"Tony didn't tell you?"

"Tell me what? And why should he, when it's you who this affects?"

Cassidy struggled with her guilt. "I'm sorry, Es. I didn't tell you because I didn't want to worry you, and I didn't want to argue with you about going to the police."

"Well, what did the letter say exactly?"

"I have a copy," Cassie said and pulling it out of her purse, handed it to Esme.

"Good Lord," Esme said as she read. "He appears to know everything about you. He knows about this party, about your going to Chicago...everything."

"Exactly, and this party wasn't even publicized. My returning to Chicago was, but this wasn't. I know a person could reasonably assume that there would be a going away party, but they couldn't know exactly when it would be unless they work with me."

"Did you take this to the police?"

Cassie nodded, trying to keep her cool. She was so damn tired of it all. "Yes, just like I did all the others. They kept the original letter, but there still isn't much they can do, not without there being a single clue as to who this guy might be."

Esme looked at the letter again. "What's this last little bit here? 'Beauty must suffer.'"

"I don't know, but the police seemed to really focus on that part." She'd asked them why it was so important, but they'd talked over her question, only frustrating her more.

"God, Cassie. This must be terrifying for you. This guy is a lunatic, and could come after you at any time…"

Cassidy was nodding her head. "Yes, I'm scared, but I'm pissed off too. Damn it, I haven't done anything to anybody! It's just a freaking job!"

Esme made a commiserating sound. "Yes, it is just a job, but it doesn't sound like your letter writer is sane enough to separate you from the job."

"But why'd he have to fixate on me? The police even suggested that I not attend the party, and if I did, have a police escort."

"Well, you're here, so where's the escort, then?"

Cassidy discreetly pointed. "He's over there. I almost turned them down because I didn't want to alarm anyone, and I especially didn't want to become fodder for the tabloids. I can just see the headline now: Soap Opera Actress Cassidy Being Stalked by Crazed Fan."

"Cassidy!" Esme drew her name out in exasperation. "How can you be so bloody stubborn? How about this headline? Cassidy Killed by Stark Raving Fan. Do you like that one any better?"

Cassidy frowned back at Esme. "I'm not stupid, Esme. I did agree to it. I mean, I'm scared to death of this guy. The police also suggested that I consider personal security. I imagine that's because they won't be able to keep providing me with protection."

Esme pursed her lips in thought. "Actually," she finally said. "Getting a bodyguard is not a bad idea. Perhaps you should."

"For the last two days that I'm here, Esme?"

"That's two days of protection."

"Yes, I thought of that, but then I nixed the idea. I'll be sticking close to your family until I leave. I won't even be leaving your house, and I've got my stuff in the trunk of my car as we speak, so I won't even have to go back to my flat."

"All right," Esme said skeptically. "If you're sure."

"I'm sure."

"Okay, then. So I suppose you haven't told Tony about this latest scare, have you?" Cassidy's face said it all, and Esme sighed. "Up to you," she said. "Now tell me why you don't want Tony at your dinner party tonight."

"It will just be easier that way, Es. If I see him before I leave, then he'll know that something is wrong, and I'll have to tell him that there have been more letters, and that I've had to go to the police again. If he gets wind of all of that, then he'll probably change his mind about us having to wait three years. He'll try to protect me, and he'd put himself in danger. I also don't want him changing his mind so he can protect me, Esme. I want him to change his mind because he loves me and doesn't want to wait."

Esme's frown said she didn't agree. "Rather dodgy bit of logic, that. It's based on what you think someone else will do, and you can't be sure of what anyone will do. It presupposes that you know Tony's mind. It doesn't really make sense, Cassie."

"Yes, it does, Es. Think about who we're talking about. It's Tony, who feels it's his responsibility to take care of everyone he cares about. If he didn't, we wouldn't be in our current mess," she muttered. Cassidy knew she was doing the right thing, but it was difficult. She wanted to run to Tony with this latest problem. She felt safe with him precisely because she knew he would do everything he could to protect her. But who would protect him?

"True, he *can* be an absolute bore when it comes to what he sees as his responsibility. Still, I don't know," Esme's tone was full of doubt. "There's another reason for your sacrifice, Cassie. There's got to be. Just tell me what it is, and I'll come along quietly."

Cassie shrugged. "If you must know, I also don't want to see Tony because I don't want him to get in trouble with his board of directors. I'm a bad bet right now because of all the bad press I've gotten recently, and if someone is really after me, well then all bets are off. I don't want Tony embroiled in my scandal. His board is already looking for a reason to get rid of him."

Esme looked stunned. "I believe you've just insulted my brother."

"No, I didn't. I know he'd choose me over the board, but I'm not going to put him in the position to have to make the choice."

He took a sip of his drink from across the room and watched her as she talked to her friend. When she pulled out the letter and surreptitiously gave it to her friend, he wanted to crow in triumphant glee. But he contented himself with a smile instead. They were clueless, all of them. He knew she'd gone to the police, but he wasn't concerned. He'd covered his tracks, and they'd never catch him. He'd been much too careful.

He continued to watch her throughout the evening, and later, he watched her leave. "That's right, little girl, run home. You can go to the ends of the earth, and I'll still find you." He was behind schedule. He should have killed her by now, but a curious thing had happened. He'd found that he'd enjoyed torturing her too much to just stop.

Cassidy lay on the sofa in the library of the Carletons' Mayfair home, and tried to make herself get up and go upstairs to bed like the Carletons had done. She was just so tired that she didn't want to move. She'd been running around for weeks now trying to get everything ready for her return home. And that coupled with her worrying about the stalker had put her on the brink of exhaustion. She was grateful that the dinner with the family had been a quiet affair. It had just been the Carletons and her, with one notable absence.

She tried not to feel disappointed that Tony hadn't come. Logically, she hadn't wanted him there, but she wasn't thinking logically now. She was thinking with her emotions. She admitted to herself that she'd wanted him to ignore his mother's and her wishes and show up anyway. Feeling lonely, she curled into herself and tried not to think.

"Cass?"

Cassie looked up to see Tony standing over her. "Hi," she said, glad that he was there, but still feeling cautious about it.

She could tell that he was angry, but she only stared back at him.

When she didn't move to get up, Tony simply bent to pick her up. He took her spot on the bottom, lying down with her on top of him.

Cassie adjusted her body to fit his, sighing in contentment when he wrapped one of his arms around her and raised the other to stroke his fingers through her hair.

"Mum told me that you didn't want me to come to your dinner. Why didn't you?"

She shrugged one shoulder and kept her face buried in his neck so he wouldn't be able to see her face, and she wouldn't have to look at him while she hedged. "I just thought it would make things easier, that's all."

"Easier for whom?" he asked in a hard voice.

"For both of us, I guess."

"Well, it wasn't for me. I was all set to ignore Mum's suggestion, but then an emergency meeting was called."

Cassie stiffened. "Of the board?"

"What? No, it was an internal team," he said.

Cassie relaxed against him. "Is everything all right?"

"Yes," Tony said impatiently. "But I don't want to talk about that. I want to talk about your trying to leave the country without saying goodbye."

"I already told you. I just thought it would be best."

"And I already told you, it wasn't best for me," he said impatiently. "How could you think of leaving without saying goodbye? For God's sake, Cass, it's already been almost two weeks since we last saw each other. I know we've talked on the phone, but as you're leaving and will be gone for some time, I wanted to see you again."

Cassidy said nothing; just nestled closer and breathed in his familiar scent.

Tony stifled his impatience at her continued silence. "I'm going to need an answer this time, Cass. Did you really want to leave without saying goodbye to me?"

"No." Her reply was soft, reluctant and miserable.

Tony wasn't aware that he'd been holding his breath until it came out in a whoosh at the sound of her voice. When he felt tears trickle on his neck, he tightened his hold. "It's all right, love. Just let me hold you." He lifted her chin and kissed the tears from her face. "Just let me hold you," he whispered again when she'd tucked her head back under his chin.

Chapter 22

Cassie maneuvered her car through the slush and sleet of November in Chicago and wished fervently for spring. "Burr," she murmured happily as she found a parking spot right in front of the theater. After several auditions, she'd gotten the lead role of Clarice in the play called *Milk and Honey*. She'd done as Paul had suggested and had come into the audition with padding and makeup. The padding had added a good twenty pounds and the makeup made her look less attractive, and at least ten years older.

Her mistake had been in getting out of her costume before she left the theater. The extra padding was heavy, and the makeup had made her hot, so she'd done a quick change in the bathroom. Unfortunately for her, the director had wanted to see her again, and she was out of disguise. He'd refused to believe that she was the same person who had auditioned ten minutes before, so she'd had to audition all over again.

At that time, however, the playwright had walked in and she hadn't been present during Cassie's first audition. She'd taken one look at Cassie and had turned her down flat. It had taken some doing, but the director had finally convinced the playwright that Cassidy was a viable candidate for the role of Clarice. But because there were other people waiting to audition, and time was short, Cassie had been asked to return the next day in full makeup and audition again.

She'd auditioned in front of the playwright, the producer and the director, and she'd been hired. So the way Cassie figured it, being made to jump through hoops wasn't such a bad thing sometimes. Success or failure depended on how skilled a person was at jumping, and she jumped like a pro.

Whistling as she skipped up the stairs, Cassie pushed the doors open and went inside. Opening night was a mere two nights away, so rehearsal went on for long hours, sometimes without a break. Cassidy didn't mind the hectic schedule, or the bad pay. She was doing what she'd been born to do.

She did miss her life in London, but she talked to Esme almost daily. According to Esme, the family was well, *P&P* wasn't the same without her, and the whole of London also suffered without her presence. The Midnight Strangler was still at it, even though the weather was bad, and the police didn't seem to be any closer to catching him.

Cassidy missed everyone and everything, about London, but her life was in Chicago for the time being. "And maybe for the foreseeable future," she mumbled happily. She was just thrilled to be on the stage again.

"Hi, Cassie."

Cassie looked up at the stage to see her cast mate Lucy waving and smiling. "Hi, Lucy. What's cooking?"

"Me, I'm afraid," Lucy joked. "I can't seem to cool off, and I know the heat in here is fine. No one else is suffering. Are you hot?"

"No, but I just came from outside and it feels wonderful in here to me," Cassidy said.

"All right, people," the director said with a clap of his hands. "Enough chit chat. Let's get to work."

Cassie rushed to put her things away, and waited for her cue. When it came, she sailed happily onto the stage.

"Is that you, Cassie-doll baby?"

"Yes, Mrs. Washington," Cassidy called to her neighbor as she closed her car door. She walked over to the chain-link, waist-high fence that separated Mrs. Washington's yard from her driveway. "How are you, ma'am?" she asked the elderly woman who had been one of her grandmother's closest friends.

"I'm good, child. Good." She smiled when Cassidy bent to

kiss her cheek. "Have you eaten? Mr. Washington and I would love for you to come over."

Cassie had a million things she had to do, and had planned to heat up some soup and curl up with her lines, but she only said, "I'd love to come over, Mrs. Washington. What's on the menu tonight?"

"Beef stew to warm your bones."

Though it was a difficult thing to do, Cassie maintained her smile. It would be the third time that week that she had beef stew. Mrs. Corley had served it to her on Monday, and Ms. Potts had given it to her Tuesday.

"Don't worry," Mrs. Washington said shrewdly. "My stew is much better than Beatrice's or Josephine's. Bea always did put too much pepper in hers, and Jo's is always too thin."

"Why, Mrs. Washington," Cassie teased. "Are you competing with your friends for my time and affection?"

"I'll only say that my stew is the best stew within twenty miles of here."

"Well, then it's a date. You go on in out of the cold, and I'll come over as soon as I've washed and changed. Will a half an hour be okay?"

"That will be fine, honey."

"Okay, I'll see you then." Cassidy waited for Mrs. Washington to go inside before she let herself into her own house. She headed straight upstairs to her old bedroom. She'd never been able to move into her grandmother's room. It felt disrespectful to even think about trying. Grabbing fresh underwear from a drawer and clean clothes out of her closet, she went to the bathroom for a shower.

Thirty minutes later, Cassie found herself sitting in Mrs. Washington's bright green and yellow kitchen, chomping on a green salad, beef stew and hot, homemade bread. The kitchen hadn't changed one iota since she'd been a girl and had come over for cookies and milk. "I will see you two on opening night, won't I?" she addressed the elderly couple that sat across from her.

"Of course, honey," Mr. Washington said. "We wouldn't miss it for the world."

"Bea and Tim, and Jo and her new beau will be coming, too. We're all so excited."

"Good," Cassie said. "Now don't forget, I'm sending a car for you guys so you won't have to worry about getting around in this crazy weather."

"We remember, honey," Mrs. Washington beamed. "I'm so proud of you, doll baby. I always knew when you were just a little bitty thing—walking around the yard spouting Shakespeare and such—that you'd grow up and be something special. Didn't I used to say that, Ben?"

"She did, you know." Mr. Washington grinned at Cassie. "She'd say, 'Ben, come here and look at Jessie's grandbaby. Lord, she is something else!'"

Cassie's smile was more than a little misty. "Thank you, Mr. and Mrs. Washington. It's good to hear about the good times that I don't really remember."

"Well, like I said," Mrs. Washington began, "we're proud of you. And if Jessie were alive today, she'd be bursting with pride. Don't you ever doubt it."

"I haven't," Cassie assured her. "She was always telling me so."

"Jessie was proud of every little thing you did. Even before you came to live with her, she bragged about you something awful. Why honey, we knew about every little accomplishment you had, sometimes even before you did, I bet."

Cassidy laughed. "Yeah, Granny was the best. I was proud of her, too."

"She knew you were. The whole neighborhood knew that you two had some little mutual admiration society going on. Once, you sat right here in my kitchen, gobbling up my sugar cookies and telling me, very politely, mind you, that while my cookies were very good, your granny's cookies were the best."

Cassie's look was sheepish. "I'm sorry. I must have been a real pain."

"Not at all. You were a little girl who loved her grandma, that's all. And she couldn't get enough of you, either. She was as crazy about you as she was about her two boys. How is your Uncle Charles, by the way?"

Cassidy spooned up the last of her stew. "Oh, he's fine. He'll here Friday for opening night."

"Where did this latest assignment take him?"

"Peru," Cassie replied. "Machu Pichu, I believe."

"That boy sure does get around," Mr. Washington commented.

"He certainly does. I'll be sure to remind him to come over here for a visit during his latest trip. The last time he was in town a couple of weeks ago, it was really just to breeze through," Cassie said.

"It's a wonder he hasn't settled down and gotten married," Mrs. Washington stated. "A man needs a wife, just like a woman needs a husband. And what about you, Miss," she pinned Cassie to her seat with a look. "You thinking about settling down soon?"

"Oh, I'm thinking about it, all right, Mrs. Washington," Cassie replied as she thought about Tony. "I should be ready to do that soon, in oh…say three years, or less," she muttered.

"Here, now, old man. I brought you to this club to bring you out of the doldrums, not to sink you further in them."

"It's a nice place, Shawn," Tony told his friend. "I'm just not fit company lately, I'm afraid."

"And why is that? Could it have something to do with a certain leggy American girl who left our shores several weeks ago to pursue a career on the Chicago stage?"

Tony looked at him in surprise. He hadn't mentioned Cassidy to any of his friends because the relationship was far from a sure thing, and because by nature, he was simply a private person.

Shawn shook his head. "And what are you so surprised about? You're in love with her, aren't you? It was ruddy obvious to me that day you brought her to my studio. You couldn't keep your eyes off her."

Tony sighed. "Well, now I can't keep my mind off of her, and it's driving me mad."

"So, then do something about it," Shawn said impatiently. "Take a trip to Chicago. Surprise her; women love that kind of tripe—makes you look romantic and thoughtful. She'll fall right in your arms."

Tony laughed at his friend's cynicism, but made no comment on it. "That's not a viable option right now, Shawn. I can't go to Chicago."

"Why not?"

"Because I'm supposed to keep away from her."

Shawn's brows rose in surprise. "By whose say so?"

Tony snorted in self-derision. "This is where it gets complicated. You're not going to believe this, but it's by my say so." He'd never had cause to regret a decision more in his life, but he was determined to stick to it. It was the right thing to do.

"Yours? *What*?"

"Yes, mine." He exhaled a breath. "It's a long story, Shawn. I'm not sure you're up to hearing it."

"Yes, I am. Of course I am."

"That's unfortunate, then, because I'm not up to telling it."

"Well, it's too bloody late to pull back now, mate, as I'm up to the hearing of it." The more upset he got, the more Shawn's Irish heritage shone through in his speech.

Tony gave in, and started from the beginning. And once he got started, he couldn't stop. Surprisingly, he found that he didn't want to stop. He went back to the very first day he'd met Cassie, telling Shawn of his reaction to her. He ended it with the very last time he'd seen Cassie—their platonic interlude on the sofa in his parents' library. When he finished his story, Shawn was quiet for so long that Tony finally looked at him.

Shawn was staring at him in utter amazement. When he finally spoke, it was to say, "Three years? You're making her wait three years? Even more stupid, you're making yourself wait three long years to have her? What are you? Some kind of bloomin' robot?"

"It's not like that, Shawn—"

"Oh, I know what it's like, all right, you imbecile. Have you no baldy notion then?" When Tony just gave him a blank look, he elaborated, "Have you no notion of what you're jeopardizing? For fuck's sake, Tony, she's got the looks of a super model, a brain that she actually uses, and legs that are long enough to wrap around a man twice, and she wants your sorry arse! And you, brilliant tactician that you are, tell her that she as to wait three years to have you. Thank God you weren't needed in the war," he said pityingly with a shake of his shaggy head. "England would have lost, hands down."

Tony was furious and let Shawn know it. "Fuck off, Shawn. I know what I'm doing."

"Oh, you do, do ya? Well, even if you don't, I do, and I just want to ask you one last question, mate. What the effing hell have you got against being happy?"

Chapter 23

Cassie's time in Chicago was flying by, and she was making the most of it. She'd gone shopping, played tourist and done some site seeing of familiar places and she'd visited — both with her grandmother's friends and her own friends. Most of all, she worked. She worked until she was too tired to do anything but rest.

Milk and Honey had gotten rave reviews, and she herself had become the critics' favorite. She should have been happier, and she knew it. "I miss, Tony, damn it," she mumbled to herself one Sunday morning as she lay on the couch watching morning talk shows that discussed American politics. She liked to switch channels and watch one after another after another. It was something she used to do with her grandmother. Her grandmother would rant and rave at the television while Cassie laughed and teased.

Cassidy smiled as memories assailed her. "I miss you, Granny," she said aloud to the empty room. She felt her grandmother's presence all throughout the house, especially since she hadn't changed one thing about it after her grandmother had died. Cassie wondered if her grandmother were alive if she'd like Tony. *Not if he's the one whose making you hurt like this.* Cassidy chuckled, liking the fact that she knew exactly what her grandmother would say.

Tony had stopped calling her all together, and she didn't want to even guess what that meant. The one thing she didn't want to do was jump to conclusions — painful, dreadful conclusions. So she tried not to feel anything one way or the other regarding her

.ack of contact with him. Figuring that he'd made his choice, she didn't call him, and she never asked Esme about him anymore. She even went so far as to tell Esme not to share any information regarding her with him.

Cassidy pulled the blanket tighter around herself and let her mind drift back to the last telephone conversation she'd had with her friend.

"Cassidy! It's so good to hear your voice."

"You're a nut, Esme. We just spoke two days ago."

"So? That doesn't make it any less exciting to hear your voice. We've gotten the clippings you've sent us, by the way. Well done, Cassie! They love you!"

"Thanks, Es. I can hardly believe it myself, but the show hasn't gotten one bad review. We haven't even gotten a mixed review. It actually kind of makes me nervous."

Esme laughed. "Of course it does. You wouldn't be you, if it didn't. So, tell me how everything else is going."

"I visited with Susan Pinkney the other day. You remember her, don't you? She was in our dorm sophomore year."

"Yes, of course I remember her. What's she up to these days?"

"Law school. Apparently, she got in at the University of Chicago. She plans to work at her mom's firm when she finishes. Now it's your turn. I don't suppose they've caught the Midnight Strangler yet, have they?"

"No, they're not even close. There was an exposé on him in the paper the other day—well, as much as an expose there could be without having any idea who he is. I guess it was more like a profile. Anyway, he's killed twelve girls now, Cassie, and he strangles them with leather. Everyone's on high alert, wondering whom he'll get next. It's a scary time to be in London."

"I'll bet," Cassie said with a shudder. She'd be leaving for London again in a little more than a week. "And your mom and dad? How are they? I'm so sorry Lord C. was too sick to travel when you guys had planned to come over."

"Yeah, so am I," Esme said. "He's better now, only now with the party planning and everything, it's a bad time again to travel."

"I understand. We'll just wait for you guys to come to my

debut on a London stage. How's *P&P*? Anything interesting happening?"

"No, not really," Esme stated in a bored voice. "Sir Wickham's back to being a dirty old man, and Jocelyn's back to doing her good works. They keep showing you in the coma, though, so you know that they're planning on waking you up soon. Have you gotten any more nasty letters?"

"No, they've actually petered out. I'm not getting much fan mail now, but what there is of it is mostly positive—people saying they wish Brooke well and that they miss seeing her on the show, you know. So I guess that means that my leaving did the trick, and it was just a fan who had lost some of his marbles."

"That's fantastic news, Cassie. I'll be sure to tell the family."

"Yes, do. But do me a favor, Es? Don't tell Tony."

"Whyever not, Cassie? He's the one who's worried the most."

"I haven't heard from him, Es. He's being strong about it, so I need to be, too. Don't even tell him about the reviews I've gotten."

"It's too late, for that. I've already shown them to him."

"Okay, but don't tell him about the letters. Promise me you won't."

"Oh, all right, I won't."

The remembered telephone conversation reminded Cassie that she'd picked up a bundle of London mail from her Post Office box two days before. She hadn't had the opportunity to read them, and she started to rise to retrieve them. Just then, she heard the key turn in the lock to the front door and looked over to see her uncle walk in. She shivered from the cold air. "Burr," she said and scrunched down back under the cover. "Shut the door. It's freezing!"

Charles laughed and playfully swung the door back and forth several times so the cold air would permeate the room.

"Hey," Cassie protested. "Stop that!" She noticed that he was dressed rather nicely. "What are you doing here? Did you decide to stop by on your way home from church?"

Whenever he was in town, Charles attend the church his parents had raised him in, despite the fact that it was twenty miles away from his suburban home. "Yeah," he said in answer to her question. "Just thought I'd check in and see how you're doing."

"I'm fine. How was church? Good sermon?"

"Yes, it was. You should have come," he said as he took off his coat and laid it on the back of a chair. "Why weren't you there?"

Cassidy shrugged. "Granny wasn't as into going to church when she raised me as she was when she raised you and Daddy. Sometimes we went, sometimes we didn't. That's the way I am now: sometimes I go, and sometimes I don't."

Charles knew that his mother had lapsed because she had lost some of her faith when her son and daughter-in-law were killed. He, on the other hand, had gotten more faithful. He'd needed something to help him understand the senselessness of it all.

"Della didn't go with you?" Cassidy asked. "Wait, I'm not missing anything, am I? You two are still together, aren't you?"

"Yes, we are," Charles told her as he sat down. What he didn't tell her was that it was very tenuous. Della and he had argued again that morning. It had been the same argument that they'd been having for years. It was that argument that kept her from accepting his many marriage proposals. "She decided that she didn't want to go to church this morning."

"Oh, that's too bad. I really would have liked to have seen her."

"You just saw her last week when we came to your play, for the fourth time, I might add."

Cassie shrugged again. "I just enjoy spending time with Della. She's a cool woman."

"I know. Why do you think I love her so much? What are you up to today?"

"Nothing. I'm not performing the matinee today. Since the show is winding down, they're giving understudies a chance to shine."

"Oh, that's too bad. You shine under those lights, baby," he told her. He was so proud of her that every time he looked at her these days, he felt he could burst with it. It was obvious when she was on that stage that she was meant to be there.

Cassie smiled back. His opinion had always mattered so much to her. "Thank you, Uncle Charles. I'm having a great time with it. Plus, I've got great material to work with. Isn't the play wonderful?"

Charles nodded. "What I don't understand is why such a great show that gets such stellar reviews is only playing for six weeks."

"You and everyone else, but it was the playwright's idea. She wants to leave the audience wanting. That way, she says, they'll be begging her to come back and they'll never get tired of her when she comes back year after year. It's not the best idea if you ask me, but hey, I'm just an actress."

"I can kind of see her logic," Charles said. "But in my opinion, you should always strike while the iron is hot." He looked around the room. It looked the same way it had looked when his mother was alive—big sectional sofa, floor model television, old-fashioned China cabinet and doilies everywhere. He didn't know how Cassie stood it—it was definitely decorated to suit an old lady. "Hey, since you've got no plans, do you want to go to brunch? You could call Della and invite her. We'll pick her up on the way."

He tried not to show it, but Cassie knew her uncle so well that she could tell that there was something wrong. And judging by the hopeful look he was giving her, the something wrong was between Della and he. "Okay, I'll call her, but let me make brunch. I've got to get rid of food before I leave next week. Do you think Della would mind driving over?"

"No, not for you she wouldn't," Charles said with a relieved grin on his face.

God, he's hopeless, Cassie thought with a shake of her head as she dialed Della's telephone number.

"So, anyway, my next assignment is in Rome," Charles said over brunch. "And you know I'm leaving in two days. But, I figure since we'll both be overseas during Christmas, and in the same general vicinity, maybe we could spend it together. Della's coming with me. And we could be persuaded to stay over to bring in the new millennium with you."

"Oh, that would be great, Uncle Charles," Cassidy said with enthusiasm. "When will you get into London?"

"We figure to fly in about three days before Christmas."

"Lovely," Cassie said after swallowing some pancake. "It will be good to have you there."

"So, tell me more about this Tony fellow. Is he smart? Is he rich? Is he funny? And most importantly, is he good enough for you, baby girl?"

Cassidy looked up from her scrambled eggs to smile at Della. Short, pleasantly plump, funny and outspoken, Della Jamison had a dark, lovely face, dark brown eyes, dyed blonde hair and plenty of attitude. Cassidy absolutely adored her. "God, yes, Della. He's all that and more. Plus, he's gorgeous and in love with me," Cassidy said, ignoring Charles' snort.

"She's forgetting to mention that he's also fourteen-years older than she is," Charles put in.

"No, I'm not," Cassidy sniffed. "I don't care about that. Only you and he do."

Della frowned. "What do you mean that he cares that he's older?"

"He thinks he's too old for me, and he wants to wait until I'm twenty-five to start seeing each other. He says he wants me to be sure that he's what I want. He also says that he doesn't want to steal my youth, and have me regret it later."

"Well, if that isn't a bunch of bullshit, then I don't know what is," Della stated. "How dare he try to tell you how you feel and what you know? That's an insult, honey!"

"See!" Cassidy slapped her hand down on the table. "That's what I said. But just like Uncle Charles, all he keeps saying is that he wants to protect me, and he doesn't want me to get hurt."

"Ha! You're a grown woman. You can make your own decisions. And besides, what good is being alive if you're not willing to take a few risks? And love almost by its very definition is risk. You have to be willing to put yourself out there, and just by doing that, you're risking getting hurt," she finished softly and looked at Charles, who shifted uncomfortably in his seat.

Brows raised in question, Cassidy thought it was probably a good time for her to exit the room, which she promptly did.

Cassidy finally got around to opening her mail from England three days later. The pile was a meager one, but she was grateful nonetheless. There was one thick envelope, however, so she chose to open it first. It wouldn't be the first time a fan had sent her photographs of her or himself, or of their children. It was usually men who sent her pictures of themselves posing to their best advantage and asking her out, but sometimes women did it too. She'd gotten several nude photos from woman. She usually got a good laugh out of them.

And figuring she needed one now after several days of saying goodbye to people, she eagerly upended the envelope so that the pictures spilled onto her kitchen table. She saw that the first one she picked up was of her. Frowning in confusion, she picked up another one…and then another one… and then another. They all were of her. Realization dawned, and horrified, she looked more closely at each picture. There were at least a dozen and each one showed her going about her business. In one, she was coming out of the grocery store. Another caught her having lunch with a friend and still another one was of her actually on stage.

Shakily, Cassie came to another realization. He was in Chicago. Her stalker had followed her to Chicago. Frantically, she dug through the pictures, scrambling until she found what she was looking for. It was a scrap of a note with eleven simple words written in a familiar hand. *You can run, but you can't hide. I'll find you anywhere. Remember, beauty must suffer.*

Cassie covered her mouth with a trembling hand. Panicked, she pushed back from the table, tripping over her chair and almost falling to the floor in her haste to get away from the ugliness.

"Damn it!" she said angrily. "Why can't he just leave me alone?" Several options were thought of and quickly discarded. She didn't want to call anyone and have him or her worry. No one could do anything anyway, except worry about her from thousands of miles away.

"Come on, Cassidy. You've got to do something," she told herself as her panicked gaze flew to the clock on the wall. Paul had set up a meeting for her with an L.A. casting director, and she had to be there in a little less than two hours.

Deciding that a visit to the police was in order, she rushed upstairs to change so she could go in before she met with the casting director. As she changed, she tried not to think about the stalker, and she prayed that he hadn't figured out where she lived, somehow knowing that her prayer probably wasn't going to be answered. She dialed Mrs. Washington.

"Hi, Mrs. Washington, it's Cassidy...good...good. Yes ma'am...no ma'am...uh huh...yes. Listen, will you do me a favor? For some reason I've been getting a bit of the willies lately. I'm getting ready to leave out for a couple of hours, and I was wondering if you could watch the house for me, and if you see anyone sort of lurking, will you call the police...no, I'm not expecting anyone...yes, I'm fine. I just have had a weird feeling lately. You'll do it...thank you. Thanks, so much. I'd really appreciate it. Also, will you ask Mrs. Corley and Mrs. Rivers from across the street to do the same? I'd call them myself, but I have to hurry out...yes ma'am, I will. Thanks again. Bye."

"So you're saying that this whole thing started in London, in August?"

"Yes, Officer," Cassidy answered the stern-faced policeman.

"It's detective. Detective Carson," he said looking up from the notes he was taking.

"Oh, I'm sorry, Detective Carson. I'm just a little rattled." She was more than just a little rattled. She was scared down to her bones. She'd broken all speed records getting to the station, only to have to wait for a half an hour before someone could see her. During that time, her imagination had gone wild conjuring up things the letter writer could be doing.

"It's all right, Ms. Hamilton. Tell me, were you in contact with the British police regarding this?"

"Yes. I've had a couple of meetings with Inspector Collins. I have her number here if you'd like to call." Cassie pulled a card out of her purse and handed it to him across the small desk.

After studying the card, he lifted his eyes to her face. "And what do they say about all of this?"

Cassie's smile was weak. "The same thing that I imagine you'll say. There isn't much to go on, but you'll check for fingerprints, and all the usual stuff."

Detective Carson smiled apologetically. "I'm sorry, but that's the way it is. I wish there was more I could do for you, but at this point, there isn't. We'll have to check things out. I'll keep these pictures, and contact Inspector Collins and share the pictures and the note. Why don't you give me a number where I can reach you?"

Cassidy parked her car on the street, trying to calm down after her encounter with the police. She was furious. The stalker was ruining her life. Detective Carson had offered her protection until she left town. They recommended a bodyguard, which she was seriously considering. Detective Carson had even given her a name.

"They won't find anything on those envelopes," she said as she walked to the address of her appointment with the L.A. casting director Paul had set her up with. She stopped in front of a small, squat building and pulled the door open. The lobby was deserted, and after only taking a few steps, Cassidy stopped dead in her tracks, every instinct in her screaming for her to get out.

She started to turn to go, but felt herself being shoved from behind. She fell to her knees, and heard the lock turn in the door behind her. Panic began to rise and not giving herself time to think, she rose as quickly as she could, ran to the door and pushed, but it wouldn't budge. "Let me out!" She banged on the door with both fists and then she resorted to kicking it. "Damn it, what the hell is going on?"

When the lights went out, she kicked, screamed and banged even harder.

"You're going to die, Cassidy Marie Hamilton Edwards."

The eerie, obviously manufactured voice slid into the room, filling it up and making her jump and cower against the door.

"You're the daughter of a murderer, and you're going to die just like your father's victim," the voice continued and Cassidy turned away from the door.

"My father was not a murderer, damn you!" she contradicted, feeling the anger as much as she was feeling the fear.

"Watch and see how she died, and learn how you'll die. You're going to die the same, Cassidy — exactly the same."

Helplessly, Cassidy stared at the wall across the room as

pictures began to flash. They were all the same. Each picture showed a girl, obviously dead, and lying on a slab with a deep red mark around her neck.

"Name: Theresa Campbell. Date of death: June 11, 1981. Cause of death: Killed by Cassidy Marie's father."

"No, no, no," Cassidy moaned, her mind rejecting what she was seeing and hearing. The anger took a back seat to pity and despair as she was forced to remember all the horror from that time. "She killed herself...she killed herself," she whispered.

"I loved her, and your father killed her. He took her away from me, and now you will suffer for his sins. He will suffer. Beauty must suffer."

The pictures continued to flash over and over again. The voice continued to repeat its message over and over again, and Cassidy began to scream...over and over again.

Once again, she turned to the door, and praying that someone would hear her, she began to beat on it again with her fists. A click sounded, the lock released, and Cassidy pushed her way out, her screams now no more than weak little whimpers.

From the back of the room behind a false wall, he watched as she clumsily ran out the door. "That's right, run, little girl. Run as fast as you can. I'll find you, wherever you go," he sang softly, his hatred for her and her family swelling inside him to burn bright and ugly.

Chapter 24

Cassidy stepped off the plane at London's Heathrow Airport and headed straight for baggage claim. After collecting her luggage, she went outside and sat and waited for Esme. Exhausted, she pulled her legs under her and rested her head on the back of the chair. She was a basket case, and she knew it. She looked a mess, and she knew that, too.

"Excuse me," a young voice said. "Aren't you Cassidy?"

Cassidy looked up to find herself surrounded by four teenage girls. Embarrassed, she straightened in the chair and pulled her sunglasses off. "Yes, I'm Cassidy."

"I knew it!" The girl who appeared to be the ringleader screeched, making Cassie wince and almost put her aching head in her hand. "We almost didn't recognize you, did we girls?" she asked the other girls and got an excited chorus of varying answers of no in return.

Cassidy winced again. She hadn't tried to hide from fans (she hadn't been expecting any); she'd been trying to hide from her stalker. That's what the huge sunglasses and comfortable clothes had been for, anyway.

"Oh, I know what's different," one of the girls screamed excitedly. "You've cut your hair, haven't you?" she stated, looking at Cassie's newly shortened hair. "Oh, it's lovely," she finished. "But you'd probably look beautiful with any cut. You've just got one of those faces."

"Thank you," Cassidy said softly in an effort to get them to lower their voices. She was nonplussed by the attention and wished for anonymity.

"Can we have your autograph?"

"Of course," Cassidy replied and looked expectantly at them.

"Oh, we don't have paper. We were hoping you'd sign our jeans or our bags," another girl said apologetically.

Cassidy laughed in surprise. I'll sign anything you want."

The girls left and Cassidy stood up to look for Esme. She spotted her, and smiled, ready to call out to her, when Esme looked right at her, walked past her a couple of steps, stopped and backtracked. Stunned that she hadn't recognized her at first, Cassidy all but fell back into her chair and covered her face with her hands, willing herself not to cry. It was all just too much.

"Oh, Cassidy," Esme tsked in sympathy from above her. "What's happened to you, love?"

Cassidy stood and hugged her friend. "It's so good to see you."

"You too, even if you are nothing but skin and bones. And what's happened to your hair?"

Cassie's fingers flirted with the short curls. "I cut it for the role. I could either wear a wig, or cut it. I decided it was time for a change, and I cut it."

"Come on, then," Esme said, leaning down to pick up one of Cassie's bags. "Let's get you home. You look like you could use a nice strong cuppa."

Cassidy sat facing the Carletons in their kitchen. She was so glad to be back with them. She'd just finished telling them about what had happened in Chicago.

"Oh, you poor child," Lady Carleton said. "Why didn't you tell us, Cassie?"

Cassie shrugged one shoulder. "I didn't want to worry you because there was nothing you could do from thousands of miles away."

"That's highly debatable, but we'll let it go for now," Lady Carleton said sternly.

"So, after you got away from the madman, you went directly to a hotel and checked in?" Lord Carleton asked.

"Yes. I didn't want to risk going home again. I called the police, and they came to the hotel, took my keys and went to my house and brought me back everything I needed, including my luggage. They assured me that they weren't followed. So, stayed at the hotel until it was time for me to leave for London."

"But, Cassie," Lady Carleton began, "why are you just getting here today when this happened days ago?"

Cassie frowned and shrugged as if the answer were obvious. "I had two more performances." When they all just looked at her like she was crazy, she said, "What? I'd made the commitment and I had to keep it. I know you're thinking that it was stupid, but I had to do it. They were counting on me, and I needed to do it to prove to myself that I could." She stopped talking to gather her thoughts. "I know it's hard for you guys to understand, but I didn't want him to completely take over my life. I had to be able to perform, otherwise he would have won."

"But what did the police think?" Esme asked.

"They advised me against it, of course, wanted me to leave for London that day. But I hired the bodyguard that they recommended, and he always took me back to my hotel. He made sure that we weren't followed, and I never left the hotel during the day. I was fine."

Lady Carleton waved her hands impatiently when she saw that Esme would argue further. "Never mind, Es. The deed can't be undone, can it?" She sighed. "And you say the police checked out the building where you were held, and found nothing?" She looked at Cassie.

"Right," Cassie said with a nod. "They said the place was wiped clean, and there was no sign of anyone there. They're trying to track down the owner, but it seems that there's so much red tape because it's owned by an affiliate of a company that's an affiliate of another company and so on and so on."

"Oh, Lord, we forgot to call Tony! He's going to absolutely flip when he gets wind of this!" Esme made to stand from her chair.

"No, Esme!" Cassidy said and took a sip of tea. "I don't want Tony to know. You have to promise me you won't tell. All of you," she shifted her gaze so that it encompassed all three of the Carletons.

"But why not, Cassie?" Esme protested.

"For the same reasons I told you before."

"But surely this changes things!"

"No, it doesn't," Cassidy persisted, exhaustion catching up to her and making her feel weak and empty. "Please, all of you, promise me you won't tell."

Seeing the desperation in her eyes, Lady Carleton patted her hand. "All right, dear. We won't tell him."

"Thank you," Cassidy said, feeling that she could finally breathe a sigh of relief.

"I suppose this means that you didn't tell your uncle, either, right?"

"No, I didn't tell Uncle Charles. He'd just worry. Besides, I'm going to see him for Christmas. I'll just tell him then."

"All right, that's enough chatting for now," Lady Carleton said as she rose. "Cassidy, I want to see a clean plate when I come back here. Is that understood?"

Cassidy grinned, feeling safe and normal for the first time in days. "Yes, ma'am."

"Good. Come on, then, darling. Let's leave the girls to catch up." Lady Carleton left the kitchen, leaving her husband to follow her.

"I don't see why you agreed not to tell Tony," Lord Carleton said as they walked into the library. "He has a right to know."

"I agreed because I didn't want to upset her any further. She's already fragile. Did you see how thin she's gotten? She's all eyes and hair, Richard," Lady Carleton said, as she remembered how Cassidy had looked with her sleeves hanging over her hands and her big eyes shining fearfully out of her face. "That poor, poor girl."

"I still say we should tell Tony."

"I feel the same way, but we're not going to tell him."

"And why is that?"

"Because she's asked us not to, and this is her story."

"But he loves her."

"I know he does," Lady Carleton said sadly.

The Carleton Christmas party was in full swing by the time Cassidy left her room wearing a black velvet pants suit with wide legs and sleeves, and a frilly white blouse. She'd been late

leaving the set of *P&P*, and had had to rush to get ready. She'd been back in London a full week, and had yet to get back on an even keel. The stalker had her constantly looking over her shoulder and jumping at shadows, even though there had been nothing from him since Chicago.

She spotted Esme, and made a beeline for her through the crowd. "Hi, you look great," she told her as she took in the long sweep of a green dress. "That dress really brings out your eyes."

Esme widened said eyes coquettishly. "Exactly why I bought it," she said smartly, making Cassidy chuckle. "You look great, too. But then again, you always do. God, I thought the waif look had gone out of fashion ages ago, but if anyone can bring it back, you can."

"I'm not trying to. It's just taking a while to put the weight back on."

Esme studied the big eyes, the more prominent cheekbones, and the wide mouth and shook her head. "Well, the look is certainly working well with that outfit. You look stunning."

"Thanks," Cassie said wryly. "I think."

"Where's your bodyguard?" Esme asked.

Cassie hadn't needed the police to tell her a third time to hire personal security. She looked around. "He's never far behind. There he is," she said and nodded her head at a large man who looked like he was just any other guest.

"Good. Do you think his presence is what's keeping your stalker away?"

"I don't know, but I do know that I feel a lot safer when he's around."

"I swear," Esme said, changing the subject as she took in the crowd. "This crowd gets bigger and bigger every year."

"Well, your parents are pretty popular," Cassidy said as she looked around.

The Carletons lived in a 19th century mansion, and they'd tried to keep its original design when they'd modernized it after purchasing it in the 1970s. The house still had an actual ballroom, which was where most of the crowd was congregating. Some of the guests had spilled out into the large hall and entryway. The old mansion had enthralled Cassidy when she'd first seen it and she was still amazed by it now.

She studied the delicate chandeliers and the old-fashioned wainscoting that adorned the walls and smiled with appreciation.

"Cassie? Are you listening to me?" Esme's voice was filled with exasperation.

"Oh, sorry, Es," Cassie said with a smile. "I was just admiring the decorations. What were you saying?"

"I was saying that the party was originally meant for Carleton employees only. Now, we not only get the employees, but we get everyone else as well."

"Hmm," Cassidy said noncommittally as she tried to think of a way to broach the subject that she really wanted to discuss. Deciding that there was no easy way, she blurted, "Has Tony arrived yet?"

"Not that I've seen," Esme told her. "Why?"

"Why do you think, Esme? I've missed him. I want to see him."

Tony arrived at the party two hours later, and was hoping that he could sneak in without anyone seeing him. His mother would consider him unforgivably late. It had been unavoidable, though. There had been another crisis at work, this time it had been a defective product. He'd stayed late with the Public Relations team coming up with a strategy to minimize the damage.

"What a lovely home your parents have, Tony," Amanda said as they stood looking at the crowd that was spread out before them.

"I'll tell them you said so," Tony said. She'd begged a ride off him, saying that her car was being fixed. He knew her game, though, and had told her she'd have to get a taxi or a ride with a co-worker home, because he'd be staying at his parents, as he customarily did after one of their parties. She'd been trying for months to get him interested in her again. But he'd not thought of her since Wimbledon.

"Why don't I just go with you and tell them myself?" Amanda suggested and latched onto his arm.

Seeing no way to get out of it, Tony turned to look for his parents and ran right into a frowning Esme.

"You're late," she accused.

"It was unavoidable."

Esme's eyes flicked to Amanda and back to him again, where they stared accusingly into his. "Yes," she said slowly. "I guess it might have been."

Tony narrowed his eyes at her, and when he bent to kiss her cheek, told her, "You have a dirty mind, Esme Carleton. You just watch that nothing slithers out of it to smear me," he warned.

A snort was Esme's only response.

"Where are Mum and Dad?"

"About," she said dismissively. "I'm sure you'll find them if you look hard enough."

Tony left her and went off to find his parents, one of which soundly chided him for being late. He was able to ditch Amanda with the excuse that he needed to talk to his parents concerning a personal matter. And then, he was lost to the crowd, with everyone wanting a piece of him, particularly members of his board.

Exactly twenty minutes later he was able to escape to the library where he hoped to find a few moments of peace and think about Cass, whom he had yet to see.

"There you are, Tony, darling. I've been looking for you."

Tony turned to find Amanda gliding gracefully toward him. She reminded him of a cat. "You've found me. What can I do for you, Amanda?"

"Darling," Amanda chuckled low in her throat, "I was beginning to think you'd never ask," she finished and threw her arms around his neck, pulling his head down for a steamy kiss.

Tony stood stock still as she pressed her mouth to his, thinking that Amanda had never been one for subtlety.

Cassidy was tired. Tired of people asking her about *P&P*, tired of feeling like everyone was staring at her and just tired, period. She opened the door to the library with the thought of sneaking in for a little peace and quiet. Peeking guiltily over her shoulder, she started to ease into the room...and was struck dumb and motionless by the sight before her.

Her horrified gasp is what brought Tony out of his stupor. He looked up in time to see Cassidy staring at him in shock. There was just enough light for him to see her clearly. "Cass? Hi. It's not what—"

After staring daggers at him, Cass turned on her heel and walked determinedly away. But Tony wasn't fooled. He'd seen the quivering of her mouth, the furious blinking of her lashes to hold back tears, and most importantly, he'd seen the devastation in her eyes.

Disentangling himself from Amanda, he pushed her away. "Fuck," he said, knowing he'd never find Cass in the crush of the crowd. She'd hide from him and he knew it. None of this knowledge, however, stopped him from rushing out of the room and into the crowd to look for a cap of brown curls and a narrow back covered in black velvet.

"Tony."

Tony turned to his mother. "Hello, Mum."

"Darling, I must insist that you stop neglecting our guests. Tim Flannery and Henry Fitzsimmons are looking for you. They mentioned something about a chip acquisition...?" Lady Carleton's voice trailed off in confusion.

Chip acquisition? Tony got a good look at her eyes. "A little too much wine, Mum?"

Lady Carleton smiled. "Maybe just a bit. Now come with me, I'll take you to them."

Tony frowned. It sounded like the two board members wanted to discuss his wanting to acquire the computer chip manufacturer. He was actually pretty close to persuading them. He sighed. He'd have to find Cass later. "In a moment, Mum," he said, and turned back towards the library. "I have to take care of something first."

Chapter 25

Cassidy threw another shirt into her suitcase. Devastation wanted to surface, but she fought it back and went on automatic pilot. She didn't want to think about what she'd seen earlier; she just wanted to act. And act is what she did. Within fifteen minutes of slamming into her room, she'd changed her clothes, and she'd packed a suitcase.

She looked at her watch. Not wanting to make a scene, she'd waited for the party to end and had helped to organize clean up before coming upstairs to her room to pack. She'd stayed away from Tony for the duration of the party by finding various corners to mix and mingle in. She'd noticed that he'd been busy with his board members, so it hadn't been too difficult to escape his attention. He and those same board members had closeted themselves in his father's study towards the end of the party, and she assumed that they were still there.

Patting the last blouse down, Cassidy took a look around trying to see if she'd forgotten anything. "Makeup case," she muttered and went into the connecting bath.

"Cassidy!" Tony walked into her room without knocking. He wasn't going to let her hide from him any longer. He noticed the suitcase on the bed and walked further in. "Cassidy!" he said again. "Where are you?"

Cassidy hurried out of the bathroom with her makeup bag. *Damn it! A few more minutes, and I'd have been gone.* "Keep your voice down; you'll wake your parents," she said calmly and walked over to her suitcase to toss the makeup bag inside. Slamming it shut, she lifted it from the bed and prepared to leave. "Excuse me," she said when Tony blocked her way. She kept her eyes on his chest. *Hold it together, Cassie. Hold it!*

"Where are you going?" he asked angrily and tightened his hands on her shoulders when she tried to jerk away from him.

"It's no business of yours," she tried to say haughtily. The effect was ruined by the fact that she wouldn't look him in the eye. "Excuse me, please."

"No. You're not going anywhere until we talk this out."

"There's nothing to talk about," Cassidy said, her gaze locked on his Adam's apple now. "Actions speak much louder than words, Tony," she finished, and couldn't resist a soft, "Just ask Amanda."

Furious because she sounded so cool and wouldn't even bother to look at him, he grabbed the suitcase and threw it so that it bounced once on the bed and then fell to the carpeted floor. "You are going to listen to me, Cass. You're not leaving here until you do. In fact, you're not leaving this house, period."

Cassidy's head swiveled to look from the disappearing suitcase and then back to him. She struggled not to let her shock show. *Keep it together, Cassie,* she thought to herself again. *Act like nothing matters.* "I don't want to hear anything you have to say. It doesn't matter."

"It bloody well does, and goddamn it, you're going to listen!"

"I'm afraid that's your opinion, Tony," she said with a shrug, and made to walk away so she could get her suitcase from the floor on the other side of the bed.

"Just hold it," he demanded and grabbed her wrist. Trying to calm down before he said anything he'd regret, he looked at her, taking in the oversized white sweater, white leggings and flats. His hand lifted to touch her newly shortened curls, and when she jerked her head away, he swore and looked into her eyes. There was so much pain and anger in them, he couldn't stay mad. She just looked so fragile. "Damn it, Cass. It's not what you think," he said with a sigh. "Will you listen to me?"

"No, Tony. Like I said, there's nothing to say."

When she tried to pull away, he tightened his hand on her wrist, noticing how bony it felt. Distracted, he said, "What the hell, Cass? What have you done to yourself? Why have you lost so much weight? And why did you cut your hair? Is this some new fashion trend?"

Cassidy's mouth formed a stubborn line. "Leave me alone, Tony. Please, just leave. I'm too tired to fight with you."

"Well, that's just too damned bad, because we're going to have this out—"

"No, we're not."

"Yes, we are," Tony contradicted and turned on his heel to leave the room, dragging her behind him. "And since this is bound to get loud, we'll take it to another part of the house."

"Stop it, Tony," she said between gritted teeth as she struggled to get away while at the same time trying to be as quiet as possible so as not to disturb the rest of the house. "Let go of me!" she said as he dragged her down the hall. "Where are you taking me?" she asked, afraid she already knew.

"To my room," he said and dragged her down a set of stairs.

Since they were no longer on the same floor as his parents, Esme and other guests, Cassie intensified her struggle. "I'm not going," she said and grabbed onto the post at the bottom of the staircase just as he stepped off the last stair and tried to turn the corner.

Tony looked at her over his shoulder. "All right, if that's the way you want it," he said, and turned towards her. He stooped, and leading with his shoulder, lifted her so that she was thrown over his shoulder with his arm trapping her thighs against his chest. Straightening, he said, "Then that's the way it will be."

Cassidy bucked against him. "Put me down, Tony! This is ridiculous," she said in outrage as he made his way towards the kitchen.

"I agree," he said and slapped her on the behind when she managed to kick him in the thigh. "Behave," he told her mildly. "Hello, Ms. Potts," he said to the housekeeper. "Ladies," he nodded to two maids. "Don't mind us. Cass and I are just going to have a little chat in the privacy of my borrowed room." He always slept in the room after his parents' Christmas party, giving up his old bedroom for guests.

Cassie, who had become stone quiet and deathly still when she realized there were actual people around, moaned and covered her face with her hands in mortification.

"You all right, love?" Tony asked with studied nonchalance as he picked up a bottle of champagne he'd noticed. "This might come in handy," he said to the housekeeper and maids, who simply stared at the scene taking place before them. "Thank you," he said with a smile when one of the maids rushed to give him a corkscrew.

"Now," he said after he'd carried her into the room and shut the door behind him. "I'm going to put you down, Cass, but no funny stuff." Cautiously, he bent and put her down so she was sitting on the bed.

She came up swinging. One of her fists caught him on the side of his head and the other got him in the shoulder before he was able to grab her, turning her so her back was to his chest. He caught her up in a bear hug.

"Oh, I'm furious with you!" she said. "How dare you!"

Tony continued to hold her, lifting her off her feet when she kicked her legs. His hold tightened and he pressed his face to the back of her neck. "Calm down, Cass."

"I will not calm down! You manhandled me!" She struggled even more, desperate to get away from him after feeling his soft breath on her neck. The heat that curled in her stomach was unbearable.

Tony sighed in resignation and tightened his hold. "I guess we'll have to have our discussion this way, then. I was not kissing Amanda, Cass, I'd never do that to you," Tony chided softly and was gratified when she stopped struggling. "She was kissing me, not the other way around, I swear it," he said simply, and waited.

Cassie stood in silence; trying to remember what she'd seen when she'd burst into the library earlier that night. "Do you mean it?" she asked quietly.

"Yes. I'm telling you the truth."

"Let me go," she demanded, and when he did she walked away from him. Arms crossed, she turned to face him. "Why did you go back in the library? I saw you."

"I went back to tell her to leave. I gave her money for a taxi, that's all."

Cassidy digested his statement, mulling it over in her head. "You stopped calling me when I was in Chicago," she accused.

"I thought it was for the best," he said and studied her

through narrowed eyes. Something was going on in that head of hers that he just couldn't figure out.

"I was miserable when I didn't hear from you, and when I walked in on that scene with you and Amanda tonight, I realized why you hadn't. You said you weren't going to have sex with anyone—"

Furious that she was actually accusing him of having sex with Amanda, Tony took his hand through his hair and wished he could shake loose some sense. "I didn't! Damnation, I haven't even thought about anyone else! I told you that Amanda was kissing me, not the other way—"

"I know what I saw," she maintained stubbornly. "If you weren't kissing her, then why were you standing there?" A part of her—a very large part—believed him. But there was also that part of her that remembered what it had felt like to walk into that room and see him in another woman's arms. She'd thought her heart would burst from the pain.

"She surprised me! We were just having a conversation and she threw herself in my arms. That's all there is to it."

"How am I supposed to believe you?"

"Hell and damnation, Cass, because you know me! I'd never do anything of the sort—"

Cassie's shrug was jerky. "How am I supposed to know anything? After all, you're the one who came up with this cockamamie idea to wait three years before we can see each other."

"It's not cockamamie, whatever the hell that means. It's a perfectly logical course of—"

"No, it isn't. It's a stupid idea!"

"Damn and blast, will you close your mouth, and stop interrupting me?"

Cassie's mouth closed with a snap, and she turned her head in offense so that her nose was in the air. "I don't see why you have to be so rude."

Tony stalked over and stood directly in front of her. "No, be still," he said when she moved to walk around him. "We're going to finish this—right here, right now."

Cassie looked at him, folded her arms across her chest and made a sound that said 'that's what you think.' "I'm finished with this conversation. Good night!"

Tony feinted to his right, stepping in front of her when she once again tried to walk around him. "We're not finished, and you're going to marry me. Not in three years, but in three months or three weeks or six months or six weeks, I don't care which."

Cassie's mouth fell open in astonishment as she stared at him. *Where did that come from? Why would he be giving in so sudden — oh, no way!* "No. I'm not going to marry you just because you feel bad. I won't be married out of pity, or guilt!" she declared. "No, I'm going to marry you in three years, or not at all."

Tony watched as her eyes filled and scowling, he pulled out his handkerchief and gave it to her, shoving it into her hand. "Don't you dare start crying," he told her and paced away from her

Feeling thoroughly driven to madness now, he told himself that he shouldn't yell, and he tried everything in his power not to. It didn't work. "Bloody hell, Cass! It's got nothing to do with guilt. I'm doing this for my own sanity! I can't wait the three years. For Christ's sake, it's driving me mad! *You're* driving me mad! Hmph!" Surprised, Tony could do nothing but put his arms around her after Cassie had thrown herself against him.

"I'm so glad," she whispered, the relief she felt making her feel weak. She kissed his throat, his jaw, his chin — wherever she could reach. "I was hoping you would come to your senses, but I could never be sure if you would. It's been so hard all these months."

Tony tipped her chin up and pressed his mouth to hers, feeling everything fall into place as she opened her mouth for him. He kissed her slowly and thoroughly, taking his time to savor and treasure. "I missed you, baby," he said.

Cassie could say nothing, only putting her heart and soul into the kiss.

"This means you're going to marry me." Tony demanded.

"God, yes, as soon as possible," Cassie said, smiling as she gently pushed the hair off his forehead.

There was no more room for talking after that, as if by mutual agreement, they moved towards the bed, stripping as they went. He moved beneath her, his hands gripping her hips tightly while she rode him, savoring the feel of him and mewling her pleasure with each stroke. Relief and joy overcoming her, she began sobbing and leaned down to lay against him. "Tony, I missed you," she cried the words against his mouth. "I just missed you so much and you feel so good," she gasped as he moved within her. "Don't stay away again," she begged. "Please don't."

Tony kissed her hungrily, and gathered her close against his chest. Turning so that their positions were reversed, he gentled his strokes into her body, making them long and deep. He bent down to kiss her lips. "I won't, baby, I won't," he promised before rocking them both to completion.

The next thing Tony heard after the three brisk knocks on his door was the sound of the door being shoved open. "Bloody hell, Esme!" he said without even opening his eyes. He knew it was her, even before she appeared after walking the short hall that actually led into the room. "You're supposed to wait until I invite you in!" Making sure the blankets covered his waist; he sat up and leaned against the headboard.

"I've got no time for niceties this morning, Anthony," Esme said when she finally appeared. "Cassidy's missing, and it's entirely your fault! I've been to her room and she's not there!"

Tony pinched the bridge of his nose and closed his eyes, keeping them closed because he didn't trust himself not to do bodily harm to Esme if he had to look at her. "Slow down, Esme, and keep your voice down."

For the first time, Esme noticed that someone was in bed with him. Her eyes narrowed. "Well, I like this! Isn't it enough that you humiliate Cassie by bringing this…this…*creature*," she said, pointing to the lump under the covers, "to the party? Did you have to sleep with her, too? I thought you loved Cassie. Oh, I can't believe you! You're a complete ass, Tony! I wanted Cassie for my sister-in-law, but you've ruined it! How could you be so selfish? Well, I'll tell you one thing: I'll never be nice to your little chickie there—"

Tony had had enough. "Will you shut your bloody trap for one minute, Esme?" he growled in a low, angry voice. Satisfied that he'd gotten what he'd wanted—for while Esme's mouth may have been wide open, not a sound was coming from it— Tony turned, and sliding his hand under the covers, took it gently over heated skin. "I'm afraid the jig is up. You might as well come out now, love."

"Must I?" Cassie asked sheepishly as she turned over, and pushing a curl out of her face, peeked over the covers at Esme. She laughed at Esme's look of astonishment. "Hi, Es. You won't tell on us, will you?"

"I-I-I thought you'd gone! You were so upset last night after seeing Tony with Amanda that I thought you'd left us."

"Nu-uh," Cassie said as she sat up and smoothed down the collar of the shirt she'd borrowed from Tony. "I tried to—had waited for the house to quiet and had packed my bag and everything—but he," she nodded in Tony's direction, "wouldn't let me."

"He wouldn't, would he?"

Cassie shook her head. "No. See, I refused to listen to him, told him it didn't matter what he said, that I was going back to my flat. I snatched my suitcase and prepared to make my grand exit and he took the suitcase from me, threw it at the bed, and grabbing me by my wrist, dragged me from my room. And the next thing you know, I was down here, in his room, being forced to listen to him because he blocked me from leaving. He would have had a bigger fight on his hands, though, if I weren't afraid of waking your parents, and if he hadn't promised that he'd gone back to the library and kicked Amanda out."

"But what was he doing in the library with Amanda?" Esme asked.

"I'll answer that," Tony said when Cassie opened her mouth. "She was kissing me, I wasn't kissing her. And I didn't bring her to the party as my date, she asked for a ride from the office. It's as simple as that."

"Yep," Cassidy agreed with a nod. "It's as simple as that. And guess what, Esme! We're getting married! Tony proposed!" She held out her hand for Esme to see.

Esme screeched and jumped onto the bed, landing in a tangle of legs on Tony's thighs. "Oh, my God. Let me see! Let me see! Let me see!"

"Esme!" Tony pushed her off of him so that she landed against Cassidy.

"Don't worry about him," Cassie told Esme in a loud whisper. "He's just embarrassed because he's naked," she finished with a wink.

"Oh, for the love of—" Tony began and cut himself off to get out of bed. He was gratified to hear the horrified gasps of "Tony!" behind him, and climbed fully out of bed with a smirk on his face to show off his...boxers.

Esme snickered and turned her attention back to Cassidy's finger. "But it's only a type of foil of some kind," she said in confusion.

"I know," Cassidy said excitedly. "Isn't it adorable? Tony made it from the foil from a champagne bottle. He wasn't prepared, but he still met the challenge."

"Well, one can only hope he challenges himself a little more and makes a trip to the blooming jeweler," Tony heard Esme mutter as he walked into the bath.

"So, tell me how he proposed," Esme demanded as soon as the door was shut behind Tony. "Was it romantic?"

Cassidy grinned. "He shouted it."

"Shouted it?"

Cassie nodded. She did her best impression of Tony. "Bloody hell, Cass. I can't wait the three years!"

Esme snorted. "That's not romantic."

"Yes it is, Es," Cassie disagreed. "Don't you see? He reneged on his own plan, and nobody made him. He did it himself because he couldn't take us being apart any longer."

Esme's patented smirk appeared and she snorted. "It was a ruddy stupid plan anyway."

"Yes, we can all agree on that," Cassie said. "But let's not bring it up anymore. It upsets him."

"All right, then," Esme said as she climbed from bed. "I'm off for some breakfast. Where's your bodyguard, anyway?"

"Bodyguard?" Tony asked with a frown as he came out of the bathroom. "What bodyguard?"

Esme looked from his furious face to Cassie's guilty one. "Uh-oh. Looks like it's time for me to exit," she said and beat it from the room.

"Now, Tony," Cassie said as he strode towards the bed. "Don't start."

"Damn it, Cass!" Tony said angrily. "I asked you a question, and I don't want you to avoid it. What bloody bodyguard?"

Cassie stopped trying to stall and explained. And as she explained, Tony found that he was too weak to stand. By the time she was finished explaining, he was sitting on the edge of the bed with his face in his hands. All he could think about was how scared and alone she must have felt, and how close she'd come to being hurt.

Concerned at his silence, Cassie put a hand on his shoulder, rubbing it gently. "I didn't want to worry you."

"I love you, Cass. I want to know when there's a problem. I *need* to know when there's a problem. I'm entitled to worry."

"I know, but I just thought it would be best if you didn't find out, seeing as how there was nothing you could do. You were an ocean away, Tony."

Tony turned to look at her. "There bloody well was something I could have done, Cass. I could have, and *would have*, flown over to Chicago and gotten you, that's what I would have done. Don't insult me."

"I'm sorry. I really am," Cassie said sincerely as she realized how careless she'd been. Keeping it all from him had been stupid. Wincing, she shrugged and caressed his cheek. "In my defense, I really thought I was doing the right thing. I also didn't want to tell you because I didn't want you to change your mind about the three years just because I was in trouble and you wanted to protect me. I wanted you to change your mind because you didn't want to be without me, just like I don't want to be without you. I wanted us on the same wavelength, that's all."

"Damn it to hell, Cass! You were in a lot of trouble, and you didn't let me help you! When I imagine you holed up in that hotel room and scared to death because there was no one there to help you, my heart wants to stop. I look at you now, and can still see the damage. It's the reason why you've lost all the weight, isn't it?"

Cassidy nodded. "All I can say is that I'm sorry that I didn't tell you, Tony. It won't happen again. But I had another good reason for keeping things from you. I didn't want to get you in trouble with your board of directors. The last thing they want is their CEO tangled up with someone like me, fodder for all the gossip sheets."

"Hang the board," Tony said angrily and pulled her around so that she straddled him. "I love you. I'd do anything for you."

Wanting to soothe, reassure and take away the hurt, Cassie took his face between her hands and leaned down to kiss him, moaning when he devoured her mouth with clashing teeth and a rampaging tongue.

Tony was a man mad with emotions as he gripped her hips in his hands. He needed her — needed her now. Needed to feel her moving around him, needed to feel himself moving within her — he needed her like he needed to breathe. *I could have lost her* was the only thought raging through his mind as he pushed her borrowed shirt out of the way and slammed her down on his erection.

Cassie's head fell back in pure ecstasy and she came in a surprised rush of feeling while he ravished her throat with his tongue. His hands were everywhere, and she couldn't keep up. "More," she heard him say as she felt herself being laid on her back. "Take more."

Conquered, she moved her hands weakly to his arms. "I can't, Tony, I can't," she wheezed.

"More," he said again as he reached between them and fondled her clitoris, making her come again in one long stream.

"Oh, God," Cassie said as she arched off the bed. She was losing her mind. "I can't, Tony," she said again. "I can't."

"All of me, take all of me," Tony demanded as he plunged into her again and again with long, hard thrusts. Taking her mouth, he emptied himself into her, the pain and the fear for her finally lessening.

All Cassidy could do was kiss him back.

Chapter 26

Tony stood offstage on the set of *P&P* and watched Cassidy work.

"She's brilliant, isn't she?"

He turned to Cassidy's bodyguard who was smiling to beat the band. *Another one bites the dust*, Tony thought before answering. "I think so, yes," he said wryly. "But of course, I'm biased." Tony had started coming to the set whenever he could. After Cass had told him what had happened to her in Chicago, he didn't really trust anyone else to protect her—at least not as well as he would.

"Okay, children," the director called. "Break for lunch!"

Tony watched Cassidy walk towards him. She smiled when she saw him and his heart automatically lifted. "Hi, honey," she said and kissed him. "What a nice surprise!"

Tony searched her face for strain. "Are you all right?"

Cassidy let her exasperation show. "Yes, I am, and no, nothing arrived today—no letters, no pictures."

"Nothing yet," Tony muttered as he walked with her to her dressing room. He heard the bodyguard fall into step behind them. Opening the door for Cassie, he walked in after her and turned to shut the door. "We'll see you in an hour or so," he said to the bodyguard right before he closed the door.

"Tony!" Cassidy chastised as she stepped past him to open the door. "I usually invite him in to have lunch with me."

Tony waylaid her with a hand on her arm. "Let's not do that today. We've got some catching up to do, remember?" he whispered in her ear, making the fine hairs along her nape stand up.

Cassidy shivered and nodded. "Just let me send him to lunch," she whispered, and opening the door, she did just that. "Tony?" she whispered as she went into his arms.

"Hmm?" Tony was too busy enjoying sucking her lips to pay much attention.

"Remember when we were in my apartment in New Haven and you almost made love to me against the wall?"

"Yes," he said cautiously.

"Well, I was wondering," she said as she began to undo his buttons. "If we could finish what we started."

Tony pulled back to look at her with a confused frown. "We did finish what we started, remember? It was at your flat, and we were... And you're shaking your head 'no,'" he said quizzically. "Why is that?"

"Because we didn't finish, Tony. Not that specific act. Don't you remember?" she asked when he still looked confused. "You had your fingers inside of me, and I was riding them and we almost finished, but then Esme came."

"So, let me get this straight," he said as he sipped kisses from her lips, and his hands wandered underneath her skirt and up her thighs. "You want to come with my fingers inside of you. Well, that hardly seems fair, does it? You'll get to have most of the fun while I'll get to do all the work."

Cassidy shivered and pressed against him when his hands slipped under her briefs and caressed her behind. "That's not what I meant," she said and tried to suppress both a chuckle and a moan at the same time. "I thought while you were doing me, I could be doing you," she whispered.

"I'll admit, the plan does have some merit," Tony said as he boosted her up until her legs were wrapped around his hips.

Cassidy hummed her agreement. It was all she could do, seeing as how he was both sucking her nipple through her blouse and rubbing her cleft against his erection at the same time. She heard a zipper come undone, felt her panties being pushed aside and surmised what was going on. "Oh, no fair," she moaned and threw her head back when he entered her in one forceful thrust.

"All is fair in love and making love, sweetheart," Tony said right before leaning in to nip at her neck.

"Tony?"

"Yes," he mumbled against her skin as he slowly took her.

"D-d-d-d-don't...ahh...leave a h-h-h-hickey, okay? I... ahhhhhhh...still...ahhhhhh...have a scene to film this afternoon."

Tony concentrated on kissing her instead, his mouth covering hers just as he plunged deep, making her scream as her orgasm took over her senses.

"That was a sneaky trick," Cassidy said later as she lay in his arms on her dressing room sofa.

"Yes," Tony said without guilt. "It was, wasn't it?"

Laughing, she kissed his chin. "Yes, it was. Lucky for you, we both benefited."

"We always benefit when we're together, love. Everyone seems to be happy for us, including some of those curmudgeons on my board."

Cassie leaned up to look at him. "Really?"

"Yes. I had a couple of them to come up and congratulate me after our engagement was announced in the papers, and ad nauseam for several days on the telly," he said wryly. "It was announced, and nothing catastrophic has happened, or did I miss the clashing of the titans?" he teased, softly kissing her lips. "And you'll be happy to know that the deal to acquire the computer chip manufacturer will be going through soon. I've finally brought the majority of the board around to my thinking."

"Oh, that's great," Cassie said excitedly. "Congratulations! I knew you could do it."

Tony kissed her again before looking down at her. "You know we have to talk about it, Cass, don't you?"

Cassidy stiffened in his arms. "Talk about what?" she hedged.

"Talk about what the police said."

She shrugged. "As usual, they didn't say much."

"They said plenty. Like, how this stalking may have more to do with what happened to your parents, than it does your being on the show."

"I don't want to talk about it, Tony."

"That's too bad, because you have to. You said that in Chicago, the man kept showing you pictures of Theresa Campbell and saying that your father killed her. He blamed your father for her death, even though she killed herself and she did it after your parents were already dead." Tony fell silent as he tried to piece things together.

Cassidy was nodding the whole time he was talking and when he was finished, her brow puckered. "See? It doesn't make any sense. How can he blame my father when everyone knows that she killed herself? It's obvious that he's not sane."

"Maybe he means your father killed her metaphorically, you know? Perhaps in his mind, the fact that the girl is dead at all is your father's fault."

Cassie ruminated on it. "I don't know. I guess that could be it."

Absently, Tony continued to rub her arm. Remaining silent, he thought about everything she'd told him about her parents' deaths, and the aftermath. He was missing something, he was sure of it. He went over the details in his head again, and feeling Cassie slump against him, looked down and saw that she was asleep. He went back to the details.

"It still doesn't make sense," he muttered. "Cass's father is dead, so how will he suffer if something happens to her?" He jerked in surprise as it all fell into place. "Bloody hell," he said in disgust.

He looked down at her face. She looked so peaceful, something that was rare these days, even in sleep. He frowned, loathed to bring any more misery into her life.

The pictures came the next day. Cassidy was sitting in the Carleton library with Tony, mindlessly going through her fan mail when her hand closed over a fat envelope. Recognizing what it was, she froze and told herself not to panic. "Damn. Tony?"

Tony looked up from the paper he was reading, immediately rising and walking over to her when he saw the look on her face. "What is it?" he asked and picked up the envelope. Ripping the seal, he snatched the pictures out. "Fuck me," he said incredulously as he stared at picture after picture of Cassidy going about her life in London.

"It's just like Chicago, isn't it?" Cassidy asked from behind him.

"I'm afraid so," Tony answered grimly, still going through the pictures.

Cassidy bent to pick up the note that must have fallen to the floor when Tony had pulled the pictures out. She recognized the handwriting immediately. *You're going to die, Cassidy Marie Hamilton Edwards, bodyguard or no* was all the note said, and it was signed simply: *Midnight Strangler.*

Cassie's blood chilled. "Oh, God," she moaned in despair. She pulled at Tony's arm, the fear she felt blocking her vocal chords and rendering her speechless.

Tony took his eyes off the pictures long enough to see what was wrong. The look of fright on her face made him more tense. "What's the matter?" he asked her as he pulled her into his arms.

Cassidy found that she still couldn't speak. Her mind was frozen in fear. She tried lifting her arm to give him the note, her hand moving against his chest. "Tony!" she finally got out urgently, and pushed against him when she tried several times to give him the note without him taking notice.

Tony released her, his eyes falling on the note in her hand. "Christ Jesus," he muttered in stunned amazement when he read the note.

"He's wants to kill me," Cassidy said in full-blown panic. "Oh, my God," she said slowly, as if it had suddenly dawned on her, "he is going to kill me."

Tony pulled her to him, holding her tight and burying his face in her hair. "No, he's not going to kill you," he said angrily. "He'll have to go through me if he wants to get to you."

"Don't say that," Cassidy murmured, growing even more afraid at the thought that something could happen to him. "We have to take this stuff to the police. They said that I was to bring them whatever came in."

"All right, then," Tony said and tunneled his hand through the hair on the back of her head to gently pull her head back so he could see her face. "We'll take them to the police. And you're going to be safe. Do you believe me?"

Looking into his fierce eyes, she couldn't do anything but believe him. "Yes."

"I'm sorry, Miss, sir," Inspector Collins, a small, polished woman said to Cassidy and Tony. "But that's all I can tell you. And all I can do is take the photos and the letter. Hopefully, he will have left some clue this time."

"That's it?" Cassie asked. "So you're telling me that I've been getting notes from the Midnight Strangler all this time, and you knew this, but didn't warn me?"

"We only suspected from the last note you received here in London before this one, but we couldn't be absolutely sure. It was the mention of beauty that made us suspect it. All the notes he's left with the girls' bodies say that beauty must suffer. "

"But isn't there anything else?" Cassie said in frustration.

"I'm afraid not, Miss Hamilton. Unless he's left something behind, we won't be able to find him. As with all the notes he's left behind with his victims, the ink and paper are quite common and can be gotten at any shop that sells stationary in London."

"But what about the pictures?"

"Yes, the pictures give us hope of the possibility of a mistake. There are so many of them, you see. Perhaps, he made a mistake and touched one of them without gloves."

"Let's hope," Tony muttered.

Like most organizations with large groups of people, New Scotland Yard had people who talked about things they shouldn't talk about at times whey they shouldn't have. When word leaked from one department that Cassidy had gotten a note from the Midnight Strangler, it didn't take long for it to leak to others.

When the leak hit the outside world, the press had a field day, feeding off the story for days. Cassidy's name could be found on the front page of at least one city newspaper for three days running. Cassidy herself was again a basket case. She couldn't sleep, she couldn't eat and she'd stopped working altogether.

She stayed huddled in the Carletons home; afraid to make contact with anyone she hadn't known before moving to London. She just didn't know whom she could trust.

She may have never left the Carletons, but she kept in touch with the police daily—sometimes hourly—to find out what was going on. That's why it came as a complete shock to her when Tony walked in late one evening with an update that she hadn't gotten.

"The police have arrested your agent, darling," Tony said to her when he arrived at his parents' home from work. The family, including Della and Charles, was gathered in the small parlor.

"What?" Cassie said. "How do you know? I just talked to Inspector Collins no less than two hours ago."

"I stopped in on my way home," Tony said. "I told them I'd tell you."

"Paul?" Esme asked incredulously. "They've arrested Cassidy's agent? He seems perfectly harmless."

"They've arrested him, you say, Tony? Why?" Lady Carleton asked.

"Apparently, he was in Chicago when Cassidy was being terrorized," Tony said and seeing that all the chairs were taken, he plucked Cassidy out of hers, and sat down with her in the same chair.

Embarrassed, Cassidy moved to stand. "Tony, don't," she said in a stifled voice.

"Hush and be still. I'm entitled," he said happily. The relief he felt at having the stalker caught was bursting from him "I've not seen you all day. Wouldn't you all say that I'm entitled to share a chair with my fiancée since I've had to be apart from her all day?" he asked the group and got a chorus of yeses in reply. Even Charles and Della joined in. "See?" he inquired of Cassidy. "Now make yourself comfortable, why don't you?"

Cassidy looked at him. He wore a big, sappy smile and she knew that he'd been hanging on by a thread. It had been hard for everyone. Understanding, she cupped his chin in her hand and pressed a reassuring kiss against his cheek before settling against him.

"Now that we've settled where Cassidy's to sit," Esme said dryly, "Do you think you could finish telling us what happened?"

"There's really nothing much to tell. His credit card receipts show that he booked a flight to Chicago twice while Cassidy was there—each time staying for at least a week and a half. Also, he's the one who called Cassidy with that fake story about a meeting with a Los Angeles casting agent."

"Actually, I didn't talk to him directly. It was just a message left by his office," Cassidy said with a frown. "But that doesn't matter now. I can't believe it of Paul," she said, feeling completely betrayed. "Why would he do such a thing?"

"They're trying to find that out now," Tony said.

They were all quiet as they each mulled this latest bit of news over in their minds.

At dinner that night, for the first time in days, Cassidy found that she actually had an appetite. She also realized with relief that she didn't have to be afraid to go out anymore. She was ready to get back to work, and decided to get started as soon as possible.

"Where are you going, Cass?"

Cassie turned from the door to face Tony. "Hi. I thought I'd go to my flat. I've been buying Christmas presents for everyone for months, and I want to pick them up and bring them here."

"Can't it wait?"

"Christmas is in two days, Tony, and tomorrow I'll be too busy helping your mother with last minute stuff to go out. It has to be tonight."

"Where's your bodyguard?"

"I let him go home this afternoon to be with his family. It is Christmas, you know. And, besides, I don't need him anymore now that they've arrested Paul."

"I'll go with you. Wait right here while I get my coat."

Chapter 27

He heard the key turn in the lock of the door of her flat, and he stood still, his heart racing with anticipation. It was about time she showed up. He'd been waiting for days, hoping against hope that she'd eventually find some reason to come home.

"Will you get the lights, Tony," Cassidy asked as she pushed the door open with her hip. "My hands are full."

"Yes, Tony, do get the lights," Andrew Garrett said, stepping out of the shadows when the lights clicked on.

"Andrew? What are you doing here?" Cassidy asked, the scripts she'd been carrying falling out of her hands. She just managed to hold onto her purse as it caught on her bracelet on its slide down. Unfortunately for her, she noticed two things at once. He had a gun, and there was also a loop of leather hanging from his pocket. It didn't take long for her to make the connection. "You're the Midnight Strangler?"

"That's right," Andrew said. "I've been planning this for years, Cassidy. And here you are, right in my city. Who would have ever imagined it? It couldn't have been more perfect."

Tony moved towards Cassidy, wanting to shield her.

"Ah, ah, ah," Andrew said, waving the gun back and forth. "Get back over there. She's mine."

"But why, Andrew?" Cassidy asked over the sound of her own heart beating in her ears. "What have I ever done to you?"

"You? Oh, you've done nothing. Nothing except live when my niece is dead because your father killed her. It's your father I want to punish now."

"You're Theresa Campbell's uncle?"

"That's right. She was my sister's child, and my favorite niece until your father killed her."

"My father didn't kill her," Cassidy stated definitively. She refused to let her father be blamed for something so horrible. "It was proven that what she had written in the suicide note was all a lie. She'd been in love with my father, and when he didn't reciprocate, she planned—"

"Brent Edwards was not your father," he interrupted her with a snarl and laughed when confusion filled her face. "You still don't know, do you? Oh, ho, that's rich. I know something you don't know," he sang happily. Suddenly his face went from laughing to menacing. "Charles Edwards is your father, you bloody nitwit!

"I know everything about you and your family, you see. I made it my business to know. And I know that Charles is your father and your father killed my Theresa." His face crumpled and he looked as if he would cry.

"Stop right there!" he said, suddenly straightening and pointing the gun directly at Tony whom he'd seen move from the corner of his eye. "Move over there to the couch, both of you!" he said and waved the gun at them. Once they were seated, he sat on the coffee table in front of them.

In a daze, Cassidy tried to listen to what he was saying, but could only focus on what he'd already said. *Charles was her father?* That just couldn't be. It was impossible.

"Now let me tell you a little story, Cassidy Marie," Andrew said. "It's about a little girl named Theresa. Theresa was a beautiful girl, and she loved her uncle. She loved her uncle so much that she never told anyone the secret they shared. Theresa was her uncle's favorite person in the world. He loved her, and whenever he could, he showed her just how much he loved her."

Rotting bastard, Tony thought angrily. His fists clenched at his sides, he made sure he was sitting as close to Cassidy as possible. He studied Andrew as he talked. Unfortunately, he held the gun steady on them. Tony looked at Cassie, and placing his hand on her knee and when she looked at him, he tried to reassure her with his eyes.

"Here's where the story gets sad," Andrew said. "Theresa was murdered. Murdered by an overzealous reporter named Charles Edwards. Charles Edwards insisted that Theresa be put on trial for something she didn't do. Charles, in fact, manufactured evidence so that it would look like Theresa had committed this heinous crime that his brother had committed.

"A tenacious fellow is our Charles. So tenacious, in fact, that he was able to convince the Chicago police and a prosecuting attorney that sweet, little Theresa should be tried for murder. Theresa was a delicate creature, you see, and she couldn't handle the thought of being in jail, so the first opportunity she got, she hung herself. And Andrew knew then that beauty suffers, beauty *must* suffer. There could be no other explanation for what happened to Theresa.

"In walks our hero, the love of Theresa's life, her lover, her Uncle Andrew. Andrew vows to avenge Theresa's death, and he figures the only proper way to do it is to take away what Charles Edwards loves most in the world—his daughter." He stopped and looked at Cassidy here, breaking into a huge smile when he saw the disbelief on her face. "Oh yes, he's your father. Luke," he said in an imitation of Darth Vader, "I am your father." He burst into hysterical laughter.

Cassie tried to ignore what he was saying. It was too much at once. She felt as if she were in a dream world, where nothing was real.

Still snickering, Andrew covered his mouth, as if trying to push the laughter back in. "Mustn't laugh," he said gleefully. "This is meant to be a serious occasion. Okay, back to our story. Where was I? Oh yes, just like Charles had taken away what Andrew loved most in the world, Andrew would take away what Charles loved most. But it won't do to kill little Cassidy when she's nothing but a tot. No, Andrew figures it would be best to kill her when she's at the same age that Theresa was when she was killed. It was a matter of poetic justice.

"So Andrew bides his time waiting for little Cassidy to grow up. And in the meantime, he stays in Chicago, works a few jobs and waits. He waits, and he waits, and he waits. And then, what do you know? Cassidy decides to move to London, Andrew's hometown. And Andrew decides to wait some more. It all has to be just right, so that it doesn't lead back to him. All he has to do is find a way to meet her, make her trust him.

"And how convenient that Cassidy's agent should suddenly need a publicist. Andrew's the one who made this convenience possible, but we won't discuss that just now. Back to our story.

Andrew meets Cassidy, and guess what? She likes him and she trusts him—"

"You killed someone else?" Tony interrupted.

Andrew looked at him as if seeing him for the first time. He scowled. "I said we aren't going to discuss that now," he warned and looked back at Cassidy, who had moved closer to Tony with the idea of somehow protecting him.

"Let's go back a few months. While Andrew is waiting for his opportunity to finally do to Cassidy what her dear old dad had done to his niece, he figures that he'll need to practice first. So that's what Andrew does. He practices. All up and down old London town," he sang. The singing turned to laughter, which affected him so deeply that tears rolled down his cheeks.

"You're a freaking nut case," Cassie murmured before she thought about it.

The laughter stopped abruptly. "Don't say that!" Andrew yelled. "That's what they tried to say when I was a kid! But I got away when they sent me away. I got away, yes I did. And I'll get away this time, as well," he finished with a proud, confident smile.

Tony laid his hand on Cassie's back in warning when he saw she'd say something. "You can't possibly think you'll get away, Andrew," Tony told him, his mind going a hundred miles a minute as he tried to think of a way to get them out of the situation. "Don't be an idiot," he said angrily. "People know we're here."

"And they'll know you're dead, too," Andrew said with unconcern. "Now, let's get back to our story, shall we? I could have killed you so many times over these past months. But I waited. You see, I enjoyed watching you suffer. The letters terrified you, and you were a complete wreck when I planted that story about your parents in the paper," he said, laughing again. "I saw you on Portobello Road, you know," he said between his chuckles. "I've never laughed so hard in my life."

Cassie looked at Tony from the corner of her eye, and quickly looked at Andrew again. She was afraid to take her eyes off him for too long. The whole thing was too bizarre, and Andrew was obviously certifiable. She looked at the gun, wishing he would take it off them for one brief second. She'd have her chance then.

As Andrew's laughter began to wind down, he began talking

again. "So we come to where we are now—the most important part. I'm going to kill you, Cassidy, and I'm going to sit back and watch your father suffer the way I had to suffer. But guess what? First I get to rape you. After all, I wouldn't be the Midnight Strangler if I didn't."

"Not bloody likely!" Tony saw his chance when Andrew waved the gun away from the couch again. Furious, he reared up and reached for it.

"No!" Cassidy yelled when she saw the gun swerve towards Tony. Realizing she had a ready-made weapon, she swung her purse, whacking Andrew on the side of the head so hard that he fell backward and the gun flew from his hand. She lost control and clipped Tony on the back swing.

"Christ Jesus, Cass! What have you got in that blasted thing?" Tony said as he hurried to get to Andrew where he punched him in the face when he tried to get up. "Bloody psychopath!" he said and hit him again when he thought of how he'd held a gun on Cassie.

"Sorry, darling," Cassie said with a wince. "Are you all right?" And then her attention was caught by something else. "Ooh, get the gun, Tony," she squealed when she saw it lying on the floor. Andrew moaned, and frowning, she whacked him with the purse again. "Stay the hell down," she muttered.

Tony managed to get the gun, and feeling ridiculous, stood over Andrew and said, "Freeze, Garrett. Call the police, Cass," he reminded her when she just stood there staring.

"I can't believe it." Esme said later as the family sat in the dining room having cups of tea. She shook her head. "I simply *can't* believe it."

"For heaven's sake, Esme," Lady Carleton said irritably. "Can't believe what?"

"I can't believe that these two actually caught a killer."

Tony scowled. "Well, believe it, you bloody brat. Your big brother and future sister-in-law are bonafide heroes."

"So, let me get this straight," Lord Carleton said. "Andrew stole Paul's credit card and used it to buy himself plane tickets to Chicago?"

"Correct," Cassidy said. "Paul never even noticed that his card was gone. He also used Paul's credit card to rent the building, which had been sitting empty for years."

"And the police believe that Andrew killed Paul's old publicist so he could take over his job and be near you?"

"Yes," Cassidy said. "Since the old publicist seems to have disappeared, they don't have another explanation. And yes, Andrew is the uncle of Theresa Campbell who killed my parents all those years ago." Cassidy was still reeling from the events of the night. If she weren't involved in them, she'd think everything was all made up.

"It's horribly ironic," Tony began, "but Andrew's admitted to molesting Theresa when she was a child, and that could have very well contributed to her being unwell and killing Cass's parents. Andrew blamed Charles for Theresa's death and he wanted revenge for it. The whole thing is completely inexplicable, but we are dealing with someone who's stark raving mad."

Cassidy looked at her uncle. He didn't look happy. "Uncle Charles?" she waited until he looked at her, his face furrowed with worry. "May we talk in private?"

"Of course," Charles said and rose and followed her out of the room.

Tony frowned after them, regretting that he hadn't told her about Charles when he'd figured it out. He'd planned to tell Charles what he knew so that Charles could tell her himself. Unfortunately, he'd never gotten an opportunity to talk to Charles.

Cassidy chose the small parlor for privacy. "Why didn't you tell me that you're my father?" she asked him immediately.

This is it, Charles thought. Curiously, his heart lifted. It was about time things were out in the open. "I was young when you were born, Cassidy. I'd gotten a girl, a good friend, pregnant and when she died during childbirth, I took you. Only, I wasn't prepared to be a father. I traveled a lot and I didn't have a stable home. It was decided that my brother, since he and his wife couldn't have children, would adopt you and raise you as their own."

"But why didn't you tell me later? After they'd died?" Cassidy felt as if her life was turned upside down, and she had no idea which end was up anymore.

"I wanted to, but the therapist said that you were in too fragile a state to handle anymore distressing news. I wanted to take you with me, Cassidy, but I let myself get talked out of it. First we didn't tell you the truth because we thought that you were too young to understand. Then I didn't tell you the truth, because I kept putting it off, and the longer I waited, the harder it got. I'm sorry, baby, sorry that I didn't tell you, and sorry that you had to find out the way you did."

"Does Della know?" Cassidy asked.

"Yes, it's the main reason she won't marry me. She says that as long as I keep chickening out and waiting to tell you, then I've got unfinished business that needs to be handled."

Cassidy smiled. "I knew there was a reason I always liked her."

Charles smiled uneasily. "You're not mad?"

"No, I'm not," she replied as she studied his face. It was the face of a man who'd always been there for her. She took his hands. "I've got so many things in my life to be happy about, why should I waste one minute of time being angry about something I can't change? And besides, you always treated me as if I was your daughter, and you definitely loved me as if I was. How can I possibly be mad about that?" she asked and grinning impishly because she wanted to end it all on a happy note, she said, "It's going to take me a minute before I can think about calling you Dad, though. Is that all right, Uncle Cha-cha?"

"It's more than," Charles said. He was unable to hide the tears in his eyes when she stepped into his arms. "In fact, it's *more than more than!*"

Epilogue

Paparazzi surrounded the limo as it pulled up to the red carpet in front of the Hollywood movie theater showcasing the latest premiere. Everyone waited anxiously to see what fabulous celebrity they would get to see next.

Inside the limo, Cass leaned into Tony, feeling boneless and fluid. "Oh, God. We shouldn't have," she murmured.

"Ah, but we did," Tony said with a wicked grin, as he took her mouth in another ravenous kiss.

Cassie pushed against him. "Stop that! I already have to repair my makeup. Don't make it worse."

Tony only laughed, and kissed her again.

Cassidy helplessly kissed him back.

"Cass?" he murmured against her lips when she continued to lean into him with her eyes closed and a happy smile. "They're waiting."

She moaned and pushed away again. "Okay, okay," she said and rummaged through her purse for her lipstick and compact.

Tony watched her with a smirk. "No matter how much camouflage you put on, darling, you'll still look like a woman who's just been well-loved."

Staring at herself in the mirror, Cassie couldn't help but agree. "Sunglasses. Where are my sunglasses?" She found them between the seats, and put them on. "There, that's better. I'm ready when you are."

A roar went through the crowd as Cassidy, talented ingénue who'd stolen an entire movie in approximately thirty minutes of screen time, stepped out of the car with her fiancée, international CEO, Tony Carleton.

Laughing, Cassidy whispered as she helplessly leaned into his side on shaky legs. "I knew I shouldn't have let you talk me into making love in the backseat of the limo. I can barely stand."

Tony smiled, his hand going around her waist to help steady her. "Well, I had to do something," he teased. "You were as taut as a wire before." She'd been so nervous about facing the onslaught of press and paparazzi at her first premiere that she'd sat stiffly beside him and had been unable to even hold a conversation. He'd felt it was his duty to make love to her. He grinned; it was a duty he couldn't imagine ever shirking. He felt her tensing against him again. "It's all right," he said softly into her ear.

"I know," Cassie whispered and smiled nervously as they got closer to a reporter with a microphone. "Oh, God, she's going to ask me questions. I hope I don't screw up."

"Maybe this will help," Tony said, right before he bent his head and kissed her as if his life depended on it. As always, Cassidy couldn't prevent herself from responding. She twined her arms around his neck. *Ah, the things one does for love*, he thought happily when she relaxed against him and hundreds of flashes went off.

Author Bio

Lisa G. Riley's work has been called "character and issue drive; exciting, passionate and thought provoking." The author of several novels and novellas, Ms. Riley resides in Chicago where she is hard at work on her next project. Please visit Ms. Riley at www.lisagriley.com